REAPER'S GATE

By

daniel storm

REAPER'S GATE

ISBN #0-9826782-1-5

Dedication

To those who have stood by me while I conjure up these stories, believing in my dreams and chosen craft, you make the concept of working at writing, my passion.

Thank you all

PS.
And Thomas R. Sniezek, who never knew how much he helped me, or cared. His resident evil became an energy source for me. Wherever he is, he is still a bastard.

Books by Daniel Storm

Reaper's Gate

Jury Duty

Praetorian Guard

Surviving the Alphabet Soup

The Apostle

Mantis

The Prey

Not Afraid to Kill, Not Afraid to Die

Masters of the Race

ALL TITLES IN SPANISH, TOO!

Chapter 1

Despite the constant cleaning, buffing, shining and antiseptics, death row smells of fear, anxiety, psychotic disorders and death itself. The men await their dates with justice and the contemporary form of euthanasia for aberrants, lethal injection. The electric chair and its hair-raising mythologies of condemned people on fire to the Devil's dance as eighty thousand volts courses through them are just a bad memory. It is a simple matter now. You just lay down on a table and some quack pushes chemicals into your body and stops your breathing and pulse. All painlessly. Just like that. Or is it?

The "row," as it is called, at Thames, the maximum security prison in southern Illinois, is home to the most violent and predatory men Illinois has to offer. They await their date with fate. Among the condemned is Johnny Lee Childress. In less than twenty-four hours the convicted child molester and murderer will die.

"Hey pervert," one of Childress's peers hollers out through the iron mesh hole in his otherwise solid steel door, "the newspaper here says your sick, fucking ass has no hope of a stay or clemency. Looks like you're a dead man walking, you piece of shit. If I could get my hands on you, I'd save the taxpayers their hard earned money." The other convicts began laughing and banging on their doors in support.

"Fuck you!" Johnny said, as he thought about tomorrow. Of course he didn't want to die. Only a fool claims otherwise. Yet, death is inevitable to all life forms. Nothing lives forever. Especially child killers. There is no empathy with Judges or politicians in such cases. Even convicts despise them and make their life behind bars a living hell, if they can get at them.

Johnny had not been on the row for very long, when compared to most cases. In his mere three years while his appeals were swiftly denied, unlike some who have been there upwards of fifteen years, he has never given thought to the reality of tomorrow. Statistically, most executions are stayed by either the courts or the Governor of the state.

When the circuit Judge sentenced him to death, it seemed

like only words. Johnny was a media star then. Not one newspaper in Chicago failed to have his now famous mug shot adorning the front page. He didn't care what the Judges said. At that point he was the center of attention, and besides, his lawyers assured him that he had solid grounds for his appeal and would probably prevail. That was only three years ago and here he was, less than a day away from dying.

The newspapers today show pictures outside the Thames prison where marchers are encamped. At first he believed they were there to protest his state authorized and sanctioned murder! However, several of the convicts around him began to read articles to him and he discovered that the people outside were in fact cheering for his forthcoming date with the executioner.

The permanent protestors who held candlelight vigils outside of prisons everywhere when an execution was about to take place, intentionally found other things to do when it came to child killers. They learned the hard way after revelers beat them senseless or destroyed their Winnebagos with fire in the parking lot, because of their belief that only God could take a life. Instead of changing their deep beliefs, they distracted themselves when a case like Johnny's appeared. Even the Bible condemns harming a child. That justified their selective absence at the death of child killers.

There was still the Governor, who had commuted the last two executions. He has only been in office a short time and ousted a multi-term Republican who wanted to avoid federal prison himself. He wasn't concerned about murderers unless they had money, according to reporters.

The new Governor was a long shot for Johnny. His attorneys, the same two who represented him at trial and appeals, said that the hearing with the Prisoner Review Board and the Governor's clemency counsel went well. Johnny has been told that a phone hangs on the wall in the execution chamber, where the warden would wait for a last minute decision for reprieve or death from the Governor himself.

Although he was found to be competent by the Judge to stand trial, and to assist his counsel in preparing a defense, the clemency petition could encompass other factors such as diminished capacity and psychological disorders which could tend to reduce culpability and invoke compassion.

The authority to commute a death sentence to life or any specified term is statutorily vested solely in the executive authority of the State's highest position, the Governor. It is not reviewable by any court in the land. Prosecutors have tried that approach when they became disgruntled over a grant of clemency and lost.

No matter how sensational the case or how heinous the offense conduct, once the Governor affixed his signature and seal on that order, it was final. Johnny could always obtain clemency.

His attorneys argued that Johnny's sociopathic disorder admittedly stemmed from a rotten childhood. Johnny never made it through the eighth grade at the facility for boys at St. Charles, which in essence was nothing more than a prison for youths who couldn't follow rules. He quickly found a home in solitary confinement there after cracking one of the other boys in the head with a shovel. The boy almost died.

Another psychotic trait was the obsessive-compulsive disorder. He said he "couldn't help himself" to the Chicago police officer who arrested him, Sergeant Rachael Hart. Of course his attorneys failed to address that statement in their defense presentation that Johnny couldn't help himself because the victims were mirror images of one another and identical twins. That would have spoiled their plan to obfuscate the harsh realities of the cases. It was all about tactics and argument, after all. The hearing wasn't to decide guilt or innocence but to ascertain the prudent applicability of compassion and understanding. Hell, everyone knew Johnny was guilty. He confessed to the slayings but proceeded to trial when a plea bargain was offered. His attorneys argued that too, as if confessing to such offenses against humanity should call for some reward. They left nothing out.

So, here Johnny Lee Childress sits, less than a day to find out if there really is a God. Or worse yet, a Devil. And these awful men around him think it is so funny. They are just afraid themselves, he reckoned, using him as a means to distract them from thinking about their own time to tickle fate.

"Fuck you," was Johnny's response to everything. "Twenty-four fucking hours." These fucking lawyers or public pretenders as he commonly referred to them during visits, had to come through.

Johnny told himself that he should get some rest. "Fuck that," he told himself. "In a day I'll sleep forever." He laughed at that thought. He'd be dirt-napping in a day, "With worms eating my fucking eyes and shit." Sometimes words never came out and these conversations were carried out solely in his mind. Johnny Lee Childress was crazier than batshit.

Chapter 2

"Ben," Rachael began, "do you think there is any chance that some Judge will stop this?"

Mordeci had joined them at their Homicide offices at the Chicago Police Department headquarters at 11th and State Streets in the Loop, the heart of the windy city. Their offices are located near the top of the building and closest to the Chief of Police's suite on the top floor.

The Homicide section was remodeled recently and the detectives worked in cubicles, with padded dividers like those in the average business selling insurance and real estate. The only one who had a real office is the Chief of Homicide, Lieutenant Benedict Ori. Ori has been a member of C.P.D. for decades and worked his way through the rank and file the hard way. He earned it. He was not a bootlicker, ass kisser or politico. He got where he is today by dedication, long hours and sincerity.

Ori is best described as a lumbering giant of a man, standing six feet-five inches tall, with coal black hair and baseball mitts for hands. He carries his two hundred and sixty pounds with athletic grace and is not easily provoked. However, when someone was foolish enough to do so, they abruptly learned their grave error in doing so. He has been the Homicide Chief for almost ten years now and considers those on his team as extended family.

Among those squad members is Rachael Hart, his second in command, carrying the rank of Sergeant. Ori recruited Rachael from a smaller department in Evanston, Illinois when they worked together on a case involving a man who executed an entire jury over a period of six years, avenging his sister. He was finally executed and Rachael went to work for Ben.

Rachael stands six feet and weighs a mere one hundred and twenty-eight pounds. Her Irish lineage is readily apparent by her fiery red hair, freckles and emerald green eyes. She also possesses the hereditary temper associated with the fighting Irish. To the dismay of a number of culprits, she has not only acquired a working knowledge of self-defense, she teaches it. Rachael is an instructor in judo. She trains regularly and does volunteer instruction for women. She has a cubicle with a door, a quasi-office which affords her a bit more privacy, but not as much as a real office like her boss's. She was promoted to Sergeant over the others in her squad, but no one took offense as she had years of experience at Evanston. Everyone knew that Ben was grooming her to succeed him at his post when he retired. They respected Ben, so accepted his choices.

Rachael is single and is not carrying the baggage of a steady beau. She makes a rule not to date other cops as she realizes the futility of trying to manage time together while working long and strange hours on the job. Besides, one gun on the nightstand is enough.

Joining them this morning is somewhat of a local celebrity. Mordeci Habush is a Chicago Tribune syndicated columnist whose forte is crime, criminals and the wheels of the justice system. He appears on talk shows, both radio and televised, interviewing a variety of interesting people. He interviewed John Wayne Gacey before he was executed for murdering thirty-three boys with whom he had sex. Mordeci could not get him to confess despite his looming execution, only hours away.

Mordeci once said, "You know you're in serious trouble when they use all three of your names in the media." If you think about it, he is correct.

Mordeci, or "Mort" as he is customarily referred to by those who know him, has been married to the same girl he dated in high school thirty years ago. Their kids are grown and their hair is a lighter shade, his white and hers "blond" as she calls it, while resembling her husband's more than Pamela Anderson's, but the fire of their romance has not faded with the passage of time.

Mort interviewed Johnny Lee Childress shortly after he was arrested and again after being sentenced to die. It was the most disgusting interview he had ever done. Mort concurred with prosecutors and the Judge that there was no redeeming factor that Childress had that would alleviate the absolute need to put him down like a rabid dog. Childress displayed no sense of remorse whatsoever and actually boasted of the horrific things he perpetrated on those two little girls. When he left Childress the last time, having interviewed him at Thames, where he would die, Mort went into the staff restroom and vomited.

Today, the three of them were preparing to drive to Thames to act as official witnesses to the execution. The law requires public witnesses to attest to the humane conditions, professionalism by prison staff and the effectuation of the Death Warrant itself. Rachael, as arresting officer, was guaranteed a seat in the gallery. Her guest was Ben, who was more than a boss and mentor to her, he was like a father. Mort on the other hand, had to pull some strings to get a chair at the limited seating. He bested some huge names in broadcasting, including network "heavies" like Rivera and King. Mort has been in this business a long time and is a journalistic icon in Illinois.

Mort's Jewish faith did not prohibit him from being a witness to an execution. Retribution is acceptable for crimes against humanity. Ask the Nazi members who happily executed throngs of Jews, only to whimper when facing the gallows themselves. Then there is Mossad, if you don't believe the Jews carry a grudge. So, Mort is not religiously constrained from watching Johnny Lee Childress die.

It was Mort who answered Rachael's question about any last minute reprieve. He was staying on top of the efforts by Childress's attorneys to salvage his miserable existence.

"Rachael, I have it on good authority that the Judges in the Seventh Circuit Court of Appeals have directed all federal Judges in Illinois to refrain from any more action on an eleventh hour petition. And I don't see our new Governor reaching out to him, either. So I don't think so."

Ben listened to Mort and his explanation. When Rachael looked at him, he merely raised his eyebrows as if to say, "Who am I to disagree with this guy?"

They decided to drive down to Thames together and take turns driving and acting as prisoner in the back of Rachael's unmarked squad which had a security divider behind the front seat. Rachael had just been issued the brand new Crown Victoria in pastel blue and it still had that new car smell. She was proud of her new squad and wanted some highway miles on it before it got mean ones from responding to emergency calls.

They planned to arrive at the prison around eight o'clock. The execution was scheduled for one minute after midnight. She wondered why they always seemed to pick that time. Why not later? Does the Reaper only ride at midnight?

Rachael would take the first watch and get them through rush hour traffic. It was three o'clock and time to leave. All their files were taken care of and the necessary requisitions approved for expenses for their trip. The trio would return to Chicago just after the execution, stopping only for meals and gas.

The scuttlebutt was that Johnny's lawyer had exhausted all options in the courts but had pitched their claims to the Illinois Prisoner Review Board, to seek clemency. Mort had not confirmed that yet, but the maneuver was standard procedure with executions looming on the horizon.

Ben wanted to talk about anything but Johnny Lee Childress and what brought him to this day. Rachael wanted nothing else but to revel in the satisfaction at watching him put down for good. Mort pretended to be their prisoner, and exercised his right to remain silent in the back seat.

Chapter 3

The building is an old clapboard structure which housed three apartments. It had one of those subterranean levels referred to as a "garden apartment" because every window was at ground level where flowers were planted. The walls were concrete and represented the foundation for the building above. It was the sturdiest unit and also the quietest one because of those concrete barriers.

This particular building is located in the Polish sector of Chicago's city limits. The dividing lines for the Polish community are as bright line as wood markers. Ethnically, it was over ninety percent Polish-American and it showed. They would have "block parties" where streets were blockaded by the neighbors, tables carried to the middle of the street and a cornucopia of Polish traditional dishes was set up banquet style for everyone. The festivities would last all day and would include live music and recordings of their favorite songs. Sometimes it would get loud, but no one seemed to mind. After all, they were celebrating.

The men would consume too much alcohol and make fools of themselves, dancing like children. They worked hard to support their families and deserved the respite from the doldrums of their jobs. They were not executives, but worked with their hands in mills and factories. It was difficult and dirty work, but they maintained. Most of them retired from the first job they had ever gotten. They were valued employees and treated their jobs like a second home or family.

No one ever figured out how Johnny Lee Childress came to be there that fateful day. Whether it was just blind luck or some evil hand that guided him would elude every investigator's grasp of understanding. They all agreed though, that evil was his motivation.

The concrete walls, along with the abrasive level of music outside, worked in concert to conceal the screams of those twin girls, Samantha and Sarina Polachek. They were common girls, not beauties yet. They were only nine years old. They were also identical twins. It was difficult to tell them apart. Sometimes they would wear identical clothes, which confused people. Only their parents could discern one from the other. Today they wore identical outfits of white dresses, made of cotton by their mother, white nylon stockings and black shoes. They looked like angels, as their black hair cascaded to the middle of their backs, as straight as arrows. All they were missing was wings. Everyone was certain that God gave them those later that night.

No one heard their screams or pleas for mercy that must have come from their injuries. They were found by the building's owner as she attempted to roust everyone for the party. The tenant of the garden apartment was at work on overtime, but the front door was ajar. The doorframe was destroyed where the locks ran home to secure the door. Someone had smashed it open and was never heard over the cheering outside.

Expecting to find the carnage left over from a burglar who ransacked the place looking for morsels he could barter for drugs, she had pushed the door open with her foot. She had never seen so much blood and immediately ran to summon help. Several men armed themselves with knives from the tables as they ran to the building. The poor woman who owned the building was lying on the grassy parkway, sobbing openly. She was certain her tenant, a quiet man of forty-eight, was in there - and dead. She liked him. Then she saw some of those hearty men vomiting around her building and she began to get scared. These men were tough, seasoned by a hard-scrabble life here in the country of dreams. They were pale and shaking.

One man came running, as he had just heard that help was needed and he would not be denied the male right of answering the call. He was literally tackled by several men and restrained, as if he had played some role in what lay inside the apartment. She saw the men talk to him quietly. She could not hear their words. But, she understood the animalistic wail of anguish that pierced the night and the man struggled vainly with his captors. Only then did it dawn on her that the man was the father of two precious girls and that the anguish he exhibited now must be related to those girls of his. She began to shake and sob again.

The first uniform car responded in minutes, its blue lights ablaze and siren yelping. The officer, a young man in his early twenties, ran into the building with one of the men from the neighborhood. A moment later, he too spewed his lunch on the ground outside. Squad cars, fire trucks, paramedics and special vans with the words Forensics and Coroner on them, filled the street. Police blockades were on each end of the block now. All of the tables and food had been carted back from whence they came.

Then, an unmarked car screeched to a halt and a tall redhead got out and strode to the building, as she flashed the ID hanging around her neck on a chain.

No one recognized Rachael, although she had been on numerous programs and featured in newspapers. She did not like recognition anyhow, as a real detective strives to be anonymous and blend with pedestrian traffic. She was assigned to this case and assumed command. When Ben had been advised of the atrocities inside the house, he took the case away from local detectives in the district which included the physical location of the home. As Chief of Homicide, he could make that call.

He assigned Rachael for three very good reasons. First, she was an excellent investigator and operated by instinct. Second, she was a woman and could relate to a grieving community with the compassion commensurate with the needs of those people and the Department. Third, was on a more personal scale. If he danced around the assignments on an unequal basis, the balance of the squad would resent the favoritism and so would Rachael. She came to his Department a seasoned veteran and no neophyte to man's inhumanity to man. She trained hard to be accepted as an equal and even more so to succeed Ben later on. She expected no partial treatment and requested none.

Rachael had heard sketchy reports on the tactical frequency so she thought she was prepared for what lay inside. She was wrong.

When she entered, she immediately saw the blood splattering the eggshell colored walls. It looked as if the Devil designed his personal Rorschach Test in blood. It ran in rivulets like morbid waterfalls. She imagined the wound necessary for such exsanguinations. Only neck wounds could spray that much blood.

The Evidence Technicians, as their jackets and jumpsuits identified them, were hard at work. Rachael was told that Dr. Jack

Farmer, the Chief of Forensics, would be there soon and Rachael felt relieved at that notion. She knew Dr. Farmer from her very first day on the job in Chicago. He was truly an expert in that field.

When the evidence people finally nodded that she could enter the bedroom, Rachael cautiously stepped over chalk marks, blood and little triangular signs with numbers which were used in photographs for identification purposes in reports and in courtroom testimony.

When she entered the tiny bedroom, she saw two bodies covered in red, with only traces of white to betray the original color of clothing. They were positioned on the bed holding hands, like Raggedy Ann dolls that the girls probably had at home on their beds. Their little heads lolled to the sides due to the savage slashing of muscle tissue and trachea which would normally hold the heads in place. The wounds to their necks were so deep that Rachael wondered what held their heads on at all.

The bedding upon which they sat was a veritable lake of blood. It was congealing on top of the spread where an occasional fly would land to feast. Their legs were splayed apart and Rachael hoped that they were positioned that way to keep their torsos upright.

The Medical Examiner himself, Tommy Dorf, was there. He was a medical doctor and surgeon, but refused to be called Dr. Dorf. Everyone knew the diminutive man as Tommy, even his subordinates.

"It's bad, Rachael," Tommy said. "I anticipate the time of death as between two to three hours ago. Someone must have seen the guy."

"How do you know it's a guy, Tommy?" Rachael asked.

"He raped them, Rachael. Then he mutilated them down there," Tommy said in a saddened tone. It took a lot to affect the M.E. like that, so Rachael assumed the worst. She did not wish to see.

Rachael was repulsed at the crime, which she channeled to resolve to find the sick sonofabitch who did this.

"I'll come by tomorrow, Tommy. Will you do the autopsies for me?"

"Certainly. Just catch the guy who did this." He said the latter matter-of-factly, as he turned away from her. His eyes were misty. She saw it.

"You have my word on it," was all she said as she turned to leave. Her own eyes were watering and she could not afford a weak appearance now. She could cry later when she was alone with a healthy shot of Jack Daniels in hand.

When she walked out front, she immediately took charge. She gathered all the detectives together and told them she wanted everyone interviewed and interviewed again by separate teams. She wanted the neighborhood searched and a knock on every door.

"This guy can still be around here. He's probably got blood on him, given the mess inside that house. Look for footprints, bloody clothing, whatever. Let's get this guy before he gets far."

There were almost one hundred officers on the scene and in the area now. Rachael wondered how far a bloody man could get in such a closely knit community.

Calls began pouring into the district and downtown at headquarters. Ben almost came to the scene himself and then thought about it. In doing so, he would be undercutting Rachael's authority. He would have to wait and see what transpired just like anyone else. As it turned out, it wouldn't be long.

"Sergeant, a uniform car just came across a mini-van that appears to have blood on the rear door. There's no one in the van now, but it's not far from here. The van was reported stolen two days ago."

"I want that area saturated right now. If it's him, he could be lurking around there waiting for a new victim. I'm relocating there right now," she told the uniform sergeant who joined her.

The uniform cop scrambled off, talking quickly into his mic attached to his jacket.

It took Rachael five minutes to race to the location where the van was found. It would take a bloody man a while to work his way there through the shadows and hiding. She felt good about the possibilities and her instincts were wired.

Several squads surrounded a cream colored mini-van and one officer was stringing yellow "Crime Scene" streamer around the entire area. An evidence tech advised Rachael that it was Type O

Positive blood on the door panel, the same type as the twins and about eighty percent of Americans.

"OK, let's spread out and search. He could be hiding in a garbage can, so don't be careless people. I'll be on foot myself. Be careful here. We never recovered the knife."

The officers fanned out. A few remained in their cars to patrol back and forth in a visible presence to help keep the fleeing perpetrator pinned down and to restrict his movement. Also, in the event officers spotted someone fleeing on foot, the cars could intercept him.

Rachael remained in her squad and cruised the neighborhood. She entered an alleyway that ended about two hundred yards away. She waited a few minutes, her car's engine idling and the radio crackling with excited chatter by uniform cars with possible hiding places. For some reason, the alley was too quiet. There was nothing moving. Not even a bird flittering around in search of food. It was like a scene from "Platoon," and "Charlie" was sneaking through the jungle in ambush. Everything was too still. She announced on her radio that she was leaving her squad and would be on foot. When she got out and listened to the stillness, she withdrew her weapon, a Glock, Model 32 and a 40 caliber man stopper. Her heart pounded and every nerve inside her was electrically charged.

Rachael began by checking garages, turning door handles to see if they were unlocked and looked into windows. She went from one side to the other, slowly working her way to the dead end. She carried her weapon in the classic two-handed grip, one hand supporting the other and her index finger resting along the slide, not on the trigger as in Hollywood movies. Placing the finger on the trigger can lead to accidental discharges. The military teaches "indexing," where the finger is straight, allowing the safety mechanism to be in the "off" position. Her weapon was carried high, next to her head, as she would use one hand for door knobs or to lift a garbage can lid. Then, she thought she heard the rustle of something brushing a metallic object on wood.

Johnny Lee Childress could not believe his luck that day. He had his pleasure with the twins, but that was hours ago and the excitement had worn off. He had to move slower than he anticipated and as he returned to the mini-van he had stolen from a mall two days before, he saw a squad car. He didn't think they could have found his twins that fast, but the stolen van was a different story. So he hid behind a garbage can until the cop left. That's when he noticed that he left a smudge on the rear door. He had not washed the blood off his hands in his haste to leave the apartment. There was so much racket in the streets, he could not hear if someone approached the apartment and that unnerved him.

While Johnny watched from around the corner, the squad car crept slowly down the alley. And then, it stopped directly behind Johnny's stolen ride. "Shit," he cursed his luck. The cop was on his radio. Johnny decided to watch a moment. Then more cops showed up and when he crouched between two houses as he prepared to cross the street, marked squad cars were cruising back and forth. He moved cautiously from yard to yard towards the end of the alleyway, as the cops didn't come his way. In almost a half hour, he had covered two whole blocks. It was slow going. When he realized the alley he was in now was a dead end, he actually smiled, as cops were notoriously lazy, or so he believed, and once they saw the dead end, they would back up and leave. So, he decided to wait awhile and make his escape when it was dark. He found a garden hose in the back of a house and used it to wash his hands and face. His clothes were soaked with blood, but in the dark, no one would notice.

Johnny saw the Crown Victoria pull into the alley and stop. Like all squad cars, it bore those special blue license plates announcing its official status as if a star were painted across the hood, doors and trunk. The bad guys could spot them from a block away.

When the tall redhead stepped out, he couldn't believe his good fortune. He was going to have this bitch too and he began to get hard between the legs. He would overpower her and put the knife to her. Women were afraid of knives. He'd take her into one of these garages and have his way with her and then cut her. He was pleased with himself for waiting. This broad looked good!

He watched her go from side to side down the alley. She carried her gun like some Hollywood queen in one of those gangsta films. He could snatch that away from her easy enough. She was getting closer now. As he moved under a porch, his jeans snagged on a nail and he used his knife to pry the cheap trellis from the stoop. The wood creaked in defiance. Damn.

Rachael circled the garage and stopped to look at the house. It was as if she could feel the presence of some evil entity. When she reached the alley again, having made a complete circle around the garage, she decided to circle it once more instead of crossing over the alley to inspect another garage and house. When she was about to turn the corner behind the garage is when she saw Johnny Lee crawling out from under the porch. He must have anticipated her following the same pattern, side-to-side.

As Johnny stood up, he saw the redhead staring at him from the garage. She had her weapon pointed directly at his chest. She didn't say a word. She just stared at him. Her finger was on the trigger and he could see her knuckle was white. "This bitch is just going to shoot me," he said to himself.

Rachael knew she had found the vermin that had mutilated those girls. Hell, he still had the knife which was in his right hand. She knew she could pull the trigger and get away with murder. He was bloody, armed and she was a woman, all alone. Internal Affairs would breeze through that investigation and recommend a citation for her. As much as she wanted to put this guy down, she was a cop first.

Johnny had seen some crazy bitches in his life, but the redhead was fucking wacko. She holstered her gun and stood there. She wanted him, like those tramps that vampires simply looked at, and they became their prey without a struggle. She wanted him inside her. Broads are crazy, man!

Rachael watched Johnny approach her. He looked confident and in control. She balanced herself on the balls of her feet. Without staring, she watched the hand with the knife. She had trained for this thousands of times. She knew exactly how she was going to do it.

When Johnny got within a yard of her, he lunged, as if to stab her just to scare the bitch a little. But he held that knife out in front of him like you always see in the movies. Real knife fighters held them close and protected. Rachael knew this guy was an idiot.

Rachael grabbed the knife hand with her left hand. The speed surprised Johnny and he watched as she placed her right hand on top of the knife, slid her thumb under his and wrapped her fingers around his. With leverage now, she angled Johnny's wrist towards his face, hyper-extending the joint and a horrible pain radiated through his arm. The knife fell from his hand. He watched it as if in slow motion, as it drifted to the ground. Shit. The crazy bitch was trying to shatter his fucking wrist and had him bent over at the waist now like some faggot waiting to get corn-holed. Then he saw the wacko's right leg flying at his face, quicker than the Starship Enterprise. With his right arm still locked in the bitch's grip, he could deflect the blow only with his left hand.

Rachael's shin landed squarely in the perpetrator's face. She could feel the cartilage snap in his nose and when she looked at her leg, blood smeared the point of impact. She gave Johnny one more kick for good measure. While Rachael watched the man spit something on the ground resembling a tooth, she planted her weight on her right leg and swept Johnny's feet out from under him with her left. He went down hard. She could see the fear in his eyes as she wrenched his right arm again and he rolled on his stomach to avoid the pain, like he was someone's bitch. Shit!

"You have the right to remain silent," Rachael began, as she gave Johnny his Miranda rights. When she had him handcuffed, (where did she have those handcuffs?) Rachael turned him over.

"Why did you kill those girls? What did they do to you?" Rachael asked quietly, almost like a mother to a son.

"I couldn't help myself. They're dolls." Johnny said proudly.

"Were dolls, you sonofabitch and I'll see you in hell for it."

Rachael removed the radio from her side, opposite her gun and summoned a wagon to come there and announced that she had the killer in custody. The homicide squad room broke out in a round of cheers and applause. Ben was so proud. With his head down in a silent prayer for keeping Rachael safe, he entered his office to wait.

Quickly, squads and vans arrived as if they materialized from nowhere. Before Rachael would let anyone move Johnny, she directed that photos be taken of him on the ground and the proximity of the knife. She also required pictures of him when they stood him up, with all the blood on him and his clothes. Then she permitted the uniform officers to place him in a paddy wagon for transport downtown. She gave strict orders that no one was to question him and they were to escort the prisoner directly to the Homicide offices and give him to Lieutenant Ori, only. The look on Rachael's face told them she meant every word.

Before Rachael returned to her office and her prisoner, she had a stop to make. She proceeded to the Polachek residence where she met the grieving parents among about twenty family members and friends. She told them how sorry she was for their loss. Rachael held their Mother's hand and told her that she had arrested the man who killed her daughters. The woman's hand squeezed her hand tightly, as if to say thank you. When she left the Polachek home, she received a hug from the twins' father, and knew that throughout the course of the trial, she would see these poor souls numerous times.

On her way downtown, Rachael finally permitted herself to shed tears for the girls. The adrenaline was draining from her now and the humanity of it all momentarily suppressed her anger. She resolved herself to make certain that the bastard she arrested would die for what he did that day.

As she entered Headquarters, every officer she encountered either applauded slowly, saluted or told her "Good job, Sarge." When she entered the Homicide offices, she was met with a standing ovation. Ben was in the middle of them, smiling.

When the place finally quieted and Rachael had shaken every hand, she went into Ben's office and told him everything.

"His name is Johnny Lee Childress, Rachael," Ben advised. "We've ID'd him from a prior arrest. Officers recognized him. He's got one hell of a rap sheet." Ben handed Rachael a stack of papers from the Federal Bureau of Investigation reflecting arrests and convictions, his "rap sheet."

As Rachael read the series of arrests and convictions, she just shook her head. So many times the justice system had failed to act and to put him away. Childress had assaults, domestic violence, drugs, carrying a concealed weapon and child enticement charge.

She made a mental note to pull that file.

Someone advised Ben that media people were outside and wanted an interview or press conference. Ben called the Chief of Police, Charles Pitts, who said he would be ready to meet the media with him and Rachael in twenty minutes. They would meet in the lobby and he would have a podium set up there.

Rachael wanted to interview Childress, not talk about the wonderful job they were doing. Hell, if they were doing such a bang-up job in protecting the citizens of Chicago, two nine year old girls would be getting ready for bed and not laying on cold, stainless steel tables in the morgue. Rachael got Ben to cover for her with the Chief of Police and headed for the holding cell where Johnny was handcuffed to the wall.

"Do you remember your rights, Childress?" Rachael said as she opened the door.

"Fucking bitch. You knocked out my front tooth. Look!" Johnny said, as he attempted to smile. There, in the middle of his even teeth, was a gap like the front end of an Edsel.

"It gives you character. How's your nose?"

"You broke it, you fucking whore!" Johnny shouted.

"You have nice language skills. Do you want medical treatment for your injuries?"

"Fuck you!"

"Great. OK, would you care to give me your official statement? Then, we can meet the reporters waiting to catch a glimpse of you downstairs. The Chief is meeting with them right now, as a matter of fact. You're a celebrity, you piece of shit," Rachael snapped, then said, "Oops, I'm sorry. That wasn't professional of me to call you a piece of shit. I'm sorry." She smiled and said, "I meant animal dung."

At that, Rachael summoned Emilio Ortiz, a relatively recent addition to Homicide and eager to solidify his prominence as a detective. Together, they set up the video equipment in their interrogation room. Rachael wanted no errors to permeate Johnny's trial and if or when he confessed, she wanted the statement ironclad.

"Come along, Hollywood," he said as he removed the handcuff from the wall. "Behave or I'll let the Sergeant whip your ass some more."

"Fuckin' bitch is wacko, man. She tried to break my fucking arm, man. And the psycho-bitch knocked out my front tooth. Look."

"I agree with the Sarge. It gives you character," Emilio said.

"Fuck you!"

For the next ninety minutes, Rachael and Emilio covered every step Johnny Lee Childress took in carrying out his goals that day. He simply saw the girls and his loins and testosterone took control. While he held Samantha at knife point, scaring Sarina into submission or see her sister slashed, he kicked the door open to the apartment. If someone were inside, he already had a hostage and they would do as he said. He parked the stolen mini-van and walked to the block party looking for free grub. When he ran into the twins between the two houses, he suddenly wasn't hungry any more.

The details of the slashing and genital mutilation enraged Emilio. His hands shook as he listened to this animal boast about his sexual prowess and how the twins enjoyed the sex. He felt like puking.

When the interview was over and Emilio had fingerprinted and photographed Childress for the booking process, he locked him in the holding cell and went to the restroom to wash his hands and face. He needed a time out. He had never encountered the likes of Childress and now knew how the officers felt who had arrested John Wayne Gacey, the notorious child killer.

As it would turn out, the mug shot of Johnny Lee Childress, smiling with that missing front tooth, would become one of the most widely published mug shots in history. That gap-toothed grin appeared on the front pages of every syndicated newspaper in the country. It made Emilio mad that they made him a household name. And for the wrong reason.

Rachael napped for a few hours in Ben's office. She intended to deliver her prisoner for his initial appearance in Circuit Court and found little sense in wasting the travel time. She kept spare clothes in the gym bag in her car and would change into those. His appearance was scheduled for one o'clock and that would give her time to meet with Tommy Dorf for the autopsy results.

When Ben woke Rachael up, he had two cups of steaming coffee in hand and bagels from the Meals on Wheels truck out front.

"I heard you were in here. I figured you'd like something to eat."

"Thanks," Rachael said as she sat up on his couch. She had spent more than one night on that couch and so had Ben. It was a comfortable piece he found at a yard sale. Made of "distressed" leather, it was made of the same tanning process as that of bomber jackets.

"So, how did the interview go with our star out there?" Ben asked as he pointed towards Childress with his blueberry bagel.

"Terrible. I mean great I mean he confessed to everything. Took Emilio and me on a virtual tour of his twisted world. Ben, it was terrible. It's all on video," she said proudly as she pointed an onion bagel at the compact disks resting on his desk.

"You did good, Rachael. I heard there was some police brutality involved, though," he said, smiling broadly.

"Sonofabitch attacked me with a knife, Ben. Crazy. I had to defend myself." At this she returned his smile and they both began to laugh aloud.

"It gives him character, according to Emilio."

"Yeah. And the broken nose like John Wayne."

Ben accompanied Rachael to see Tommy Dorf. He really did not want her alone when she heard what he had done. Tommy was waiting for them at his desk.

"Good morning you two," Tommy began. "Rachael Hart, you look like you belong on one of my tables in there."

"Thanks. I spent the night on Ben's couch upstairs. I feel like I belong on one of those tables. You have coffee, Tommy?" she asked, waving her empty cup.

Tommy pointed at the fresh brew in the corner and as Rachael was filling her cup, the M.E. produced two crisp copies of his autopsy reports for both girls.

"It seems like my sergeant here wasn't the only one working late here last night," Ben remarked.

"I have my own couch, thank you," the M.E. responded and they all laughed.

"Ben, it wasn't pretty. This guy Childress really hates the female species. A psychiatrist could write a textbook on this maniac and what he did here. Did he make a statement, Rachael?"

"It was more than that, Tommy. It was a mixture of press release and autobiography, with step by step instructions on murdering little girls. It's all on video and all very disgusting."

"He's a pedophile-necrophile-sociopathic piece of shit," Tommy barked. And, I wrote that pompous ass State's Attorney a personal note that if he does not seek the death penalty in this case, I'll resign."

Rachael and Ben stood there looking at the usually unflappable Tommy Dorf. They had never seen him this riled or use such language in any other case.

"I'll relay your message personally to Mr. Pompous Ass this morning, as I have a meeting with him after I present Childress to the Cook County deputies for court," Rachael advised and added, "I called him a piece of shit too. Just after I whipped his ass and knocked out his front tooth."

Smiles spread around the room like an infection.

"Ah, the Fighting Irish. I would have loved to watch you."

Ben, on the other hand, made a mental note to have a very personal talk with Rachael about that topic. Rachael made no mention in her report of how Childress could have gotten the drop on her before she had the opportunity to draw her weapon. In police work, if you didn't want to lie, you omitted. When defense attorneys couldn't read the unwritten, they couldn't impeach you at trial. He needed to ask her what really happened out there.

"Evidently, he liked Samantha most, as it appears that she died first. That must have been her blood all over the living room walls. Sarina watched her sister die. He raped Sarina, and then cut her. She was dead when he mutilated her genital area. Samantha's sexual assault was post-mortem. The vaginal walls were relaxed in death and there was little tearing. Her genital area was devastated with a knife as well. The pool of blood on the bed resulted in drainage from the torso. Causes of death are exsanguinations due to near decapitation. By the way, I matched the knife you caught him with to the wounds on both victims, and they are consistent, in my expert opinion."

"Jesus, Tommy, this guy raped that girl after he almost cut her head off?" Rachael asked in total revulsion.

He simply nodded. "I have already taken the precautionary measures to seal both reports. I did so to protect the evidentiary aspects, according to the court order. I really did it to protect the parents of the girls from having media trot that horrific information to sell their newspapers. Tell Mordeci no offense for me?"

"We will," Ben said as they turned to leave. There was nothing else to be said here and both cops needed some distance from what they had learned.

Ben had yet to meet Mr. Wonderful, Johnny Lee Childress, and found himself looking forward to meeting the monster who had defiled those kids.

"I'll go with you to get our media star for the trip to 26th and California," Ben said. The Cook County Criminal Courts Building was already surrounded by news vans, their broadcasting masts reaching skyward. Rachael would deliver her prisoner to deputies in Division One, the oldest yet most secure lock-up located in the Cook County Jail. There was a suite in the basement of Division One, reserved for those facing death penalties. A seven-by-ten foot cell had Childress's name on it already. At least he would be housed alone, lest the other prisoners have their way with his "mangina." Child molesters were not revered by even the most hardcore criminals and were usually raped themselves.

After handing over Childress, Rachael had a meeting with Scott Schroeder, the Cook County State's Attorney. He was a tall, charismatic, charming bag of hot air who enticed voters to give him the position. His political ambitions were lofty and he would like to be Governor some day. Recently, his career was almost ruined when the Associated Press released evidence that a man named Eddie Veins had murdered an entire jury while avenging his sister. He dodged that political silver bullet by saying that it was a federal grand jury investigation and beyond his personal knowledge.

Schroeder was dressed for success today. After meeting with the arresting officer in the Childress case, he was going to make a grand speech to the awaiting media and praise the wonderful work by the Chicago Police Department and personally shake the hand of the arresting officer. The press would love it.

Rachael arrived wearing slacks, blouse and light windbreaker which concealed her lithe figure and her weapon. She was not dressed for the media. She was dressed for work. She was not interested in media exposure. She was there to begin the process of retribution.

"Mr. Schroder," she said, refusing to call him "sir." "I have a message for you from the Medical Examiner, Mr. Dorf. He said that if you don't seek the death penalty, he'll retire."

"Thank you, detective. I received his note earlier this morning."

She tendered Tommy Dorf's autopsy reports and Schroeder never even bothered to read them. Rachael did not like the State's Attorney. She thinks he is a pompous ass!

"Sergeant, I see by your star, shall we go downstairs? I have a press conference arranged and I'm sure they want to meet you as arresting officer."

"Unacceptable, Mr. Schroeder. I work undercover and photo ops would undermine my ability to function in that capacity and compromise my position in the Department."

Schroeder knew he couldn't order her to attend a press meeting and he had seen her on talk shows about women's rights and domestic violence, so she was saying that she didn't like him and that was that.

"It's just as well. You're not dressed for it anyway," he chided.

Rachael wondered what this politician would look like with a gap in his front teeth like Childress.

"As arresting officer, I have some input into the disposition in this case. I want no plea bargain and the death penalty. If you don't announce that you're filing for the death penalty and that there will be no negotiating, you will see me in the media and hear my words. I promise!"

Without waiting for Schroeder to respond, she strode out of his office and headed for the courtroom where Johnny Lee would make his cameo appearance at one o'clock.

Mordeci found her in the hallway and took her to lunch in the cafeteria there in the building. He did not push her for information and she appreciated that. They talked about Schroeder and his ambitions, which seemed unattainable to Mort.

"Hell, he was almost beaten at the last election. He needs all the good press he can get. Your arrest is great for his personal agenda and crusade. I'm surprised that he didn't want you with him at his grandstand with the media."

"He did. I told him it was unacceptable." They both laughed like kids at lunchtime in school. It was perfect medicine for Rachael. She needed a friend right then and Mort was just that.

Mort accompanied Rachael to the reserved seating in the courtroom. Although it was reserved for law enforcement and not reporters, he was with the arresting officer, who was also a Detective Sergeant. No one voiced any objections.

The case against Childress was finally called by the clerk and a hush fell over the courtroom. Schroeder stood up at the prosecutor's table and gave his best profile for the artist and Judge.

"Let the record reflect, Your Honor, that the People of Illinois appear by their counsel, Scott Schroeder, the Cook County State's Attorney," he said in a booming voice so all could hear.

"Your Honor, my name is Nello Gamberino. I am appointed by the Cook County Public Defender's Office on behalf of Mr. Childress, who is present in open court."

Johnny Lee had been escorted into the courtroom, dressed in a bright orange jumpsuit, crimped at the bottom by the shackles that restrained his legs. He was surrounded by five burly deputies to dissuade him from flight or improper behavior. Johnny smiled at everyone, that gaping hole in his front teeth for all to see. The smile disappeared when he saw Rachael.

"Your Honor, if it please the Court, the defendant Johnny Lee Childress is charged with First Degree Homicide, Felony Homicide during the commission of an aggravated felony, namely rape, kidnapping, home invasion and murder. He is also charged with multiple counts of rape. I have just filed with the Clerk, an Information seeking the imposition of the death penalty."

"Mr. Gamberino," the Judge began, "have you received copies of the complaint and Information referred to by the People?"

"I have both, Your Honor."

"How does the Defendant plead?"

"Not guilty, Your Honor, and Not Guilty by reason of mental disease or defect," Gamberino said loudly.

The Judge enquired, "Do you request a psychological examination of the Defendant?"

"Yes, Your Honor, the motion is being filed with the Clerk at this time and is supported with my affidavit attached thereto and incorporated therein."

"Do the People object, Mr. Schroeder?" the Judge asked for the record.

"No, your Honor. We would ask that it not be delayed and the period of time excluded under the Speedy Trial Act."

"Very well. The record will reflect the plea by the Defendant, will order the psychological evaluation immediately and the period of time to accomplish the evaluation is excludable time under the Speedy Trial Act. Furthermore, the Defendant will be remanded to the Cook County Sheriff without bail. A preliminary hearing is scheduled for one week from today, unless the People have filed a True Bill of Indictment and the arraignment will be scheduled by the Clerk thereafter."

With a bang of the gavel, it was over and Childress was being escorted back to the holding cell downstairs.

As Rachael turned to look at everyone in the courtroom, she noticed the artist sketching her profile with pastel chalk, along with the Judge, prosecutor and Johnny Lee Childress with his gap-toothed smile. That drawing adorned almost every newspaper in Chicago.

Chapter 4

Thomas Kindt is the current warden at Thames, the maximum security prison recently constructed which houses death row. He is a large man, brownish-gray hair, a ruddy complexion but with a boilerplate even-handed disposition in dealing with inmates and staff alike. If an inmate was right, he would not automatically side with the staff.

As a general rule, a warden who is charged with carrying out an execution should not actively demonstrate any desire to kill another human being, no matter what they were convicted of doing. It is a solemn ritual which is to be dignified and mechanical. The men chosen for the death squad are honed in skills that meet those expectations of professionalism. However, all these rules and protocol were suspended in the case Warden Kindt faced in a few days. He was earnestly looking forward to killing Johnny Childress. He would do so with his bare hands if he could. He despised the man who was convicted of savagely killing two children who could have been the models for Precious Moments figurines. He boasted of the monstrous acts he did to those innocents and everyone anticipated his upcoming execution, including Thomas Kindt and his entire staff.

Outside the prison's security fences, marchers were carrying placards and banners, celebrating Childress's state authorized murder. It reminded Kindt of Ted Bundy and his execution in Florida. Only this was Illinois and these revelers were angry that the justice system had taken so long to kill an admitted child murderer and Kindt had added extra perimeter security just in case someone wanted to hurry along Childress's appointment to meet his maker. The place resembled Mardi Gras in New Orleans and Thomas couldn't fault their good cheer. Johnny Lee Childress was going to die and even Kindt found himself smiling.

"Warden," his Captain said on the phone, "the doc is about ready to cut Childress. I think you may want to be here in case there's a problem."

"I'll be there in a few minutes. I don't want anybody doing anything until I'm there," Kindt said as he began tidying up his desk as a distraction.

When Kindt arrived on the row, he noticed several of his staff waiting for him outside the officer's station.

Hollywood makes millions of dollars portraying "the row" in the worst possible way. At Thames, prisoners are not locked in cells with iron bars, where they can train mice to roll thimbles across the floor or where they smoke pack after pack of cigarettes awaiting their trip to the gas chamber. At Thames, the condemned are housed in an antiseptically clean environment. The hallways are brightly lit, the cells are made of concrete block which is reinforced inside by steel rods, the cells have solid steel doors and they don't sing "Swing Low Sweet Chariot" to pass the time, unless there is nothing to watch on television in their cells. However, there is the lingering smell of death in the air. Or, the smell of the Reaper.

"OK, gentlemen. Are we ready?" Kindt said.

They nodded in agreement and in unison they headed for Johnny Lee's cell.

"Mr. Childress," the Warden began after they had handcuffed Johnny from behind through the slot in the door, "the doctor here needs to prepare your leg. He needs to shave a spot on your left leg. We need you to sit on your bunk, please."

Johnny Lee complied and the doctor removed bandage scissors from his black medical bag and snipped off the left pant leg about twelve inches above the knee, turning that side into summer shorts.

As Johnny watched with some amusement at all the attention and six officers in his cell, the doctor deftly removed a small syringe from the bag and slid the needle under the skin.

"Hey, asshole, what the fuck did you just do, poison me? What was in the fucking needle?"

"Relax, Mr. Childress, it's a topical anesthetic," the prison doctor responded.

"What the fuck do I need that for to shave my fucking leg?"

An officer sat down on each side of Johnny Lee and leaned towards him. They laid him back on the bed and then placed his right foot on the floor, giving the doctor better access to the inside of the left leg. That is where the femoral artery runs and is second only to carotid arteries in blood flow. This is the artery needed to pump the quantity of lethal chemicals into the condemned.

"What the fuck is this? Get the fuck off me!" Johnny shouted. No one was listening. As he began to struggle, the officers merely sat on him.

"Relax, Mr. Childress," the Warden said, attempting to calm him down.

"What's that fucking quack doing to me?" Johnny did not feel the Betadine being spread around an area on the inside of his leg. The doctor removed a bundle from the bag and laid it on the floor. When he unrolled the linen, Johnny saw the scalpel.

"Hey, you fucking quack. What the fuck are you doing?" Johnny's demands were useless.

The doctor made a three inch incision in the skin and surface tissue in the leg, giving him access to the artery. He produced a catheter, which he swiftly inserted into the artery and began stitching Johnny's leg around it. He was using double-ought silk thread to anchor the catheter and to staunch the minimal blood flow.

"Hey, you fucking piece of shit, you cut me, you prick."

"Mr. Childress," the Warden said sternly, "this is standard procedure. This is where the chemicals are introduced, not in your arm like they used to. Just let us do our jobs, OK?"

"I'm gonna pull that fucking thing out, you assholes. My date ain't here and it's gonna get called off."

"Mr. Childress, that will have to remain where it is. If you try to pull it out, you'll bleed to death," the doctor replied.

"Fuck you, quack. Just watch me get that outta there."

"I'm sorry to hear that Mr. Childress," Kindt said. With a simple nod, Kindt started a series of moves his staff had trained for many times. One of the officers produced leg shackles and attached them to Johnny's legs. He was then placed on his back and a leather strap applied to each wrist and ankle. These straps were then affixed to loops on each corner of the metal bunk. Johnny Lee lay spread-eagled on the bunk and immobilized.

"We can't let you yank that out, Mr. Childress. You'll have to remain as you are tonight."

"Fuck you! You can't leave me like this," he screamed.

"Sue us, Mr. Childress," Kindt said warmly with a smile.

"Fuck you!"

As the officers filed out of Johnny's cell, they could hear him struggling with his restraints. The leather was thick and even sheepskin, lined for comfort. It would take a very strong man to break the two inch wide straps, or a bull, maybe.

Only the Warden remained behind. "Mr. Childress, every thirty minutes, my officers will return to turn you over. We don't want you to be uncomfortable. If they are convinced that you will not remove the catheter in your leg, they will be authorized to let you go. If they do that and you pull the catheter out, we will chain you down, re-insert the catheter and you will remain in that same position until we escort you to the...other room." Kindt had to think a moment of what he should call the room where Johnny will die. Staff and the manual refer to it as a chamber, but that might frighten Johnny Lee even more and make it more difficult for his staff.

The Warden exited the cell and the solid door was run home with a solid thunk of the case hardened lock falling into place. He took one last look through the security window with the steel mesh crisscrossing inside and tried not to smile.

"You guys know the procedure. Every thirty minutes offer to turn him over. If he needs to use the toilet, call a nurse and let him use a bedpan or soil himself. If you are convinced he'll behave and leave that catheter alone, you can let him up. If something happens, call me at the office. I'm sleeping on the couch tonight in case a Judge or the Governor's Office needs to speak to me."

"Yes sir," the Captain said. He too was spending the night in the prison. He was concerned about the goings on outside the prison and would not stand down until the threat was over.

When the Warden returned to his office, the red light on his answering machine was flashing. He listened to the message and immediately returned the call.

"I'm returning your call, sir," Kindt said.

The Director of the Illinois Department of Corrections was no politico. He had been a warden himself over one of its most violent prisons, Statesville, near Joliet. Statesville was the institution which held death row before Thames. It was also referred to as "the killing field," where bloodshed was a daily event and the three story hospital within its forty-foot high concrete walls, was generally full of wounded. He was no neophyte to such settings and wanted to assure himself that all was well at Thames.

He had been the one to assign Thomas Kindt to the Thames post. He had known Kindt for years and admired his even temperament and disposition. When Illinois courts began affirming death penalty cases and prisoners neared their dates to die, he had chosen Kindt to succeed J.D. Barhhill, who had resigned after a rather controversial execution.

"How is everything there, Tom?" the Director asked.

"Everything is under control. The people outside are not posing a real problem. They're looking forward to the execution, actually. They aren't harassing staff at shift change, except to ask questions about Childress."

"And how is the star of the show holding up?" the Director responded.

"We have him four-pointed right now. After the doc inserted the catheter for tomorrow, Childress said he would pull it out. So, we put him down."

"Make certain you follow policy, Tom. We don't want his lawyers trying to make a federal case out of this. I'll be here in my office if you need me. How are you holding up, Tom?"

"To be honest with you, I'm looking forward to tomorrow. This guy deserves to go and he has been a pain in the ass since he arrived here. I'm sorry to say it, but personally, I'll enjoy watching him go. Perhaps I should resign after this? It's wrong for me to look forward to killing someone!" Kindt exclaimed.

"Nonsense, Thomas. You're the best man for the job there and as a man and father, your emotions are justified. I know the execution will come off professionally and without a hitch."

"Has the Governor given any indication of what his decision will be?" Kindt inquired.

"The last I heard, Tom, he was planning on coming there. I'm not privy why."

"Great. If you hear, will you let me know? I'll be in my office all night, too."

After Kindt hung up from talking to his boss, the machine's red, cycloptic eye winked furiously. As he listened to the messages, he recognized a bevy of names from such programs as "60 Minutes," "20/20," "Dateline NBC," and "CNN News." Everyone wanted to ask him a myriad of questions. The most bizarre is what Johnny Lee Childress was eating as his last meal? Morbid bastards!

The reality was that Johnny Lee had requested fried chicken, sweet cornbread, mashed potatoes and triple fudge ice cream. Amazing how compassionate the justice system is to those who brutally murder someone - enough to feed them a gourmet meal so that they can soil themselves with it when they die. If it were up to him, they would get whatever prison population was eating. If they didn't want it, so be it. It wasn't like they were going to starve to death. Kindt was sure Johnny Lee had not treated the twins to Wendy's or ice cream before he ravaged them. But, policy was policy and until that was changed, he would abide by it. That didn't mean he would have to like it.

At around midnight, Johnny Lee Childress's attorneys showed up requesting to see him before meeting with their esteemed client. Someone must have let them know that Johnny was a little tied up at that moment. He would have to find out who ran their mouth.

About twenty minutes later, having been pat searched and their briefcases run through scanners, an officer showed them to Kindt's office.

"Mr. Kindt," the flamboyant Amaranta blustered, "we object to your restraining our client like an animal to his bunk. We demand that you release him immediately." He wanted to be so convincing.

"You demand nothing here, Mr. Amaranta. He is four-pointed because he promised to remove the catheter the doctor inserted into his leg which is a prerequisite for tomorrow. I will not permit him to disrupt the orderly procedure. As it stands now, your client will be executed. Unless, of course, you have a court order staying said execution or the Governor has chosen to commute the sentence. I have not been informed of either event and you, sir, shall conduct yourself in a non-inflammatory fashion or you will be removed from my facility. Am I quite clear?"

"Mr. Kindt," Nello Gamberino interjected. "Please forgive my associate's outburst. Of course we do not wish to make Mr. Childress's last hours more difficult. We were not fully advised of the totality of circumstances and completely understand your position with decorum and procedure. We offer you our assistance in making Mr. Childress aware that this is normal procedure and that you mean no harm."

Kindt liked this guy Gamberino. Smooth. Very effectual.

"Mr. Gamberino, as you know, we take no pleasure in our obligation to follow orders and extinguish a life. However, we cannot permit your client to harm himself by removing the catheter and bleeding all over the place. Further, the procedure was painless and performed by our prison's doctor. It is all part of the protocol. I will have someone escort you to his cell. We would appreciate your help in making your client understand and compliant. If you assure my staff that he will behave, I will tell them to release him. I have already advised your client of the consequences."

"Thank you," Nello said as he glared at his associate to hold his tongue.

Kindt wanted to add, "Go to hell, smart ass," to Amaranta, but didn't. Instead he phoned his officers on the row and advised them of what he had offered the attorneys.

The warden decided not to return any of the network's calls. Instead, he removed his shoes and obtained a quilt, given to him by a man who was on death row until his sentence was overturned by a court of appeals, from the closet. As he laid down, exhaustion overcame him and he was fast asleep almost instantly.

Chapter 5

Tom Kindt remembered the day that the Illinois Department of Corrections Apprehension Unit brought Johnny Lee Childress from Statesville, where the Cook County Sheriff's Department dropped him. Death row prisoners were not transported like those serving determinate sentences, on D.O.C. buses. Condemned prisoners were brought by special van, with a marked squad car behind. Johnny arrived on a Saturday night at about eleven o'clock. Everyone knew the media wanted a glimpse of him entering Thames, so the move was done covertly. Not one reporter was there.

Kindt was relatively new to Thames, having recently assumed control after Barnhill called it quits. He had not had to execute anyone yet and was not certain he was up to the task morally. Then he met Johnny Lee Childress

The Captain of his officers advised him that the van was at the sally port.

"Let's go greet our new guest then," Kindt said, as he donned his sport coat and headed for the door. The Captain was dressed in "D.O.C. Green," sort of olive drab jacket and pants, with a light green shirt, with officer's insignia and "scrambled eggs," across the bill. He was a veteran from maximum security trenches.

The scene of Johnny Lee's arrival reminded you of the big guy's arrival in "The Green Mile," by Stephen King, only it wasn't Percy hollering "dead man, dead man walking," it was Johnny Lee. He woke up everyone on the row with his antics. Most of the prisoners knew of him already and shouted at him as he passed by their cells.

"Hey, sweet-thang, why don't you come in here with me and sit on my lap. I'll show you my dolly," one convict said to him.

"Fuck you!" Johnny responded.

"Hey pervert. I got somthin' in here that belongs to you. This dick!" another con said as the place erupted in laughter.

"Very funny, you stupid nigger. Fuck you!" was the response that hushed the row that night. Yep, he knew how to make friends and make a grand appearance. And that was only in the first few minutes.

The ensuing days brought racial epithets hurled at staff and cons alike. Johnny slung insults from sexually assaulting their wives and children, including boys, to wishing he could twist his knife inside them and savor the anguished screams and the sweet smell of blood in the air.

Numerous members of the staff were physically restrained by other staff as they attempted to enter Johnny's cell and make any further appeals a moot issue, with their bare hands.

The prison psychologist, Dr. Warren Clifford, was a frequent visitor to the row, but found himself there more often after Johnny arrived at Thames. The other cons complained of not being able to sleep, more stress and uncontrollable rage. He dispensed more medications after Johnny arrived on the row. He considered forced medication on Johnny, but was advised by the Department of Corrections counsel that it was unconstitutional.

Dr. Clifford found himself meeting with staff from the row, treating them for stress and trauma. A couple of them, fine officers, too, he had to relieve from their posts on the row and have them reassigned to other positions which were less stressful.

He interviewed Johnny Lee and wished that he hadn't. He found Johnny reprehensible as a human life form, but a textbook example of a sociopath with a personality disorder. He was happy that Johnny was in prison where he couldn't defile any more children. After all, he too was a father, even if his ten year old daughter lived with his ex-wife in Wisconsin.

As a professional, Clifford tried to keep his emotions out of his captive practice there at the prison. He dressed moderately well, his suits coming from national retailers and were not tailor-made. He was in his mid-thirties, was reasonably fit and stayed active. He has coal black hair, neatly cut, with a full beard and mustache, closely cropped and meticulously sculpted. He looked like a shrink. He was gregarious and affable with everyone he met and took his profession seriously. Quite often he was summoned to the prison because some inmate attempted suicide or threatened to harm himself. He didn't mind though, as he sincerely believed he was performing a service to everyone concerned. His beliefs wavered when he interviewed the man who tortured and raped two little girls and boasted about it as if he belonged amongst the great serial killers or cannibals in history.

Warren Clifford, like the Warden, would remain at the prison in case Johnny Lee or one of the other cons became distraught over their own destiny and a needle. His office had the nicest couch of all.

Another figure who attempted to embrace Johnny Lee was the Chaplain. A Catholic priest, actually, he had found his calling in prison ministry and enjoyed the sessions with cons who devoutly studied the Bible. Father Abraham Birney is a diminutive African-American whose heritage he boasts has lineage to great tribal chiefs and warriors. He roams the halls and recreation yard without fear. He is revered by all the cons as a friend, not a "hack-in-black" as customarily associated with prison clergy. Besides the Bible and God's word, he is fluent in the history of the Chicago Bears and George S. Hallas. He has a picture of him with Hallas on the wall in his office. Since 1986 he has been waiting for them to win another Super Bowl and bring the trophy home!

"Lovie Smith is building a great team. Just watch them next year," he would always say. In 2006, they came real close and he wore Bears clothing to work and had dispensation from Warden Kindt to distribute cookies shaped like football players in Bears jerseys to every prisoner on the row. To all except Johnny Lee, that is.

"Here, my son, I have something special for you," Father Birney said as he held a cookie in the food slot in Johnny's door.

"I don't want your fucking cookie or your fucking Bible-thumping, you fucking nigger."

It was difficult even for the man of God to remain civil. He withdrew the treat, closed the slot door and made the sign of the cross. He would pray extra hard for Johnny Lee, instead of letting hatred enter is ministry.

"Father Birney, why do you even bother with that piece of...waste?" the con said. "If any of us could get our hands on him, we'd save the state the trouble. Sorry Father."

"Don't let anger and hatred enter your heart. He's afraid. If you let him upset you, he wins."

Johnny Lee Childress had been on death row less than ninety days and had met most everyone, and all were looking forward to the day he walked his last walk. God forgive him, but even Father Birney was among them.

The good Father would remain at the prison all night and day, in case Johnny Lee discovered there may be a God after all and wanted to pray for forgiveness. Only, he had no couch, but had scrounged up an old Army cot, which served him quite well. God provides.

Chapter 6

The elder statesman and bastion upon which the contemporary views and opinions of the United States Court of Appeals for the Seventh Circuit is Judge Frank J. Easterman. He has been a member of the Seventh Circuit for decades.

The Seventh Circuit covers Illinois, Indiana and Wisconsin and is responsible for reviewing all decisions by United States District Courts in those states.   The Judges in the federal system, contrary to state judiciaries, are appointed for life. Once commissioned by Presidential authority, there is little that can be done to remove them and strip them of the immense power associated with their position, unless they commit a felony or they die. Until Easterman chooses to retire, he will continue to serve, even if they have to carry him to work.

When hearing and deciding appeals, a "panel" is assigned to each case. The clerk is supposed to make random assignments, but Easterman likes to work with two particular comrades-at-arms, Judge Evans and Manlon. Research by defense attorneys indicates a non-random selection process, but the Clerk will not breach the sanctity of the office or snitch on the Judges. Without that valuable information, defense attorneys can only speculate and that is insufficient to justify intervention by the Supreme Court.

And so it is, Easterman and his cronies were the "random" panel given the case of **People v. Johnny Lee Childress**. The case came to the federal bench as a result of attorneys representing Johnny, who, having exhausted all available State remedies, had filed a "Petition for Writ of Habeas Corpus," pursuant to Title 28, United States Code, Section 2254. The petition was filed in the district court in Springfield, Illinois, which was the court assigned to the geographical location where Johnny is held. By stipulation of the prosecutors and defense counsel, the matter was transferred to the District Court in Chicago and assigned to Judge James Hinderman.

Hinderman had been repeatedly called "The Nazi of District Court," not because of his ethnicity, but because he goose-stepped to a silent agenda likened to Adolph Hitler's theme of retribution. He loves sentencing and federal prosecutors love his heavy-handed tactics at sentencing. He is "prosecutor friendly" and defense attorneys cringe when they see his name stamped on a file to which they are assigned. They especially try to avoid having hearings before him after lunchtime, where he ventures to his favorite barrister hangout and deposits several martinis down his gullet. He cannot operate a car when he returns from "lunch," but he can reign from a federal bench!

Hinderman wrote a scathing opinion in regards to Johnny Lee's attempts to curry favor with him in reversing the conviction and/or the death sentence. He was abusive in his language and in a literary method, insulted the defense attorneys and assassinated their character. He called their arguments ludicrous, meritless and frivolous. All of these terms in the legal world, represent slander against an attorney.

Nello Gamberino and Sam Amaranta posited legal theories and questions regarding Johnny Lee Childress's competence before the commission of the crime, which would negate the necessary degree of culpability to support a conviction for first degree murder. That was a matter decided by the trial Judge in Cook County Circuit Court, not the jury, until the deliberation stage.

Defense counsel accurately argued that there are distinct determinations that must be made in regards to competency. First, is the accused in a current state of mental competency which permits him to understand the charges against him, and to assist his counsel in preparation and defense of those charges? This question is answered by a Judge, not a jury, and is given great deference by courts receiving that determination during appellate review.

The second determination, was the accused competent at the time of the commission of the offense? This is a matter that remains in the purview of the jury and is not reversed, as a general rule, by reviewing courts. If a quantity of evidence existed at trial where a reasonable jury could convict, the conviction would not be reversed. The sole caveat to this rule was that the jurors also had to be given accurate, concise and constitutionally permissible instructions upon which to rely during their deliberations. This is the quagmire where the lower courts and prosecutors generally find themselves in challenges under the Eighth and Fourteenth Amendments.

Third, was the contemporary concern by the Supreme Court, that condemned prisoners must comprehend the gravamen of their actions and the rationality of their impending execution. Although "diminished capacity" may not be a complete defense to the crime, a lesser degree of *mens rea*, or state of mind, is what is called a "mitigating factor" in the penalty phase of a capital case and is considered in the validity in the imposition of a death sentence. Besides being a valid basis upon which to not impose a sentence of death, the Supreme Court has held that it is cruel and unusual punishment to execute someone so lacking in competency that he does not understand why his life is being terminated. A condemned person may become mentally incompetent awaiting execution and upon a valid psychological determination and presentment to a court, avoid execution altogether.

The posture of the appeal before Judge Easterman is the colorable issues presented by Johnny Lee's attorneys. But only in two regards, as the jury had made the factual determination that he was not legally insane when he slaughtered the Polacheck twins, but whether he was entitled to a serious and meaningful consideration during the sentencing phase of the trial, to an instruction that his psychosis and disorders were to be given weight by the jury when recommending death. Also, whether or not Johnny Lee Childress had a rational understanding as to why he was being killed himself. The attorneys alleged that he has become so psychotic while on death row and the "death row phenomenon," that he should not be put to death.

"The Death Row Phenomenon" is a psychosis whose genesis lies in the conditions of death row housing, the duration of their stay on death row awaiting execution, the degree of violence to which they are exposed, the care they are given on death row and the method of execution. Together, these conditions can create a psychosis so deeply engrained in a condemned prisoner's mind as to drive them over the edge of insanity and render them fundamentally unable to appreciate the seriousness of their respective crimes and their impending demise.

Johnny Lee's attorneys had made a showing of diminished capacity. The federal prosecutors defending the State had conceded as much, which obviated a need for another examination by federal forensic psychologists, and the expense. The dominant questions regarded the jury instructions and Johnny Lee's state of mind today. Easterman had decided a long time ago that he would deny the appeal and vacate any stay of execution now in existence. In relevant part, his Opinion, concurred in by lapdogs Evans and Manlon, read as follows:

"Since 1976, the Supreme Court has spent considerable time attempting to determine the constitutional parameters of mitigating and aggravating circumstances as utilized by the various states in the determination of whether to impose capital punishment in a particular case. *Furman v. Georgia*, 408 U.S. 238. Any statutory scheme which limits the mitigating factors to be considered is offensive to the Constitution. *Lockett v. Ohio*, 438 U.S. 586. The Appellant in this case, Johnny lee Childress, contends that the jury who recommended the imposition of the death penalty was not accurately charged or permitted to give a meaningful consideration to the various psychosis and personality disorders from which he suffers, as mitigation. This contention is misplaced.

The advisory jury was instructed that it could consider as aggravating circumstances the presence of aggravated felonies of rape, kidnapping, home invasion and necrophilia. The jury was further instructed that even if aggravating circumstances were present, the death penalty need not be imposed if the jury found they were outweighed by mitigating circumstances, that is, circumstances not construing justification or excuse for the offenses committed, but which in fairness and mercy, may be considered as extenuating or reducing the degree of danger.

The Appellant produced two psychologists during the trial who attested to various maladies he suffers from, none of which excused the commission of the underlying offenses. Instead, the Appellant now contends that the aggravating and mitigating factors were in equipoise and that the jury should have been instructed that in such circumstances, the State had not met its burden to demonstrate that the aggravating factors outweighed (emphasis added) those in mitigation.

This Court does not intend to impose that burden upon the State, but instead places that burden squarely upon a criminal defendant.

The Appellant next contends, albeit in a circumlocutious fashion, that since his arrival on death row, his psychological impairments have manifested to a degree which now renders him incompetent.

The Supreme Court has held that imposing a sentence of death upon a mentally retarded criminal is unconstitutional and violated the 'cruel and unusual' proscriptions of the Eighth Amendment. **Atkins v. Virginia**, 536 U.S. 304. The District Court rejected this argument as baseless, in that Appellant failed to provide convincing evidence to support that allegation. This court will not reverse a district court in such circumstances unless it is determined the Court committed an abuse of discretion.

For the foregoing reasons, the denial of habeas relief in all respects is affirmed."

In a separate Order, Easterman dissolved the automatic stay of execution. A new date was set for Johnny Lee Childress to die.

Both defense attorneys decided to apply to the Supreme Court for what is called "certiorari," where the nation's high court sorts through thousands of cases each year and selects approximately one hundred-fifty cases of first impression, which are cases with issues never decided before. These appeals are discretionary, in that the appeal is not a matter of right and the Appellant is simply asking the Supreme Court to please hear the case.

Each Circuit Court of Appeals has one Supreme Court Justice who acts as liaison and can hear emergency motions or requests. In Johnny Lee's case, that Justice stayed execution, as a mechanical and prophylactic measure, as a criminal does have the absolute right to *seek* Supreme Court review, they do not enjoy the right of review. In Johnny's case, the Supreme Court declined to hear his case, within four months and the same Justice who spared Johnny's life four months earlier, signed a new Order setting the stage for execution.

Nello Gamberino was alone today when he met with his

client, as Sam Amaranta was appearing in a federal courtroom defending a mob boss on racketeering charges.

"What the fuck does all this mean? Where are you guys going from here?" Johnny demanded to know.

"Well, Mr. Childress, we've presented your case to the Illinois Prison Review Board, which then makes a recommendation to the Governor's Clemency Attorney. I think the hearing went well and they'll make a favorable recommendation."

"Fuck the Governor. What court are you going to?"

"I'm sorry, Mr. Childress, but Judge Easterman has directed the District Court and his fellow Judges in the Seventh Circuit not to entertain any more motions or petitions from us unless we have newly discovered evidence. No Judge will talk to us unless we have something huge."

"It's only been three years you fucking asshole. There're guys back there who write their own shit on notebook paper and have been there ten years. You fucking hotshots can't think of something?"

"You're welcome to try writing something on your own."

"Do I look like a fucking lawyer? You're supposed to know so fucking much about the law. Are you gonna let them kill me or what?"

"I'm really sorry Mr. Childress, but we have exhausted judicial resources and means. But we've got a good chance with the Governor for clemency."

"Fuck you, fuck the Governor and fuck this place. I'm outta here." At that, Johnny rose, kicked the chair he was sitting on and sent it careening around the room. Immediately, two officers rushed to subdue him, despite his hands being cuffed and attached to waist chains.

Gamberino simply rose and left the room. He had to talk to the warden to make arrangements for him and Mr. Amaranta to attend their client the last day of his life. For those twenty-four hours, they would not leave the prison.

"Mr. Gamberino, come in. I was hoping you would stop in before you left." Kindt said.

"Mr. Kindt, I would like to know your position on our being here the twenty-four hours preceding the execution if it is not stayed again?"

"Are you expecting any more stays?"

"Quite frankly, the Seventh Circuit has closed all doors to us, unless we have something substantial. I don't think we have any recourse. I am thinking more of the Governor's Office."

"I'm informed he is planning on being here. That doesn't sound promising for your client."

"I'm not willing to concede yet. But what I am wondering is if you'll accommodate co-counsel and I for the day?"

"That is no problem. Will you be attending the execution?"

"That will be up to Mr. Childress when the time arrives." When Nello left that afternoon, he knew that the sentencing court would select a new date for the execution and the statutes required no more than thirty days. He would not tell his client it would be that soon as it would only worry him needlessly. As it turned out he didn't have to.

The Warden stood before Johnny Lee's cell door and told him that he had just received a new Death Warrant and provided him with a copy, which is required by law.

In just two weeks, he was set to die.

Chapter 7

The moment had finally arrived. The State prosecutors had fought hard for this day. Defense counsel battled on all viable fronts. It was now 11:45 p.m. and in sixteen minutes, Johnny Lee Childress was set to die. Last night the prison doctor had inserted the catheter that would introduce the rush of chemicals into Johnny's femoral artery and he had not attempted to pull it out. However, they all knew that his cooperation was subject to change as the time got nearer, and they were ready. Six husky officers accompanied the Captain and Warden Kindt to his cell. The Chaplain had tried to pray with him, but he told Father Birney to leave and not in friendly language. The Priest established a vigil outside the cell in case of a change of heart.

Johnny's attorneys were taken to the witness gallery a half-hour ago, permitting the condemned a moment of solitude.

"It's time, Mr. Childress," Kindt said as they all entered the cloistered cell.

"Fuck you!" was all he uttered and when the warden noted his hostility and aggression, he was immediately taken by the arms by two officers.

"Mr. Childress," Kindt began, "I was hoping that you would accept your fate in a manly way. If you do not wish to do so, we are prepared to act accordingly."

Johnny Lee spit directly into the Warden's face. The Warden produced a handkerchief and wiped the spittle from his face, calmly.

From nowhere, a goalie mask, similar to that worn by Jason Vorhees in the "Friday the 13th" flicks, appeared and was placed over Johnny's face.

The officers took Johnny to the floor, where his legs were shackled and his hands cuffed behind his back.

"Cocksuckers! Get the fuck off me!" he shouted as the officers methodically restrained him.

The others on the row were cheering and banging on their doors in glee and support.

"It's time to meet the Reaper, fag boy," a deep baritone voice intoned.

"See ya in Hell, gay boy. I'm gonna pimp your white ass to the Devil himself," another con shouted.

When they lifted him off the floor, he was quite a sight with that mask on and his orange blaze jumpsuit with one pant leg.

As they proceeded down the hallway, the windows of each cell they passed had a face in it which had nothing nice to say.

Johnny was struggling fiercely and sobbing while he shouted, "Fuck You!" to all the heads in those windows. He folded his legs and the officers carried him as if he were a mannequin. This is what everyone was waiting to see. The tough guy was more bitch than beast and cried like a little girl.

Tom Kindt wondered if one or both of those little girls cried and begged for their life as he was doing now? It made the cons on the row happy. At least until they realized that their own day would come and they would have to walk the walk.

They dragged Johnny to the chamber and hoisted him onto the table while he tried to kick them and screamed "No!" When his legs and hips were secured with the leather straps, they attached belts to Johnny's forearms and when the handcuffs were removed, two officers on each side stretched his arms out and away from his body before he could use them for any other purpose. Two officers began strapping his arms in the cruciform position, and his upper body was secured by the Captain himself.

"Noooo," Johnny whined as they stepped away. His eyes were bulging as if they were trying to escape the confines of his mask. Tears ran freely out the sides as he wept openly.

"If we remove the mask, Mr. Childress, are you going to behave?" Kindt asked. In truth, he would be required to remove the mask to permit the witnesses to positively identify him, but he wanted Johnny to calm down.

Johnny stared at him, and nodded. The mask was lifted from his face, but a different mask resided underneath. One of pure fear.

The doctor, who had prepared the three chemicals that lay in a compartment beneath the table, connected the line from the pumps below to the catheter in Johnny's left leg.

At midnight the curtain was opened and the gallery was able to view Johnny on the table. The gallery was dark, compared to the glaring light of the chamber, so Johnny could not see the witnesses.

In the first row, Mr. Polacheck and his brother had chosen to attend. Mrs. Polacheck declined and sent her brother-in-law instead.

Next to them were Rachael, Ben, Mordeci and a reporter from the Associated Press.

The second row contained four reporters and Johnny Lee's attorneys. The room was full.

At 12:01 a.m., Warden Kindt opened a folder and read the contents of the Death Warrant and how having been found guilty by a jury of his peers, he will now be put to death in a manner prescribed by law.

Rachael wondered if they could even find a jury of Johnny's peers and hoped not.

"Do you have any last words, Mr. Childress?" Kindt asked.

"Fuck you! Fuck all of you out there!" he shouted as he squirmed to see through the large window to the gallery.

With a mere glance at the prison doctor, a soft whirring sound was heard.

Johnny stiffened and arched his back against the straps which crossed his chest.

"Stop it. Please stop," he mewed. "I'm sorry," he said, like a child. He was looking straight at Kindt. His eyes betrayed his submissive tone. His eyes bespoke of pure evil. Kindt felt as if he were killing the devil himself.

"You sonofabitch," the father said softly. His brother had his arm around him

Rachael watched with a quiet degree of satisfaction. After all, it was a monster they were putting to sleep.

Ben had witnessed another death by lethal injection. There wasn't much to see, really. It wasn't like a firing squad where the bullets would strike the body in a mist of blood.

Mordeci made notes.

Johnny's attorneys looked on as if it was a memorial to their failure and ineptitude. They had tried their best. The Governor, who was elsewhere tonight, had phoned Warden Kindt and advised there would be no clemency and that he could not make the trip due to a more important reason than Childress's death.

Johnny was still the center of attention. He continued to glare at the Warden, but was not struggling any longer. He wasn't doing anything, really. You could barely perceive movement of his chest. It was about over now.

Ten minutes passed like that - an eternity when you're counting the seconds. Warden Kindt watched the doctor, who would pronounce Johnny dead. The whirring ceased and the chamber was deathly silent.

Johnny's attorneys looked towards the floor, as if they were ashamed of failing.

Then, Tom Kindt drew the curtain and it was all done.

Rachael believed there should be more to it. He deserved to die kicking, screaming or choking, not the peaceful sleep Johnny gently fell into.

"If I have to die, I gotta tell ya, that doesn't look bad," Rachael remarked to Ben and Mordeci on their way out. She was careful not to let the father or the girls hear her, but she believed that he would agree. In Poland, they shot their condemned.

"It's over, Rachael. You did good," Ben said as he took her arm.

Mordeci fell in beside them as they walked to Rachael's new squad car for the trip back to Chicago.

As they passed through the throng of people outside, camera lights were following the father of the girls.

"Poor bastard," Rachael said in general.

A few of the people recognized Rachael and asked how she felt about the execution.

"It's over. The whole affair is over and the streets are a little safer this morning."

The reporters were waiting for Johnny Lee's attorneys to exit, but no one saw them leave.

Warden Kindt paced the floor behind his desk, a look of consternation upon his face.

"Doctor, how do I tell this guy's attorneys when they get here, that their goddamn client isn't dead? How do I explain to the

Director that we pumped enough chemicals into this sonofabitch to embalm him, and he's alive?" Kindt demanded.

"Warden, there is no way humanly possible that the man still lives. He's in a coma and will likely stop breathing any moment. His body can't survive."

"Where is he now?"

"He's still inside the chamber. When his heart stops, I pronounce him dead in there."

"You had better hope so. I have to tell his lawyers and they are gonna scream cruel and unusual crap. Let me know as soon as he's dead."

"Yes, sir," the doctor said. On his way out, he saw the lawyers coming towards the Warden's office with the Captain escorting them. He wouldn't look at them as he scurried away.

"Come in, gentlemen. Please take a seat. We have a matter to discuss," Kindt said.

The lawyers sat down and the Captain leaned stoically against the office door. "This otta be good," he said to himself.

"Gentlemen," Kindt began and was interrupted by Amaranta.

"If it's about the body, we're not claiming it. He has no family that we could find, so the State will have to bury him."

"That's not why I sent for you two. You see, there's been a slight glitch in the procedure here. Your client still has a heartbeat."

"What!" Amaranta shouted as he stood up so quickly his chair fell backwards.

"What the hell are you doing Kindt?" Amaranta shouted.

"He's probably deceased by now. He' still in the chamber and our doctor is next to him."

"Mr. Kindt," Gamberino began softly, "let me get this clear. There was a malfunction in the equipment and Johnny Childress is not legally dead?"

"There was no malfunction, Mr. Gamberino, all of the chemicals were pumped into him. I am assured by our physician that he is in no pain and is in a deep coma, but maintains a faint cardiac rhythm."

"I want to see him." Amaranta exclaimed.

"I don't wish to see him, Mr. Kindt. I would like to leave here immediately. You can phone me when he expires." Nello

Gamberino stated sternly. At first it appeared as if he wanted to wash his hands of the whole affair. Then, Kindt remembered the smooth and calculated tactician that he was.

"Mr. Gamberino," Kindt said coyly, "you're going to find yourself a Judge, aren't you? Never mind, sir, you don't have to answer that. I can't stop you. I'll call you when he expires."

"I'll stay here Nello, and make sure no one puts a pillow over his face. Get an order to move him to a hospital," Amaranta said.

The statement drew looks of disdain from Kindt and the Captain, but they would not qualify that accusation with a response.

Kindt asked the Captain to escort Gamberino to his car so reporters would not hear the sour news. At this juncture, it was in Johnny's best interests to keep it all a secret or the Courts would close their doors to him. The trial Judge could issue an Order to do it again today, as the Death Warrant gave Kindt twenty-four hours to carry out the execution.

When he reached his car, he was already calling his hotel to arrange for someone to come right now and word process his motions.

He knew what Judge he intended to approach and knew he would sign the Order.

"What the hell do you mean, he's not dead? Tom, explain this to me, quickly," the Director said as he sat up in bed.

"The doctor pumped all the chemicals into this guy and he still has a heartbeat. What do I do now?"

"Choke him or give him more. Have the doc give him more of that shit and kill the sonofabitch like you're supposed to do. Before the press hears about it. Tom, this is a huge screw-up."

"The doc is in there now and assures me that his heart will stop soon."

"Aw, Jesus Christ. This is really bad. What if he survives? You've got to give him more drugs to finish the job, Tom."

"That may be a bit difficult, sir. One of his attorneys is here with him and the other is running to find a Judge," Kindt said hesitantly.

"Shit! This just gets better as we go. Who is holding Childress's hand? The Pope? Damn it, Tom. You better call the

Attorney General, and explain this to him. He's gonna be pissed. He's got to know. I'm heading your way in about an hour. If he dies, call me immediately." Click.

Damn. Kindt did not look forward to his next call.

"Sorry to wake you, sir, but I have a problem here."

"Warden Kindt," the Attorney General said as he looked through bleary eyes at his clock next to the bed. "It's 2 o'clock in the morning. Unless something has happened to the Governor, you had better have a real good reason for calling me at this hour."

"Sir, Childress didn't die. The equipment worked fine and all the chemicals went through him, but he still has a heartbeat." There it was in a nutshell version and that paragraph was the epitaph to his career.

"Let me get this perfectly clear. You screwed up the execution and this killer remains barely alive?"

"No sir. I mean, yes, legally he's alive but I did not screw up the execution. We did everything by the book. The guy didn't die. What do you want me to do?"

"Kill him, you idiot!" the Attorney General wanted to say, but didn't. "Where is Childress and who knows about this?"

"He's still in the chamber and our doc is waiting for him to die. He assures me that he will, too. As for who knows, his attorneys are here. Well, one is here and the other ran off looking for a Judge."

"Good Christ, this will be all over the press soon. Have someone meet me. I'll be there as quick as I can. I'll get a helicopter here and be there within an hour or so. And, Warden, you had better hope he dies by the time I reach there!" Click.

Kindt was suddenly getting used to people just hanging up on him. Click.

"Any changes down there?" the Warden asked the prison doctor who remained in the chamber.

"No, sir," he said, regrettably. "His attorney is demanding that I act like a physician and do something to save him. This doesn't help, sir."

"Doctor, you will do nothing to assist in that man's recovery! Do you understand me? I have the Attorney General and the director on their way here. I don't want them to learn that you're trying to save this bastard's life. Got that?" Click.

Even the doctor hung up on him. This was starting to annoy him.

When Kindt returned to the execution chamber, he heard Amaranta's ranting about suing everyone, and torture. "Mr. Amaranta," Kindt bellowed as he walked into the room, "might I remind you that your client came here to die, not sunbathe or get a massage. We are not, and I underscore that counselor, not going to assist his survival in any respect. When the Attorney General arrives here, we will probably finish the job and stop this freak show. Until then, sir, you will act respectfully towards my staff or you will be removed. Is that clear? I don't know why he has a heartbeat, but I assure you he will cease to exist soon."

"Warden, my client is obviously in a lot of pain and that is cruel and unusual."

"Counselor," the doctor interrupted, "I assure you that your client is in no pain whatsoever."

"And why should I listen to you? You believed those chemicals would kill him and here he is as alive as you and I."

"He is a vegetable, Mr. Amaranta. He has only a faint heartbeat. He's not ready for a rousing round of golf. Now, stop carrying on like we are a hospital. He is here to die and die he shall," Kindt said.

"You underestimate my co-counsel, Warden. He is probably on his way back here already. And he's probably got Marshals with him."

Kindt just looked at the doctor, waiting for some sign that Johnny Lee had died while they were arguing, but he just listened to his stethoscope. Damn.

As it turned out, Amaranta was not too far off in his predictions. Nello Gamberino had used a hotel clerk who received three one-hundred dollar bills for her trouble, and had prepared an "Emergency Motion for Stay of Second Execution." He had his affidavit attached and had used the hotel facsimile machine to send it to the home of United States Court of Appeals Judge Joel Flaumary, with whom he attended law school at John Marshal in Chicago.

When he called the Judge at his home and explained the situation, his friend was appalled and said it was sufficient to overcome Easterman's directive. The Judge did not care much for Easterman's heavy tactics even on his brothers in the Seventh Circuit and this was a clean shot at Easterman's big mouth.

Flaumary not only signed the Order that Nello had faxed to him, under seal of course, but called the United States Marshals Service in Springfield to dispatch at least two deputies to meet Nello at Thames, to serve the Order upon Warden Thomas Kindt and to take Johnny Lee Childress into custody pursuant to the direction within the dictum of the Order. Easterman was gonna shit when he phoned him and the Judge smiled as he rose and headed for an early shower. Yes!

When Nello reached the prison, he was approached by two men in dark blue combat fatigues with U.S. Marshal above the breast pocket and in big white letters across the back. Each carried a sidearm strapped on his thigh, like those tactical holsters seen in the movies. They both had badges suspended in front on beaded silver chains. These were frontline cowboys for the feds.

"Mr. Gamberino?" one began. "U.S. Marshals Service, sir. We're here to serve a court order on the Warden and to take custody of a prisoner. We have an ambulance, as directed, and more units are responding to this location now. Shall we go inside and see what the Warden says?"

As they were admitted at the front gate, leaving their weapons and ammunition in the locked compartments, they heard the roar of a helicopter as it neared the prison.

"I think we have company," one deputy remarked to the other, as they continued inside the building. The Captain met them at the Administration Building entrance and escorted them through the prison to where the Warden waited for them.

"Good morning, sir, we have a federal court Order to take immediate custody of one Johnny Lee Childress. Would you kindly produce him, please?" the deputy said as he handed Kindt a copy of the Order signed by Judge Joel Flaumary.

"Gentlemen, I was just informed that the Attorney General and my superior, the director, have arrived. They will be here momentarily. While we wait, can I get you anything?"

"Coffee would be fine, sir. But we really have to get going. Our instructions are quite clear in the Order, sir. We have an ambulance at your sally port gate now. Is the prisoner sick, sir?"

"Something like that, Deputy. Please come with me and we'll take you to where the prisoner is at the moment. The others will join us there."

"Yes sir," the deputy said smartly. He appeared to be fresh from the military, Kindt supposed. Many of them from the military went into some federal service as their time in the military counted towards their federal retirement. Not a bad deal there.

When they arrived at the chamber, the two deputies looked at each other and the crucified form on the table.

"Sir, is this some joke? If it is, we haven't been made a part of it," he said towards Gamberino.

"Deputies, the Order you have is very specific. That is your prisoner and I ask that you move expediently," Nello said sternly.

"Let me see this Order," the voice said from behind.

"Gentlemen," Kindt started, "may I introduce you to the Attorney General for the State of Illinois?"

"Good morning, sir. We're here for this prisoner. May we move him now, sir?"

"Give me a minute, deputies," he said curtly as he reviewed the impeccable wording of the Order.

"Any change, Warden?" he asked.

When Kindt looked at the physician, he shook his head. "No, sir." He wondered what was keeping him alive. Satan must be helping him, he thought.

"Jesus Christ, Tom. They are to rush him to the nearest hospital for any and all treatment to preserve his life and aid his recovery from a forced overdose of chemicals," he read from the content. "This is going to get bad, Tom. However, the Order seems legitimate and we haven't much choice at the moment. Unless he expires on the way to the sally port."

"OK gentlemen. We have a gurney outside the door. We can place him on there. Do you have restraints?"

"Yes sir. We have cuffs here and shackles outside. We'll secure him, sir. We transport all the time, sir."

As they began pushing the gurney with Johnny Lee towards the sally port, the doctor continued to monitor his heartbeat. It was still there.

The ambulance was waiting inside the enclosed sally port, where Johnny was transferred to their gurney, covered in blankets and lifted inside. The last sight of Johnny Lee was as the paramedic was inserting an IV into his arm, while another began removing the catheter and bandaging his leg.

One of the deputies, who was given his sidearm by one of the numerous deputies who appeared in several vehicles with red lights flashing, climbed inside the ambulance.

In a moment, the ambulance was gone, its lights ablaze and siren piercing the sunrise. There were at least six federal squads surrounding the ambulance as it headed for the hospital.

The Attorney General was returning to Springfield in the helicopter, while the Director remained behind for "damage control" as everyone braced themselves for the aftershock of Johnny Lee Childress's feat of defying the lethal injection. Well, almost lethal, anyway.

Chapter 8

"Good Afternoon, everyone," Mordeci said as he sashayed into Homicide offices carrying bags of food for Rachael, Ben and himself.

"I have some wonderful news for you two, but I thought we could enjoy lunch together first." He had a playful expression on his face and they had learned not to trust that look.

"What's up, Mort?" Ben asked, as he placed his hands on his hips and smiled.

"I'm just inviting my friends to feast with me on the epicurean delights within these heavy bags." He set them on Ben's desk and smiled.

"Not until you tell us the real reason that brought you here. Give!" Rachael said, as she smiled as well.

When they had dropped Mort off at his car, it was around six that morning and now he returned, carrying enough food to feed a family, but the giveaway was that he wore the same clothes from when they attended the execution and dropped him off. He hadn't bothered to go home to sleep or change yet.

"Come on, then. I'll tell you while we dine." Mort had picked up a variety of items from "Peking House" and the dishes were delicious. As they each enjoyed helpings of their favorite foods on their paper plates, Mort broke the silence.

"It's about the execution we attended last night or this morning."

"What about it, Mort? Was Childress spotted this morning with Elvis someplace?" Rachael chided and smiled.

"Very good, Rachael. You're getting better at this. And you're very close." He let that statement hang in the air.

"What do you mean?" Ben said as he loaded up his plastic fork with cashew chicken.

"Well, we saw the execution, right?" Mort quizzed.

"Go ahead, Mort," Rachael said as she quit eating.

"Well, the bottom line is that Johnny Lee Childress did not die."

Rachael jumped to her feet. "What the hell are you talking about?"

"A sealed court Order was signed a couple hours after we left which directed the U.S. Marshals to take custody of him, transport him to a hospital for care and remain under their protection pending further orders."

"What does it take to kill this guy? What the hell is he, the devil? Do we have to drive a wooden stake through his heart or use silver bullets?" she said as she paced around the room.

"What else do you know?" Ben asked as he too set down his fork.

"He's in a hospital under a false name and is in a coma. He also remains under the control of the Marshals and they aren't saying anything."

"Are you breaking the story?" Ben inquired.

"It's in the afternoon edition that will hit the streets about now. I thought you two would like to hear it from me personally."

"Thanks, Mort. Did your sources have any explanation how this happened?" Rachael asked as she returned to her seat.

"It's speculative, but someone who read the supporting documents for the federal Order, says that despite the lethal dosage of chemicals that were pumped into him, he continued to maintain a heartbeat. His attorney, Gamberino, woke up a Judge on the Seventh Circuit, who signed the Order and the Marshals took over from there."

"Any idea where he is, Mort? This guy who won't die?" Rachael asked.

"We have the destination sheet for the ambulance the Marshals hired. The hospital isn't far from the prison. We drove past it on our way home."

"I'm not hungry any more. I'm gonna see what I can find out. I'll call the Marshals. We certainly have an interest in this guy, if anyone." With that, she closed the door behind her as she headed for her own work space. She was not happy with the news and was determined to get answers.

Ben was not hungry anymore either, and pushed his plate to the middle of the desk.

"Mort, what happens now? Obviously, they're spending

money on this guy to keep him alive, so it's safe to assume they're not just going to kill him, right? Has this happened before?"

"When I contacted his attorneys, they said they were meeting the press later this afternoon," Mort continued after a brief pause. "However, I contacted a couple of criminal attorneys and they said a scenario like I set for them would trigger a new round of habeas reviews and appeals. If they can kill him, it won't happen for years to come." He let that notion settle on Ben.

"Is there any chance he could avoid the death penalty or get off free?"

"He could avoid the death part, but it would turn into life in prison."

"Rachael's not going to like all this," Ben said. He was concerned for her and how hard she had worked on that case.

When Mordeci left, Ben had another thought strike him. What about the Polachecks? Shit!

"Mr. Polacheck, I'm afraid I have some disturbing news for you, sir..." Rachael had decided that it should be her who contacted him. He had taken the day off from work, as the long drive would not have permitted him any sleep, and watching the man who had butchered his daughters die was more important than one day of vacation time. His anguished scream tore through Rachael's very soul.

At exactly 4:00 pm, as promised by the attorneys for Johnny Lee Childress, they strode into the meeting room set up for them at a Holiday Inn. The show was about to begin.

Samuel Amaranta, his jewelry sparkling and his Armani suit perfectly tailored, began the chronology of events. He held up the court Order for all to see and proclaimed it as the "ticket to life" for his client.

It was Nello Gamberino who fielded the questions.

"What's on the judicial horizon now? Are you planning to file a new action regarding your client's sentence?" the reporter from channel 7 News asked.

"At this moment, we are filing a Petition for a Writ of Habeas Corpus in Springfield, where the horrendous events occurred. We are seeking our client's release, or in the alternative, that his sentence be reduced to life." Nello announced.

"Mr. Gamberino, do you really think you can get Childress off completely?" the hottie from CBS News then asked.

"Absolutely. We have case law that supports our position," Nello responded.

And so the questions went back and forth like a boring tennis match. Only the stakes were higher.

Later that evening, Cook County State's Attorney, Scott Schroeder, accompanied the Illinois Attorney General to the podium in the Capital Building and together they faced national reporters from Associated Press and CNN News, now that the whole country had heard what happened. Or, in this case, what didn't happen.

The Attorney General did all the talking, while Schroeder bobbed his head in agreement behind him, like one of those stupid toy animals you see in the rear window of cars. Up and down, like his head hung on a concealed hook under his suit coat.

The Attorney General fired back on every question. "No, Childress will not get off. Yes, he is alive, in that he has a heartbeat but is otherwise legally dead. No, Childress will not avoid the death penalty and I will handle this case here in federal court, myself."

In all, he was pretty convincing. He did not realize it then, but some of his words were going to haunt him later on.

For security reasons, the Marshals removed Johnny Lee Childress from that tiny hospital and flew him away in the night. He was going to a federal medical facility in Minnesota.

Chapter 9

The Federal Medical Center in Rochester, Minnesota, resembles a college campus, if it weren't for the security fences and miles of razor wire strung around it. The Center was a haven to Jimmy Baker, the televangelist who was convicted of fraud and sentenced to serve seven years in federal prison. Violence is a rare instance and the majority of the population is there for medical treatment, while a small force of inmates, called cadre', are there as a support mechanism for the facility.

The more important element to this facility is its contract with the famous Mayo clinic, one of the most renowned hospitals in the world. Kings, queens and presidents travel there for care and the Bureau of Prisons has their services at the prison.

It was decided by the Marshals that security, both protecting Johnny Lee from extrinsic matters and preventing his escape, was far too difficult at the local hospital. In a meeting with the Judge in Springfield, it was decided that he would be safer in Rochester, receive excellent care and be secure in his confines.

Johnny Lee was in a single cell in the three story hospital there. An officer was stationed at his door at all times. His status with the Bureau of Prisons mandated maximum security, while his status with health care professionals from the Mayo Clinic considered him a medical miracle and case study. Specialists from the clinic came to see him. No one had ever encountered a case where someone survived the dosages of the drugs injected into him and if he came out of the coma, he could enlighten everyone about what he had endured. Johnny was the buzz of the Clinic.

At the moment, all he was to the world was a lump under the sheet. He had undergone a complete dialysis and transfusions to cleanse the blood and filter out residual chemicals. He was given massive doses of medications to counteract the execution drugs and draw them out from the muscle tissue and organs. Johnny's otherwise lifeless form lay under a sheet, tubes, hoses, monitors and IV bottles which nourished him and flushed his body. His pulse was steady now and what was amazing to Clinic physicians, his blood pressure rose almost overnight to a normal range, 60/110.

This was like a tsunami at the Clinic and after a plethora of cardiac and respiratory specialists examined Johnny, a consultation was ordered for a neurologist and neurosurgeon to examine him to determine the viability of his brain. The question was, could his brain survive the chemical overload which was designed to destroy it?

An electroencephalogram, EEC, was performed and the brain waves and impulses were fairly flat, indicating little or no stimulus or action. Or, a brain at rest and healing.

The ganglia, a bundle of nerve endings which is located at the base of the skull, is the true epicenter for impulse transmission. Sort of the hub of an airline or rail system. Destroy that, and it's lights out, as they say. The drugs given to condemned prisoners shut down the respiration and heart. As an ancillary effect, it will destroy the synaptical ability of the brain and the ganglia.

If Johnny Lee's brain was destroyed and he could only exist on life support and maintain a heartbeat, the judicial system would be faced with a new and unpleasant round of appeals and pleadings. The country waited and daily reports were given by a spokeswoman for the Bureau of Prisons in Washington, D.C.

"Is he dead yet?" Or, "Is he alert?" Or, "Will the Court order him off of life support?" - were the repetitive inquiries of reporters. Truth was there was no life support to unplug. Johnny Lee was breathing and maintaining a pulse on his own. The medical staff only did monitoring, but every day, the country wanted to hear if Johnny Lee Childress vicariously clung to life.

For ten days, he lay perfectly still in that bed in Rochester. And then he moved. It was the officer who happened to see it while doing a routine check on him. He could have moved before, but no one saw it and the monitors indicated nothing unusual. The officer advised the nurse and quickly, Johnny was surrounded by physicians. The neurologist watched in amazement as Johnny responded to reflexes at the knees and elbows. He tapped with is little rubber gadget all over Johnny, and his limbs would jerk in response. This meant that the motor nerves of the brain and ganglia were not destroyed. Now they wondered about the cerebral cortex and cerebrum. Was Johnny cognizant of his surroundings?

Could he reason or communicate? He seemed to be quite a study case and the neurologist and neurosurgeon, both of whom made copious notes, were planning a book about their treatment of him. It was astonishing in all respects, likened to a miracle.

It was more than a prison guard who stood vigil over Johnny now. He had at least one specialist there at all times and the neurologist and neurosurgeon were on a stand-by to rush to the prison if some event occurred of significance.

"Doctor Janis, your patient just opened his eyes," was all that was said and the place got hectic at two o'clock in the morning on the twelfth day. Scores of physicians converged, along with the Warden of the facility who reported to Washington and to the Marshals.

His eyes were open, but dilated, yet his eyes followed the penlight from side to side. He was healing!

"The craven monster from Chicago, Johnny Lee Childress, is out of a coma and is alert!" is how a nationwide newspaper described the event.

The Bureau of Prisons issued a boilerplate statement which read that Johnny was no longer in a coma, was responding to external stimuli and was apparently recovering.

Johnny's attorneys flourished in the national spotlight, which incidentally was not bad for business and required a few new suits in their closets. They too were celebrities.

To Warden Tom Kindt and the Illinois Department of Corrections, the news was the manifestation of a nightmare, even though the prison doctor had resigned his position, unable to sustain the intense media attention and personal anguish at having failed to perform somehow. It was not certain if Kindt could survive the fallout, but the doctor who was charged with executing Childress and failing, would never weather such a storm.

To Rachael, the news sickened her. She could not fathom some of the descriptive words used by responsible members of the professional media. "Miracle" was the most offensive to her. That word was reserved for religious, faithful people who believed in God, Allah or Jesus. Applying it to Johnny Lee Childress was a desecration of its historical definition and meaning.

To the United States Marshals Service, it meant time for action once again. As soon as Johnny was stable and able to move, they would return him to Illinois. A hearing was scheduled for just that determination.

The courtroom of Judge Lucius Echols was filled to capacity. Lucius has been on the federal bench since Jimmy Carter appointed him and stood beside him that day when he became the first black man to assume a federal Judgeship in southern Illinois. He attended law school at Southern Illinois University and served an internship with Justice Thurgood Marshall of the Supreme Court. Considered a bit to the left in his beliefs and rulings, it was insufficient to label him a liberal. He has a deep, baritone voice similar to that memorable voice of Darth Vader in "Star Wars," in real life known as James Earl Jones. Strangely, he bore an uncanny resemblance to the actor as well and suffered the constant chiding from friends. When he is on the bench, he is all business.

"Johnny Lee Childress versus Thomas Kindt and the State of Illinois," the clerk announced.

"Good morning gentlemen, your appearances are on file and I know who you are. We're here to determine a location where the Petitioner can be housed during the pendency of these proceedings. I have read the submissions by both parties and I am prepared to rule," Lucius said clearly.

"I am concerned about one point you raise and the safekeeping of the Petitioner. I must admit that the gravamen of that issue is not lost on this Court."

As the State's attorney rose to voice his objection, concern or opinion, the look on Lucius' face told him to shut up and sit down.

"I am cognizant of the serious issues relating to this case. I am also aware that the State of Illinois has a vested interest in the Petitioner as well. This is a hearing, gentlemen, not a trial and I am given wide latitude in considerations. Moments ago, I spoke with Warden Thomas Kindt at Thames Correctional Facility and he has assured me that if the Petitioner is returned to that facility, he will receive whatever care this Court deems reasonable and proper. Given the fact that he is a State prisoner and because I have had prisoners present their cases from within these same confines, I find it compelling to return him to the care of Warden Kindt."

The looks that defense counsel gave each other and the Judge were not lost in obscurity.

"That is not to say, gentlemen, that there are no provisos here. I have mapped out a detailed Order, appointing local physicians here as monitors over his medical care. I will hold a weekly status hearing to make sure that the Petitioner is receiving the medical care commensurate with his needs. If at any time I find that he is not receiving that level of care, I have advised Warden Kindt to bring his toothbrush with him to court here because I am locking him up for contempt."

Reporters were moving towards the exit, some already dialing their editors to relay the news.

"I am directing the U.S. Marshals to surrender physical custody of Mr. Childress to Warden Thomas Kindt and only Thomas Kindt. I might add, the custody transfer will take place when Mr. Childress is medically fit and able for such transfer. That decision of suitability for travel will rest with his caregivers in Minnesota. If there is nothing more, gentlemen, this Court stands adjourned." The gavel struck and in a tornado of black cloth, Lucius was gone.

There is no clear victory for either side.

The Awakening

Chapter 10

His eyelids fluttered, shuttering out the glaring overhead light from the five foot long, multiple tube fluorescent fixtures, making his first glimpse of his surroundings similar to the first cinematic movies that were pictures of motion which flapped before the eye. What he saw was a thousand pictures of white. Even that had a patina of mist or fog at the edges. It required immense concentration on his part to force his eyelids to cease their attempt at flight and he forced them into a squint. The light was sharp and overpowering, but slowly his eyes accepted the burden of ultraviolet exposure and he was able to hold them wide open and see.

Seeing did nothing to abet his body in attempting to suppress the lightning bolts of pain which shot down his neck or the thunder threatening to separate his brain into more than two sections. Little by little, as he lay there, the cognition associated with sight was encroaching upon his awareness. An infant sees yet has no cognitive ability to associate the vision with recognition. He saw lines across the sea of whiteness above him. They were perfectly parallel and perpendicular. He concentrated his focus, the aperture of the corneas set to adjust the correct amount of light needed to establish the distance. After a few moments, he realized that he was looking at ceiling tile. He was alive!

He permitted his head to tilt slightly to his left, and heard a beeping noise begin. He did not recall hearing the rapid beep before, but he distinctly did so now. The light was less painful to him now and he saw another sea of white, with lines parallel and vertical, only the vertical lines were different. Staggered, and ended at the parallel lines. Bricks, he finally determined.

He turned his head slowly to his right, and he saw electrical things mounted on thin metal posts, lights blinking on and off. One beeped every time the orange light flashed on and off. More brick. He tilted his head towards his chest and not only was the pain in his neck intensified, forcing his fists to clench in rebellion, but someone stood there looking at him.

"So, you decided to join us after all?" the man said.

"Can you hear me?" the man asked. He was dressed in one those white coats that almost reached his knees. He wore a white shirt and a brilliant red and silver striped tie. Johnny's first taste of real color. The man had coal black hair and a beard, sort of like Abraham Lincoln.

"I'm Doctor Clifford. If you can hear me, would you nod your head?"

Slowly, he pushed his head back to where it was before and back down.

"Great. If you can, would you nod if you recognize me?" No movement.

"Would you like to sit up a little?"

He needed a change of position, so he forced another slight nod.

There was a mechanical hum and he started to bend at the waist. His upper body was creeping upward and towards the man. His head pounded like herds of water buffalo charging across the Serengeti Plains. "Stop!" he yelled in his mind and the punishing movement ceased.

"You can speak, I see," this Clifford guy said. The command must have actually come from his mouth and not just in his head.

"Would you care for some water?"

He held a glass with a straw with a bend in it so that it is easier to drink. The doctor placed the straw to his lips and he began to suckle.

The water was sweet to his tongue and throat and Clifford had to pull the glass away before he emptied it.

"Whoa, take it easy. Don't overdo it at the first trip." Clifford smiled at him. He had a soothing voice, one that could hypnotize a person.

"Feel better?"

""Yes," squeaked out. "Thank you."

"When you started wiggling around, you set off the monitor. That's when I came in. Will you be all right for a while if I leave?"

"Yes."

Clifford backed away from him and produced a large, flat key which appeared to be constructed of solid brass. The key was flat, but a hundred times larger than a regular key, with an oval head where he held it. He inserted the key into what must be a door and turned a quarter of a turn and the door swung open. When Clifford left, he heard a solid thunk as the locking device secured. He was alone.

The room in which he found himself was about twenty feet square, he guessed. It was completely white, except for the floor which was a battleship gray and looked painted, not tiled.

In the corners was a gleaming stainless steel commode, which was attached to a box-like structure and a basin rested within the top portion. Other than that, the room had no chairs or furniture, except for the bed where he found himself.

He had seen hospital beds before, with those pole-shaped railings on the sides. On each side of him were plastic bottles with clear liquid in them and transparent lines that ran into his arm. He had seen these, as well. "Intravenous," or "IV," he said to himself. There were gauze patches where the needles must be inserted.

He wiggled his toes and was delighted that he was not a paraplegic. He lifted his arms and moved his fingers. Everything seemed to be working fine. He lifted the sheet that covered him and looked at his naked body. Everything appeared normal, except that his penis had a transparent tube running out of it and into a bottle which held yellowish liquid on the side of the bed. He had seen these before as well. They are called catheters and are inserted into urinary tracts of people who are unable to ambulate to a bathroom and urinate. He must have been supine for some time for a catheter to be inside him. Otherwise, there was a full complement of limbs, feet, toes and more control. He felt lucky.

However, luck had no recourse against the pain that buffeted his brain. He closed his eyes and laid his head back against the bed. That seemed to help.

Moments later, a woman in a nurse's uniform, a cap with a black stripe resting on her head, entered and approached him cautiously. She was pretty, in a simple way. She wore her hair short, like a boy, but the hint of blond hair was there. She wore no make-up or lip gloss and made herself unattractive. Otherwise, he thought, she would be quite pretty. He wondered why.

"It's true," she said. "You are awake. Can I get you

anything?"

The black stripe on her hat meant that she was a Registered Nurse or RN, he knew that. Her name tag said "Frye, RN."

"My head hurts," he croaked.

She reached into a packet and produced a clear plastic bottle with "Bayer" on the label. Aspirin. That would help him.

"Here you go, take these." She handed him two white tablets and then picked up the water from the tray next to him. She did not hand him the water, but brought the straw to his lips. He plopped the aspirin onto his tongue and took a gulp of water to chase them down.

"Thank you," he said. Better now than before, as the water seemed to be helping his larynx.

"Excuse me?" she asked.

"Thank you," he said with a touch more clarity and authority.

She looked at him quite strangely as she backed away like the doctor did earlier. She went to the door and produced a similar key that Clifford had and left the room.

He laid back and forced himself to relax. He was alive! He was really alive! He made it! He dozed. It had been a long journey and he was tired.

The opening of the door awoke him. Two men entered his room. One was the Clifford guy, still in that white lab coat. The other was dressed in a blue suit, with a light blue shirt and striped tie in blue, red and thin lines of gold. He was a big man, but had a ruddy complexion from drinking or maybe acne when he was younger.

"Well, Doctor Clifford just gave me the news that you were alert. Are you in any pain?"

"No."

"Good. We're going to be moving you back to your old home. You're quite the celebrity now. I have some phone calls to make." At that, the big man spun and left the room. Only Clifford remained.

"I'll stick around in case you have questions."

Two men entered the room now. Both wore uniforms of light green shirts with dark green trousers. They had a wheelchair with them and with Clifford's help, set him in the chair. Then one of them placed handcuffs on his right wrist, and to the chair.

The nurse appeared now and began unhooking all the electronic gadgets. All that remained now were the two IV bottles and the bottle attached to the catheter.

As the three men watched, the nurse donned latex gloves and removed the sheet that covered him. He sat there stark naked, the men watching closely. The nurse lifted his penis and inserted a syringe into a bulb and withdrew the plunger. She pulled the needle out and gave the catheter a slight tug, then steadily pulled it out. Urine dripped on the floor, but he was not looking. He was never treated so crudely in a hospital before. It was as if he were nothing more than a practice dummy.

The sheet was returned over him and while one officer pushed the chair, the other pushed the frail stand which held an IV. Nurse Frye did likewise. Dr. Clifford preceded them, opening doors and announcing passage. Doors clicked open and a set of bars opened electronically as they rolled through them, then closed behind them. It was all maddening to him and his head began to hurt again. He closed his eyes and just went for the ride.

They made a series of short turns. He heard the rustlings of numerous people, but he kept his eyes closed. They bumped to a halt and he heard the hum of something moving and he was pushed into a small room. He opened his eyes to verify what his mind told him. It was much smaller than the first room, but constructed the same way. The walls were all painted brick. There was even a commode similar to the other, mounted in his left corner. To his right was a bed. Well, a steel rack with a blue mattress on top. Blankets appeared to be rolled up at the head of the bed. Other than that, there was nothing in his new quarters.

"Welcome home," one officer said and began to chuckle. "Didn't think you'd see us again, huh?" They removed the handcuffs and lifted him from the chair, guiding him towards the bed.

"Don't pull these lines out. I'll be here to check on you in a couple of hours. Maybe we'll remove them then. OK?" The nurse said as she pushed the wheelchair together, making it about six inches wide now and wheeled it out the door.

"Reminds you of home, doesn't it asshole," the officer said

who removed the cuffs. "Oh, my bad, it is your home." That seemed to be hilarious to them both. They ceased laughing when Dr. Clifford turned the corner.

"We'll wait outside, Doc," the last officer said and they left.

"If you need to speak to me, I'll be here for the next few hours."

"What kind of doctor are you?"

"I'm a psychologist," Clifford said skeptically.

"Am I in an asylum?"

A smile etched his face and he said, "No, you are not in an asylum, John."

"You know who I am?"

"Yes, John, we know who you are. You're a celebrity now. I've got to go. I'll be around later, too."

When Clifford left the door ground shut and the thud of the lock mechanism clunked. He was in a cell!

"Hey, welcome back, fag boy," he heard outside. He wondered who they were talking to or about.

He needed to find out where he was and for how long. But for now, he needed rest.

True to her word, the nurse returned some time later and removed the IV needles. Inside the rolled up blankets, he found an orange jumpsuit, a T-shirt, a pair of briefs and a pair of socks. His clothes were pink, but he was naked, so he tried them on and they all fit.

He found the two sheets, or what once were sheets, and were now tattered remnants, and made up his bunk. He tied the bottom sheet on both ends. The top sheet, he tied on one end and placed it at the bottom where his feet would go. Next, he spread the gray blanket over the top and folded the corners under "hospital" style and bloused the end where his head would rest, about six inches. The other blanket he folded neatly and placed it at the foot of the bunk. It looked as if a Marine had done the bed, preparing for inspection. He laid back down and fell asleep.

When he awoke, there was a newspaper lying on the floor by the door. He sauntered over and picked it up. The cover page bore a story of a "psychotic monster" who had shocked the country

and survived what was supposed to be a lethal dose of chemicals as payment for his crimes. There was a picture of the man who was supposed to die. His scraggly hair, beard and missing front tooth mirrored his own.

When he walked to the polished steel mirror anchored to the wall above his commode, the realization struck him. He was that man on the cover. He stumbled backward and came to rest harshly, on the bunk. He couldn't take his eyes off the cover. He began to read the story below. Tears started flowing down his hairy cheeks, freely. Before long, he was sobbing loudly.

The prisoners on the row listened. Most of them just laughed, except for the man with the deep voice. He thought about it.

The next morning, Doctor Clifford bounced into his cell, as if he were a gift to him from the psychology gods above.

"I'm told you had a rough night? Do you need something to help you sleep?"

"No sir. I would like to shave and lose this tangled mess of hair. Could you arrange that?"

"Yes, I think I can, Johnny. Want to look good for court?"

"No sir. I just don't like all this hair on me. And, Dr. Clifford, please call me Jonathan."

"Well, that is your legal name. If that's you wish, sure. Jonathan. I'll arrange to get a barber over here. I'll see you later on."

Two hours later, he was shorn, shaved and looked like a marine. Of course you could see the pasty areas where hair had once blocked the sun from tanning his face, but time would handle that.

He had lunch of oatmeal, toast and orange juice, as the nurse had said that he could not eat solid foods yet. It tasted just fine to him.

Warden Kindt stopped in afterwards, and abruptly stopped when he entered the cell. The bed was perfectly made again and there sat the recently barbered celebrity. Only you wouldn't recognize him if you didn't know him upfront and personal.

"Good afternoon, Johnny. I like the haircut. A little sprucing up for court?"

"No, sir. All that hair was a mess. And please, sir, call me Jonathan?"

"Sure, Jonathan. You're a new man now. It's not going to work in court, but I'll go along for now. Your attorneys are here. I have a wheelchair outside. Are you ready?"

"I'd like to walk if I may. Would you mind?"

"I'll arrange that." He was gone in a flash and two officers stepped into the cell carrying chains and leg shackles. He was bound hand and foot like some animal. Then again, according to what he had read, he was supposed to be exactly that. A monster.

Both attorneys looked in disbelief as he hobbled into the little visiting room, not sure they had brought the right prisoner.

"Johnny, you're looking much better. The Judge will love the new look. You feel ok?" Sam Amaranta asked.

"Ah, my lawyers. Are you going to get me out of here, gentlemen?"

"Of course. Nello and I have a status hearing in a few days and we are amending the petition. He looked at his co-counsel to take over, but Nello was looking at their client.

"Oh, yes, I have copies for you. I'll leave them with the officer and he can put them with your other legal materials. Are you all right?" Nello asked apprehensively.

"I'm a little unsteady, but I'll manage. You said I have other legal materials here. May I ask where those are?"

"They keep them in a room someplace. Why?" Nello asked. Johnny Lee had never asked about such things before. He didn't read well and quite frankly, didn't give a damn.

"I would like to read them. Could you arrange that?"

"Certainly. Would you like to take these with you?" Nello asked as he held the papers for him to grasp.

"Thank you."

"We've got a long drive back to Chicago. It's good to see you up and around," Amaranta said.

"Please call me Jonathan. And yes, I'm ok for now. I look forward to meeting with you again."

"Jonathan? A new image, huh? I like it." Amaranta nodded. But Gamberino just watched as the officers escorted "Jonathan" away.

"We need to talk, Sam. I think he's giving us new argument. I'll explain in the car." On the way back to Chicago, Gamberino explained and his co-counsel loved every word of it.

A cardboard box was sitting on his bunk when he arrived back in his cell. All the time while the officers removed chains and cuffs, he looked at the box. He figured he knew what awaited him in that container and had mixed emotions. The true story was in there, but so was his challenge. When the officers left and he was alone, he opened the box and began arranging the documents in piles on his bunk. An hour later, he began reading from the start. He read through dinner, instead drinking just the apple juice.

"May I have some paper and pens or pencils, please?" He enquired of Dr. Clifford when he showed up just before going home.

"Certainly. May I ask why you need them now?" Clifford asked and then added, "Jonathan."

"I'd like to make some notes for my attorneys."

"Are you all right? Is there any pain, I mean?"

"I'm a little stiff." When he used the word "stiff" he looked amused, and Clifford smiled.

"I guess I shouldn't use that word here, huh?"

Clifford joined him in a brief laugh and left. A few minutes later, a writing tablet and a Bic pen slid under his door.

He studied the transcripts from his trial and sentencing. He devoured the opinions from his appeals and the condescending words of Frank Easterman. He wrote furiously. He wanted to be prepared for his attorneys. And so he was. He had gotten their names from the bottom of the petition they intended to file on his behalf and he knew which one was which, too. He did not care for the abrasive nature and manner of the Amaranta fellow. He liked the suave style of the Gamberino gent, but didn't know if he would follow his lead.

A few days later, Jonathan met with his attorneys again. The officers who escorted him carried his tablet and the sheaf of papers from his cardboard box.

"Johnny, I mean Jonathan, how are you?" Sam Amaranta asked. A wide smile spread across his face like a glacial fault.

"I'm much better, thank you. And how are you gentlemen

doing, Mr. Amaranta?" Jonathan enquired, looking directly into Sam's eyes.

"We have a surprise for you. Over the weekend, we came up with a new petition and we believe it's a winner. Nello, tell him about it, will ya?"

"I have a copy for you. Would you like to read it over, Jonathan?" Nello had carefully planned this test. He wanted "Jonathan" to read it and ask him questions. Whether the ruse was going to work in court, was a different story.

Jonathan began to look over the pages. He turned the pages quickly and his eyes appeared to scan the lines, but Nello knew he couldn't understand most of the words. Nello had inserted words he had calculated would confound Jonathan. After all, he never graduated from eighth grade.

When the last page was flipped, which was nothing more than a signature line for Nello, he asked his client what he thought. Here was the punch line to the joke.

"Mr. Gamberino, I don't agree with your cavalier approach. These chemicals did not substantially affect my cognitive thinking and I am quite lucid. I'm not insane and therefore unfit or unworthy of being executed again."

"Jesus Christ," Sam said.

"Jonathan, would you turn to page six and read that to me, please?" Nello asked.

"Certainly," he responded as he leafed through the pages. "Paragraph 17. Petitioner's counsels, having had significant contact and communication with the Petitioner before, during and post-trial, attest that they have consulted with two forensic psychologists who have concluded that the detrimental affects of the narcotics administered to Petitioner during the defective attempt to execute him, have most likely impaired his cognition to the degree where he no longer comprehends the seriousness of the offenses or the basis for his execution."

"Goddamn!" was all Nello could say. He could read every word.

"Mr. Gamberino, I do not agree with the approach you seem to be taking. I am not insane! I do believe the premise on which you pitch this claim, comes from the Supreme Court case, *Atkins versus Virginia*, where it's cruel and unusual to execute the retarded? I assure you, I am neither insane nor retarded. You will not file this petition of yours. I want to appear before the Judge. I want you to arrange that. Can you do that?"

Before Amaranta could voice an objection, Nello said, "Sure."

Both attorneys appeared before Judge Lucius Echols that afternoon and they advised him of their client's request. However, based upon the assurances of both counsel that he would find the encounter as rewarding and in conformity with their petition, he scheduled a hearing for that Wednesday.

Dr. Clifford relayed the message for the lawyers and the Warden that he had the hearing and would be taken there sometime beforehand.

He had about thirty-six hours to prepare. He wondered if they would believe him.

Early on Wednesday morning, Marshals moved him to the federal courthouse and through the bars on the van's windows, he could see those cube vans with various numbers on the sides; Channel 7, Channel 5, and CBS News. The country was poised to hear the truth.

His case was called by the clerk and the room fell into a sepulchral silence.

"Your Honor," Gamberino began, "if it pleases the Court, the petitioner appears with counsel, but requests the indulgence to address the Court."

"That's unusual, counsel. Is there a compelling basis for this request?"

"I've just read his pro se pleading, Your Honor, and I believe there is."

"Does the Respondent have any objection?"

"No, Your Honor."

"Mr. Childress, would you like to say something?"

All eyes were on him as he stood. He wore a bright red jumpsuit with "prisoner" emblazoned across the back in black letters. "Your Honor, may I use the podium?"

"Certainly."

"Your Honor, my name today is Jonathan L. Childress, the Second. I will explain that 'today' part for you as it will have a dire bearing on these proceedings." He arranged his notes and began again.

"Johnny Lee Childress was convicted of heinous crimes of monstrous proportions and was sentenced to die in retribution. He did die." He let that set in a moment. He watched the gallery. Frantic notes were being taken by reporters. They would love this.

"As you know, he was strapped down and a variety of chemicals were pumped into him. When those chemicals are combined, they are lethal to the human body. They performed exactly as expected that morning and Johnny Lee Childress expired.

His spirit, or soul as you will, moved on. It was taken by an entity. Call it an angel, Spirit Horse, Allah, or The Grim Reaper, but that entity collected that spirit or soul and carried it to an ephemeral place. Sort of like a holding cell I was in this morning, only much, much larger. When that entity opened that gate to deposit Johnny Lee's soul or spirit in there with all the others awaiting judgment, I came out in that nano second and assumed the body I appear in today. I am not Johnny Lee Childress."

The Judge's mouth hung open in amazement. The reporters were breaking for the exits, rushing for their crews to interrupt the normal broadcasts. A few people made the sign of the cross. He could hear the whispers behind him.

"I am willing to prove those contentions, Your Honor. I will submit to any battery of tests this Court desires. I have prepared my own Petition in this case, which is based solely upon the truth. I am not the man the court sentenced to die and I request my release from custody. Thank you."

The gallery was awash in comments and it required the Judge banging his gavel repeatedly, to re-establish order.

"Mr. Gamberino," the Judge began, "were you aware of the content of your client's statement before today?"

"No, Your Honor, not until a few moments ago."

"Your Honor," Jonathan interjected, "I want the record to reflect that I hereby terminate both counsel and elect to proceed on my own."

"The Respondent has no objection to that motion, Your Honor," Schroeder said. He was enjoying this circus act by Childress. "He who represents himself has a fool for a client," the old maxim says.

"Are you sure you understand the implications of that request, Mr. Childress?" the Judge enquired.

"This is a civil proceeding, Judge. I have no absolute right to counsel, unlike in criminal proceedings. Basically, these gentlemen have been appearing as friends of the court, or 'amicus.' Yes, I can handle this myself."

"Your Honor, for the record, Mr. Amaranta and myself wish to appear as amicus curiae' in this case, friends of the Court, as Mr. Childress avers. I think it would be prudent, since we are most familiar with the case and our services would benefit this Court in its decision."

"Mr. Childress, do you object to that?"

"No, Your Honor, so long as I am my own attorney and present the truth."

"O.K., Mr. Gamberino and Mr. Amaranta are hereby relieved as counsel of record. Mr. Childress you are from this moment on, *pro se.* I will appoint Mr. Gamberino and Mr. Amaranta as amici, under the provisions of the Criminal Justice Act. I will order that Mr. Childress be examined by the prison psychologist and given a standardized battery of tests including competency and aptitude. I will see everyone back here in one month." Whoosh, he was gone!

The evening newscasts across the country all had the identical theme; what kind of hoax was the convicted killer trying to get away with in Court? Most of the stories chronicled the events and memorialized his speech before the Judge. They bespoke of his eloquence, poise and grace, compared to the vile monster who murdered children. Is he the Johnny Lee Childress or Jonathan L. Childress II? He was the topic of the country and his revelations today reduced the import of his surviving a lethal injection a hundred fold.

Chapter 11

He arrived back at the prison around midnight, escorted by State Troopers and U.S. Marshals, their sirens crashing the tranquil community around Thames. The reporters waited in vain as all they saw was a white van pulling into the sally port and disappearing behind closed gates. The prison staff discussed him in every nook and cranny. A red-line division was beginning to form in their opinions as they compared Johnny Lee to Jonathan. Some began to call him J II or J2.

The staff watched him as he ambled past them, his chains rattling at each step. They studied him to see if he was different somehow, crazy or the same white trash killer who was supposed to die.

As he approached his cell, he noticed that it was quieter. There were no insults flung at him this morning, but the windows in every cell he passed had a face watching him. He had made quite an impact in one day.

Later that morning Tom Kindt came to see him. He brought a plastic chair with him and sat down to chat.

"Jonathan, huh? If that's your angle, so be it. I'm not sure why the religious slant, but it's your plan. The Judge wanted tests done and those will begin this morning. Dr. Clifford will be here shortly. We'll see how those go. And I have been advised by my boss to provide you with things you'll need to help you in court. You will be given access to the Law Library, after normal hours of course, pens, a portable typewriter in here and plenty of paper. I would have objected more, but you've been behaving yourself lately." The Warden went to the door and stopped. "The chair is yours, too. I warn you, though, one incident and I remove everything from here but your hide. Understand?"

"Yes, sir." Was all he said in return.

Kindt firmly believed that it was all a ruse or scheme and Johnny Lee would return to his old self. He would look at the test results.

Jonathan sat in the plastic chair. It felt good on his back. He placed it so it faced his bunk like a desk or table and noticed the black lettering on the back.

"J2"

Between breakfast and lunch, he underwent a series of personality tests. Dr. Clifford showed him ink splotches, photos with colored dots, abstracts of animals and gave him a one hundred fifty question Minnesota Multiphasic Personality Inventory, or MMPI, to answer by filling in ovals on a computerized score sheet.

After dinner that night of salad, rice, beans and iced tea, he set to work. He again read every document he had.

The next morning, Dr. Clifford had someone from the Education Department, who had him answer the Stamford Achievement Test, or, SAT, which took until dinnertime once again. He reviewed his notes, and then he would ask to go to the Law Library.

"Mr. Kindt," Clifford began, "his personality screens reflect no major abnormalities whatsoever, except he appears in the passive areas. He presents no personality disorder or psychosis whatsoever. When we gave him the SAT, he registers 'post college' in all respects. We are giving him another test today, the Law School Admission Test, or LSAT. Perhaps that will tell us where we're at here."

"May I have copies of your test results, Doc? I would like to do some homework."

"Certainly."

"Let me ask you a question. Do you believe him? Can he be telling the truth? I mean, he appears and seems different, but is he?"

"From a professional standpoint, sir, I am not able to answer that. From a personal perspective though, I have to say that he seems totally different. But, it could be a game he's conjured up to deceive the courts. I don't know. It sounds like a question for Father Birney more than for me."

As Kindt watched the psychologist leave, he was thinking the same thing. Father Birney.

As Kindt was making his rounds, he finally found his chaplain. He was in Jonathan's cell and they were chatting like old friends.

"Good evening, Warden," Father Birney said. "Jonathan and I are having quite a discussion about life after death. If what he says is accurate, the Bible is one hundred percent accurate. Wouldn't you agree?"

"Father, would you stop by my office tomorrow?'" Kindt said, avoiding the question.

"Of course," the little priest said.

"How are you tonight, Jonathan?" Kindt asked in earnest.

"Fine, thank you. Father Birney and I have been discussing what it was like for me and how much I actually remember. Care to join us?"

"Perhaps tomorrow. I have to get going." When the Warden left, he saw the priest and the prisoner talking like they were family. Kindt would later believe that this was the turning point regarding Jonathan and his contentions.

Before he left for the night, he retrieved the test results Dr. Clifford had left him and the file he had received from the sentencing court in *People v. Childress*.

Chapter 12

Mr. Childress, here is a copy of our Amended Petition for Judge Echols," Nello said as he handed the multi-page document to him.

"You want me to be examined by federal psychologists in hopes they'll find me insane or impaired enough to change my sentence to life?"

"We have an obligation as officers of the court to bring our intuitions regarding competency to bar. I may believe your rendition of the events morally, but from a professional standpoint, I have to question its veracity."

"I underwent tests here, Mr. Gamberino. From what I am told, I did rather well and Dr. Clifford said I will get a stellar recommendation from him. Why is it you persist otherwise?"

"It's not personal, sir, it's my job to explore every viable avenue for relief. I would be ineffective if I did otherwise."

"I'll object," Jonathan said.

"It won't make a difference, I'm afraid. The Judge will order it anyhow," Nello said coldly.

When Jonathan returned from meeting with Gamberino, he noticed the Warden waiting for him. He carried a plastic chess game.

"You play chess, Jonathan?" Kindt felt that Johnny Lee was no match for him, having been on the high school chess team and being a champion.

"Yes sir, I do."

The Warden and Jonathan set up the chess game on the bunk and in an hour and a half, Jonathan had beaten him three games straight. Kindt had never been beaten so badly or so quickly.

"You can keep the chess set here. I'll want a re-match," he said, smiling.

"Thank you."

"I'll stop in tomorrow, J-2," he said, smiling as he left. Damn! He had to admit, J-2 did not resemble the mad dog killer he looked forward to executing a short time ago.

That night Jonathan went to the prison Law Library and

researched landmark decisions from the U.S. Supreme Court and the Seventh Circuit Court of Appeals, regarding capital punishment.

He began with the seminal case of **Furman v. Georgia**, where the Supreme Court struck down the death penalty in a sweeping decision. The Court held that capital sentences could not be applied in an arbitrary or capricious manner. He read case after case.

In 2001 the Supreme Court decided a blockbuster case regarding all sentencings. In **Apprendi v. New Jersey**, the Court ruled that any element which could elevate the applicable penalty must be pleaded in the Indictment, submitted to a jury and proven beyond a reasonable doubt.

He made copious notes until the wee hours of the morning when the officers told him they had to take him back to his cell.

Even the staff talked nicer to him now, but he could still feel the hostility in some. He sort of liked his nickname, "J2."

After only a few hours of rest, Dr. Clifford was at his door, eager to get going. He was permitted a quick shower, shave and some fresh clothes. In the Education Department, the same woman waited with a large packet.

"We don't score this here, Mr. Childress. I am only a proctor for this. Once finished, we mail this to the testing center and we receive the results back in a week or two. Because of the court and all, we're asking that the results be faxed to us. Shall we begin?"

"Yes ma'am."

And that was the beginning of a grueling seven hours for Jonathan.

When he returned to his cell, there was a brand new T-shirt on his bed. On the front it had J2. He appreciated the shirt and wore it proudly the next day.

That is also when he began preparing his brief for the Judge. The words and phrases flowed as if he had written legal briefs before. Perhaps he did. He couldn't remember what or who he was before now. He tried to remember, but try as he may, he could only recall what was said in court.

A couple of weeks later, in the dead of night, two men from the Marshals took him by car to Chicago. Despite his alleged familiarity with the Windy City, everything was alien to him. He didn't recognize one sight or building, not even the landmark John Hancock Building with its lighted ring at the top. He watched the hustle and bustle of the big city and its denizens. He couldn't recall ever being in such a metropolis like this.

Metropolitan Correctional Center is what the signs said. They were at the sally port, waiting for someone to let them inside. It is a unique bit of architecture. The building is triangular and soars almost thirty stories tall. It's operated by the Federal Bureau of Prisons and has housed some of Chicago's most notorious crime figures. He was intimidated by the building, yet he was Chicago's biggest mystery man at the moment.

When the car finally rolled inside, four men were waiting. The Marshals secured their weapons in lock boxes and when the rear door was opened, Jonathan was pulled out and literally dragged to the elevator. A minute later he was unchained in a receiving area as the Marshals traded paperwork with the staff. He was pushed into another elevator and when it reached the eleventh floor, he was prodded through a metal door, stripped naked and taken to a tiny cell with only a quilt to cover himself. He did not like his new surroundings at all.

A few hours later a gruff voice asked him if he was going to eat and he shook his head.

Afterwards, a slot opened in the door, about six-by-thirteen inches, and a voice told him to back up to the door and place his hands out to be handcuffed. After he complied, while he stood there naked with his hands behind his back, the door swung open and a man entered.

"Mr. Childress, I am Dr. Sebastian. I will be doing the exam on you for the Court."

Before he could continue, Jonathan interrupted. "Unless I am given clothing, bedding and treated like the human being I am, doctor, there will be no examination. I am not a remnant from Planet of the Apes, sir, and you will act accordingly. I am not suicidal or homicidal, despite the recent media feeding frenzy. Now, please leave here so that I may maintain a modicum of privacy. He turned away, signaling an end to the interview.

After the good doctor left, a short time later fresh clothes arrived, along with blankets and sheets. It was a start. He wondered if Sebastian would succumb to his demands. He had power. Star Power.

After lunch, Dr. Sebastian had him brought to his office on another floor. He was escorted by three officers and walked past numerous inmates who stared or pointed at him. He heard, "That's him!" a few times. He was a media star after all. History in the flesh. The only man to defy "the needle."

Sebastian asked him questions about his childhood.

"Blank. I have no idea, sir," Jonathan answered. It was the same response Sebastian received for his explorations into education, family, employment, residence and hobbies. Blank. Nada.

He pounded Jonathan regarding prior arrests and convictions. Zip. Zilch.

After almost four hours, Sebastian was ready to call it a day. Before he did though, he asked Jonathan if he would mind if his boss, the Chief of Psychology at the MMC, could examine him as well.

"Is it necessary?" Jonathan asked. "I'm getting tired of being questioned and bombarded daily."

"Yes, for reasons I cannot discuss right now, it would be clinically indicated."

The "clinically indicated" part captured his attention. "All right," he said. Later he was glad he did.

The next morning, just after breakfast, he was brought to the same office as before. Joining Dr. Sebastian was a stunning woman dressed in a black business suit, and white blouse. She had long blond hair which she wore in a ponytail, and riveting green eyes. She was almost six feet tall, he supposed, and was thin and athletic.

"This is the Chief of Psychology here, Jonathan."

"Hi," she said as she held out her hand to him. "I'm Dr. Ann Lechman. It's a pleasure to meet you." Then she added, "Finally." The name lingered in the outskirts of his mind. Then, the recollection struck him like a chunk of timber above the ear.

"You did an interview about me, didn't you? A couple of

them, actually. You're sometimes called 'Hannibal Lecter,' right? Like the psycho in 'Silence of the Lambs?' I read the comments in the paper. As I recall, you weren't flattering to my psychic profile."

"Of course, Jonathan, I didn't have the opportunity of meeting you at that time. I was making an opinion based on documents I had received. Let's start fresh, shall we?"

He had to admit she was eye candy and he had the chance to change her opinion of him. That would be a benefit to him in Court, wouldn't it?

"Sure," he said.

She didn't belabor the questions Sebastian did the day before, but she watched him as he answered. She would be deadly at a poker table.

Both psychologists made notes on yellow pads at almost every answer he gave. They took turns studying him and his body language. He had the impression that these two had done this same routine numerous times. The reporter for the Chicago Tribune, Mordeci Habush, had reported that "Hannibal Lecter" held the professional opinion that he suffered from some "fugue" state of mind and is utterly mad. He found her as interesting as she did him.

His lunch was brought to him so that they could continue virtually uninterrupted. She had a granola bar and bottled water, which answered his question about how she maintained her figure. Sebastian ate ravenously on sandwiches, Fritos and a banana. These two psychs were in a marathon and had no intention of quitting. They went through the standard battery of tests and he sailed through them with ease. And then the lethal side of "Hannibal Lecter" surfaced.

"Do you believe you should be released back into society?"

"Certainly," he began. "I have committed no crime and the killer is quite dead and gone forever."

Her eyes widened and her eyebrows arched.

"And the people of Illinois should forget that those two hands butchered two children?" she asked venomously.

"The hands merely followed the spirit and brain of a killer. They were servants. That master is dead. They serve me now."

"And we're to take your word for it that this other Childress is gone forever? We should take that chance and more children could die as a result?"

"Not exactly. That's what your tests are for. To establish that I am not Johnny Lee Childress."

"Then why do you call yourself Childress if you aren't him?" She had a point there, too.

"Because I don't know who I was before or I would use that name. I believe when I originally died and went to that limbotic place between Heaven and Hell, my earthly identity was erased as insignificant."

She studied him for almost a minute.

"Dr. Sebastian, do you have any questions?"

"Yes. Just one. Jonathan, what are your goals if released?" He watched her flip to a fresh page in the pad for this one.

"Well, I would like to discover who I was before and the purpose for my return. Otherwise, I would like to find a place where they have never heard of me and live like everyone else." Keep it simple, he had decided.

"And what if you aren't released? What if they decide to execute you again?" she asked.

"Well, my long-term goals would be limited at that point, wouldn't you say?" That drew a smile from her. Pretty, too.

"However, I have faith in the justice system and they won't execute an innocent man."

"Thank you, Jonathan. Unless Dr. Sebastian has more, I think we're finished."

When he returned to his cell, he felt that he had handled himself well and defended his position with intelligent responses. All he could do now was to wait for the report.

Once again, waking him from a sound sleep, the U.S. Marshals were back and were returning him to Thames. Before sunup, he would be back on the row.

He did very little his first day back. He slept most of the time. He needed the rest and they let him be. The following morning, however, was a different story.

"Good morning, Jonathan," Father Birney said as he walked into the cell. He carried two big cups of hot coffee and handed him one of them.

"I have a special request for you. Someone very special wishes to meet with you. He called me over the weekend and asked if I would speak with you. I told him about our discussions and he is very interested in you. Besides, he could be a great person to know."

"Sure, Father, if you want me to meet him, I will. He's not a reporter though, is he?"

The little priest laughed. "No, not hardly. His name is Cardinal John Patrick Carroll. Ever heard of him?"

"No. The name does not ring any bells. Should it?"

"He's in the news a lot. They say he could be the first American Pope. He's a very nice man. I will call him and let him know you'll meet with him and they can schedule the time."

They drank the hot coffee and talked about this limbo he had been in before returning. The priest finally garnered the strength to ask him, "Did you actually see God?"

"No, Father Birney, no heavenly visions, angels flying around or even the Devil. Just a dull white, sort of like the inside of a cloud."

When the priest left, giddy with the news that the Cardinal was coming to Thames, an officer stepped into his cell.

"My wife would like to know if you would actually sign something, J2. She believes you're special to all of us and she's special to me. Would you mind?"

"What is it?"

"Her Bible. She said you could be an angel and your signature would be like a blessing." He held out a small, red leather Bible which looked well used. A page was marked with one of those sticky notes shaped like an arrow, which said "Sign here."

He read the verse and scrawled "Jonathan Childress II, I'm no angel."

The officer left, concealing the little Bible inside his jacket, as if he had just stolen it. Jonathan could not help but smile. An angel?

It seemed his door was only closed at night, as the procession of people kept coming to him. He was like a trustee almost, going to the shower without cuffs and chains and when he went to see counsel now, he did not have leg shackles on, just the waist chains and cuffs. It made life easier for him; that's a grace in itself.

The Warden was next in the parade. He brought his own chair and sat a few feet away.

"Who or what are you?" Kindt asked.

"Excuse me?" Jonathan said as he set down his pen on his bunk, surprised.

"I was doing homework, Jonathan. I took your file home and looked at your Pre-Sentence Report. I talked to the probation officer who verified certain items. I also looked at your test scores. Have you seen your scores?"

"No, I thought my Judge would provide them at some point. May I have a copy?"

"Do you have a copy of your Pre-Sentence Investigation Report from the probation officer?" Kindt asked, ignoring the question for a moment.

"No. Should I have one? Is there something I should know from there?"

"It's pretty convincing to me. Even Dr. Clifford thinks it's important enough for his report on you and we have faxed it to the federal doctors in Chicago. All of us are mighty concerned about this. Your test scores reflect post-graduate levels in almost every area. When I say post-graduate, I'm referring to post-college, Jonathan. Is that reasonable to you?"

"I'm not sure I understand, Mr. Kindt."

"I don't - we don't understand, either. You see, I verified that you never graduated from the eighth grade. You don't have a high school education, GED, or skilled trade. See the anomaly? Hell, you're not even supposed to understand what 'anomaly' means, yet you do!"

"So, the concern is, where did my education come from? How am I able to function at this level if I never made it through the eighth grade? How could I be that ignorant child killer if I am so educated today?" Jonathan asked as he walked back and forth, looking at the floor.

"Exactly. Dr. Clifford is rewriting his whole report. The folks in Chicago want copies of everything. And by the way, your last

LSAT score came back. You can attend almost any law school you choose. Your score was 92. Not too shabby for a seventh grader. So, what are you, J2? I'm hearing whispers that you're an angel. Is that true?"

Jonathan laughed heartily now and as if an infection, the Warden joined him.

I'm No Angel

Chapter 13

"Have you seen the morning edition, Rachael?" Mordeci asked on the phone.

"No, why? Let me guess, since you're calling so early, either you're having breakfast with Elvis or maybe Childress has confessed that it's all been a hoax?"

"Leave Elvis alone, will ya? He works here in the mailroom downstairs. And no, Childress hasn't made a confession. His lawyers have made a revelation, though. And they have a pretty convincing argument that is going before the court." Mort explained about the "off-the-chart" test scores their client now consistently demonstrates, and how the criminal she arrested barely made it past seventh grade.

"It must be some psychological thing where he accumulated the knowledge subliminally, like a battery stores energy but you wouldn't know it to look at it."

"The theories are flying, Rachael. It's going to be a difficult decision for Judge Echols."

Rachael did not like hearing talk like that. To her, Johnny Lee Childress would always be the calculated killer and the sonofabitch who attacked her.

"Jonathan, may I present His Eminence, Cardinal John Patrick Carroll," Father Birney said proudly. For this occasion, Jonathan was brought to the Warden's conference room. It has a large, square oak table which appears to be a restoration project. There are a dozen chairs around it, all recent purchases from the Stateville Correctional Facility's furniture factory. The room is not austere or paneled in exotic woods. It is painted a soft white, with pictures of the State Capital Building and the present Governor adorning the walls.

The Warden was talking to Cardinal Carroll when Jonathan arrived. The Warden directed that the handcuffs be removed and stepped into his office through an adjoining door which he left open. He could still watch Jonathan, but not overhear them.

"Good afternoon, Jonathan," the Cardinal said as he vigorously shook his hand.

"Good afternoon, Sir," Jonathan said uncomfortably, as he wasn't sure what he should call the man before him.

The Cardinal wore the traditional robe, the shawl-type collar with a beautiful gold crucifix on a gold chain around his neck. He looked pontifical, only in red.

"Father Birney has told me so much about you. Do you mind if we sit down and discuss your statements to the world?"

"Certainly Sir. It's the truth," Jonathan said clearly.

"Jonathan, I would like to hear whatever you can recall about your 'journey.' Would you mind if Father Birney records our conversation?"

"Not at all, Cardinal."

For the next hour, Jonathan explained in detail, everything he could recall. His first recollection was being in "limbo" as he referred to it, the souls or spirits that were collected and how, for lack of a better name, the Reaper had made the slight mistake that permitted his escape.

"Jonathan, I have a few questions. Do you remember what form you were in? I mean, were you in a body with wings, a ball of light or something else?"

"I, or we, were energy, we had no bodies or wings, but we could ambulate somehow and we could see, hear, feel emotion, things like that."

"Did you see the Savior? I'm sorry, how Catholic of me. Did you see whatever entity brought your soul there to limbo or kept you there?"

"There was only light, Cardinal. It was brighter than our surroundings, it moved as we did. I saw no face or God as you would call Him. Just a bright light."

"Do you know what happened to the soul of Johnny Lee Childress?"

"As I said, Cardinal, we could sense or feel emotion. As I passed him, heading for the trail of light back here, I sensed pain, fear and a dread of what he believed would come. It was unlike any of the others that were there."

"Do you believe in God, Jonathan?" the Cardinal asked as

he tried to look into his heart.

"Cardinal, Father Birney brought me a small Bible last week. There is some kind of life after death, although I'm not exactly sure what it is. The body may die Sir, but a part of you, a soul or spirit, carries on. I am proof of that. Therefore, the Bible must be accurate."

The Cardinal's hand clenched on the table, but only for a second.

"Jonathan, are you an emissary?" the Cardinal enquired solemnly.

"Do you mean, as in 'angel,' Cardinal?" Jonathan returned. "If that's what you mean, I don't think so, Sir."

"I understand they call you J2? Well, J2, I would like to know if I may come back to see you, unless you don't approve, of course?"

"Any time you'd like to come to see me, Cardinal, that would be great."

"I have two favors to ask of you, then. Would you mind if I brought a guest when I return? As a favor to me?"

"As long as they're not reporters, Cardinal," he answered.

"No, he is not that. The second favor I have to ask is if you would accept a gift from me, as he had placed it on a chair under the table. Father Birney leaned over and retrieved it. It was a huge, white Bible, with gilded edges. The Cardinal handed it to Jonathan after blessing it.

When Jonathan opened the cover, there was an inscription inside:

To: J2, a very special person for the entire world.

With God's Grace,

John Patrick Carroll,

Cardinal

The Warden had already approved the Bible and the laminated bookmarkers with it. Jonathan looked at the colored ribbons that marked several pages.

"I think you'll find those pages interesting, J2," the Cardinal said. He left an embossed card with his address and private numbers.

"You may write or call me any time you like. If you need assistance, just let Father Birney know and he'll contact me. Thank you for meeting with me and I look forward to our next meeting." He rose and Father Birney joined him, as they departed. Then, the Cardinal walked back to the door and said, "I think you're wrong, Jonathan." And then he was gone.

The Warden accompanied him back to his cell. "Jonathan, I received a stack of requests for media interviews. Every top name wants to see you and interview you. What do you say?"

"No! No reporters," he said emphatically.

"It's your decision. That was quite a visitor you just had. He is the most important Cardinal at the Vatican."

"I like him," he said. "I hope he comes again. And the Bible is gorgeous. Don't you think?"

They played chess again and the results were the same.

"I almost beat you tonight, J2." They laughed.

Then after Kindt left for home, Jonathan began looking at the most precious thing he owned now. He read each page that the Cardinal had marked.*

---

* 1 Peter 2:24   **"Who his own self bare our sins in his own body on the tree, that we, being dead to sins, should live unto righteousness; by whose stripes ye were healed."**

*1 Cor. 1:9   **"But we had the sentence of death in ourselves, that we should not trust in ourselves, but in God which raiseth the dead."**

Chapter 14

Nello Gamberino came to see Jonathan two weeks after the Cardinal's visit. He brought copies of the reports from Dr. Clifford, Sr. Sebastian, and Dr. Lechman. Each wrote an individual report, and each conflicted with the other's in conclusions.

"These forensic reports are great, Mr. Childress. The Attorney General is going to have a difficult time overcoming them. You're going to win."

Jonathan scanned the first report in the stack, which was authored by the prison psychologist, Dr. Warren Clifford. In sum, the report said that in his opinion, "the subject presents a case of delusion, accompanied by an unexplainable quantum leap in knowledge." The report from Dr. Sebastian called him schizophrenic, probably due to the induction of the chemicals during the failed execution. Then he reached the one from "Hannibal Lecter," Dr. Lechman.

"This subject presents an undefined disorder on any Axis within the Diagnostic and Statistical Manual of Mental Disorders, or DSM IV. It is the author's impression that the subject is confined in a fugue state, whereby he releases accumulated and stored knowledge from unknown origin."

Before Jonathan was done, Nello told him to jump to her "conclusion" on the last page.

"In conclusion, it is my opinion, based upon a degree of medical certainty, employing the standard practices that are generally acceptable in the psychological community, that Jonathan L. Childress II is no longer a danger and will, without question, remain so for life."

"She killed them, Mr. Childress. She is the hired gun they thought would get them over the top. You must have impressed her."

"We won't use them, Mr. Gamberino. I am not insane or managed to expel knowledge that I never knew I had before."

"Mr. Childress, I must remind you that I'm no longer your attorney, technically, but I serve as a friend of the court. You cannot decide what I can and cannot use."

"You're right. I can't fire you anymore." When Jonathan said that, he got up and walked to the door where he generally entered, and rapped on it with his knuckle. An officer opened the door.

"Officer, Mr. Gamberino is just leaving now. Would you be so kind as to notify the front gate that under no circumstances is he or Mr. Amaranta to be permitted to visit me?" Then he turned back to Nello. "You're right, I can't fire you, but I can stop you from getting in here. And, I will notify the Judge. Oh, and stop the theatrics for the media or I'll hold my own press conference and ruin you two. Have a nice drive back to Chicago."

As he walked away, Nello heard him thank the officer for taking care of the call squashing any future visits.

That night, Jonathan crafted his arguments for Judge Echols. He went to the Law Library every night and filled legal pads with notes. He outlined what he wanted to say and began typing. He typed for three days. When it was finished, he was completely spent. But, it was a masterpiece. At least to him.

As he read the Federal Rules of Civil Procedure, which apply to habeas corpus actions, not criminal rules like most would expect, he was permitted to file his Reply to the response filed by the Attorney General. Basically, he gets the last word and the Judge has several options. He can deny the petition outright. He could hold an evidentiary hearing, which everyone expects in this case, and then decide whether or not to grant relief.

In either method, it would take months before Judge Lucius Echols would issue a decision, as federal courts work differently than others.

While he and the country awaited the big decision, Jonathan occupied his time reading the Bible from the Cardinal, and he began doing exercises in his cell. He enjoyed both and it took his mind off the decision over his life.

As it turned out, the wait wasn't as long as everyone thought it would be.

The door opened to his cell. He was half asleep after reading his Bible most of the night. Warden Kindt was there, with Father Birney. Neither smiled.

"I'm afraid I have some bad news for you, Mr. Childress". The Warden was there on Saturday morning and had the priest with him. There were two officers at the door.

"Well, what, Mr. Kindt?"

"Judge Echols issued a very long decision in your case. He said he found no reason to hold an evidentiary hearing. His clerk faxed me a copy, although a copy is being mailed to you. Also, one of the attorneys tried to visit you. He can't, at your request." They stood there looking at him.

Jonathan took a deep breath. "So, this is what it feels like to know you're going to die. Again." He thought to himself. He wondered how Johnny Lee took the news.

"I thought you would want to hear it from us first, the priest joined in."

"Thank you," Jonathan said as he laid back on his bunk.

"We haven't told you everything yet, Mr. Childress," Kindt said.

"I can tell, thank you, though."

"I guess I'm obligated to tell you. That's why they faxed it here."

"OK, Mr. Kindt. I'm ready," he said as he swung his feet onto the floor and sat up.

"Let me go to the Judge's conclusion and get to the point," he said as he cleared his throat. He read:

"It is the finding of this Court that based upon all three psychologists appointed by this Court, the Petitioner does and has suffered an undetermined degree of mental impairment. The record in the Trial Court reflects that these forensic determinations were not put before the jury at trial or sentencing, which violates the Supreme Court holdings in **Apprehendi v. New Jersey**.

Therefore, this Court, having considered the premises and merits, along with the pleadings filed by the parties, hereby Orders that the conviction and sentence in the Circuit Court of Cook County, Illinois, is hereby vacated and a new trial shall commence within one hundred eighty days or the Petitioner shall be released from custody forthwith.

IT IS SO ORDERED.

Honorable Lucius Echols
United States District Court"

Everyone was smiling at him. One of the officers at the door produced a cupcake with a candle in it.

"Congratulations, J2, you've beaten the odds again," the Warden said.

"Jonathan, I believe God is protecting you," Father Birney said as if he wanted no one to overhear him.

A few of the cons on the row actually cheered, not because it was Jonathan who won, but because it renewed their hopes of avoiding their own untimely death. "What does all this do for me now, Mr. Kindt?"

"Well, the Cook County Court has to vacate the conviction and sentence. Until then, you are still going to be here with us, but you've won a major victory. Of course, the State may appeal the decision. All you can do now is to wait. We wanted to let you know the decision and Father Birney was so excited. I have to be going now. Congratulations!" Kindt turned and when he left, the two officers joined him outside the cell.

"Jonathan, I have a message here for you from Cardinal Carroll. I called him with the news last night. He says that you're a man with many victories and says that you are the luckiest man alive or God is watching over you. And he said, 'Congratulations'."

"Tell him 'thank you' for me, will you, Father?"

He sat there looking at the decision from Judge Echols and realized that of the thousands of petitions like his, only a handful are granted. He had read that often in the cases he researched. Was there some extrinsic force helping him?

"I'll leave you alone now. I know this is all a bit overwhelming right now," Father Birney said and headed for the door.

In Chicago there were mixed feelings. The State's attorney was holding a press conference on a Saturday morning at his office.

He didn't want to wait until Monday and let the media get the jump on him.

In an office at the Cathedral, Cardinal Carroll was privately discussing the matter on the telephone and was faxing a copy of the decision he received from Father Birney, to the party he was conferring with on the matter.

The Attorney General issued a written statement for distribution through his media representative. The statement was a bit overbearing, but he didn't care at that point. He called the decision unconscionable, preposterous and utterly without a reasonable foundation. He also said he was appealing and felt certain that the decision would be reversed.

Mordeci called Ben at home and gave him the news.

"Mort, could this guy get off at a new trial?" Ben enquired.

"He's picking up a lot of support, Ben. There are a lot of unknown factors in this. He could be found incompetent or not guilty by reason of insanity, but he would be placed with mental health then. If he is no longer a danger, he'd walk."

"Rachael isn't going to like this."

"That's why I'm calling you, Ben. She should hear it from you before the media tells her. Don't you think?"

"I'll call her. Unless you'd care to call her and tell her?"

"Are you nuts? The woman teaches self-defense and I have no desire to be her test dummy," Mort said as he began to laugh and Ben joined him.

Sam Amaranta was hailing the decision as one of "their" greatest victories. P.T. Barnum had nothing on this guy. He and Nello were holding their own press conference that morning. Their law practice was steadily improving now and they were asked questions by lawyers, Judges, friends and well-wishers wherever they went. When Amaranta read a letter to the Editor in the Chicago Tribune from a woman in Waukegan, asking if the Editor believed that Jonathan could be an angel, he began to formulate a plan. He had a great marketing strategy. He needed an artist, though.

Back at Thames, Jonathan paced the floor of his cell. He had already requested to go to the Law Library. He was not entirely happy with the decision after all.

Mordeci's story was front page news. The decision was a blockbuster, which both shocked and pleased the legal community. He had interviews with some of the top attorneys in the Chicagoland area. He had no interest in interviewing the State Attorney General, but he would like Rachael's slant on the whole case. He doubted she would co-operate though, but he would contact her later on after the news settled in. He would give a month's salary to interview Jonathan, but he doubted that would ever happen.

In a little house in the Polish community, the mother who would never see her twin daughters grow and give her grandchildren, wept openly. The Father of those little girls did something he never thought he would do. He bought a gun.

Chapter 15

As promised, the Attorney General filed a Notice of Appeal, which is a simple, one-page document, filed in the District Court. By filing it, the court in Springfield no longer had jurisdiction or power to enter any more orders regarding Jonathan's case. Only the Seventh Circuit Court of Appeals had any power now. What confounded appellate lawyers was the news that Jonathan, the victor in the District Court, had filed his own notice and was seeking appellate review.

A phone call was surreptitiously made, and the same panel composed of Easterman, Evans and Manlon was quietly assigned the appeal.

The process of an appeal in federal cases is not much different than in the states. The Clerk of Court assembles the file, including all pleadings filed by the parties and any Orders or decisions by the trial Judge. The parties can purchase transcripts of any hearings or trials and the court reporters will file the original in the Clerk's office and send the requesting counsel a copy. However, the only copies of transcripts in this case originated in the trial court, when Judge Echols found no reason to hold an evidentiary hearing.

Once the District Court file is transmitted to the Court of Appeals, the panel will issue a Briefing Schedule, which establishes exact dates for the filing of the briefs, where issues and arguments are presented, with the Clerk.

As a general rule, the Appellant, or loser in the District Court, files his Initial Brief, which sets the tenor of the issues he contends entitles him to a reversal of the conviction or other relief. The Appellee, or winner in the lower court, files a brief responding to the issues raised in the Initial Brief of the party initiating the Appeal. The last brief is filed in reply to the Appellee's brief. The Court of Appeals panel of Judges then decides if oral arguments are to be scheduled. At oral arguments, just the attorney's appear before the Judges to present additional points and legal authorities which they believe will persuade the Judges to rule in their favor. Also, they answer the questions put to them by the appeals panel. The contemporary notion among top appellate lawyers is that oral argument is merely fluff or extraneous effort, a waste of time.

In Jonathan's case, the process becomes more complex because the lawyers, as "friends of the court," get to file their own briefs which may or may not follow the same vein as the other parties.

To muddy the waters even more, Jonathan has appealed himself, and can raise issues beyond those raised by the State in the Initial Brief.

The legal analysts agreed that the appeal in this particular case would be complex and interesting. Every one of them wondered what Jonathan disagreed with in his sweeping victory.

The first step in the appellate journey according to Jonathan's marching orders was to file a request that the panel of Easterman, Evans and Manlon, recuse itself. He would premise this request on two primary principles of law. First, they had heard the initial appeal and issued a scathing opinion, which clearly manifested a predisposition in the case. In layman's terms, the legalese filtered away, it means that the Judges are biased and can no longer be impartial.

The second issue Jonathan intended to raise is a bit more difficult to substantiate. It is called "steering," where the Clerk assigns cases to Judges who are not in the random order of selection, according to statutory provisions. This is a serious allegation to make and implies that the Clerk or an employee thereof violated established procedure in assigning Jonathan's case to Easterman's panel.

Jonathan had an idea though, and asked Father Birney for a little help and he was delighted, playing sleuth!

Jonathan began his research. It became rote that every night the lights would burn in the prison's Law Library, signaling his struggle against the finely honed machine of the Attorney General's office and his desire to cling to life. It was the Proverbial David versus Goliath battle and in some eyes, assumed Biblical proportions. It was destined to be an epic legal battle and without question, on a fast-track itinerary for the Supreme Court. The country could hardly wait.

"Good morning Jonathan," Father Birney said as he entered his cell.

"Good Morning, Father."

"I received faxed copies of what you asked for from the Court," he noted as he handed them to J2.

"Thank you. Let's see if my hunch was correct. Give me a minute, Father."

The priest looked over his shoulder and waited. "What are you looking for?" he asked.

"If I am right, Father, we should see a departure from the sequential assignment of appeals as they come in."

"I am fluent in Latin, Jonathan, but none of what you just said made much sense to me."

"When an appeal is received in the Clerk's office, it is given the next available number for a file." He showed the priest the notice he had received from the appellate court which told him his appeal number, which is a new appeal case number, different from the one he had in the District Court.

"What you just gave me are copies of the Assignment Log, which is public record if anyone cares to ask, and is maintained by the Clerk. Let's get my notebook and write down the progression of assignments. If there is a departure in that normal progression, we have a case of *steering*."

"How do you know all of this stuff?"

"I've read a lot, but I'm not sure of how I know the rest."

The priest made the sign of the cross. Jonathan only smiled faintly.

As Jonathan read the names, the priest wrote them down and at J2's exacting guidance, assigned the first rotation numbers. The names of the Judges were cyclical. That is, until Jonathan's case.

"You see here, Father? The panel assigned to my case jumped nine spaces, then returned to the regular sequence and then skipped them in the rotation. Someone manipulated the assignment."

"Oh, I see. You're a genius, J2."

"Now I have hard evidence. Would you tell the Cardinal

thank-you for sending someone after these copies?"

"Certainly. May I convey to him what we found?"

"Sure, but he should keep it quiet until I get my motion filed."

"Can we send him a copy of your motion?" the priest asked shyly.

"Sure", although Jonathan doubted that the Cardinal would fully understand it.

While Jonathan was hard at work, so were the publically funded forces in the Attorney General's Office and the Cook County State's Attorney's office. There were numerous assistants working in a syncopated harmony befitting gold medal teams.

The gist of their arguments was myopically focused on an abuse of discretion and the clearly erroneous application of **Apprendi v. New Jersey** to this case. They believed the Judge was far out of line in ordering a new trial. They had no idea about the steering allegation, but were quite pleased that Easterman was back on the case.

After Jonathan filed his recusal motion in the Seventh Circuit, which the State's Attorney General responded to in a two-page defensive, a bombshell found its way into the epicenter of the controversy. A "recusal" basically alleges judicial bias and requests that other Judges be assigned to decide a case.

The President of the American Bar Association, which represents the legal community and defines ethical standards, along with the National Association of Criminal Defense Lawyers, the NACDL, representing thousands of prominent defense attorneys nationwide, petitioned the Chief Judge of the Seventh Circuit, to intervene as *amici*.

The petition substantiated not only Jonathan's claims, but documented almost seventy additional instances where steering has occurred and the Easterman & Co. Panel got assigned to cases out of rotation. It further called for a thorough investigation by the United States Attorney in Chicago, with prosecution of those responsible.

The ABA issued a scathing statement and its president appeared forceful and confident on the news.

The cat was out of the bag as they say, and the mice were scurrying for cover. Frank Easterman and his cronies, attired in their judicial robes, made a conciliatory statement denying any involvement in any steerage of cases and due to the appearance of impropriety, they ordered the Clerk to reassign the appeal to another panel. Very sanctimonious.

"Hey, counselor," one of the cons on death row hollered out his door to Jonathan. "Hey J2, it says on the TV the Judges on your case have quit or not hearing your appeal. Did you do that?"

Jonathan thought about the panel removing themselves from his case. Then he thought he had a viable answer, but thought that the con wouldn't understand. "I don't think so." It appeared that he couldn't lose. He was doing better than most attorneys.

Jonathan was notified of the new panel assigned by the Clerk. They were fresh names and to his knowledge had never heard anything even remotely associated with his case. He was quite pleased.

The country held its breath waiting to see what Jonathan wanted to complain about on his appeal. He began receiving books from advocates and well-wishers. His cell began to shrink as the books piled up. He had a ravenous appetite for knowledge and wisdom they held for him. An empty cell began as his personal Law Library, but he insisted that the others on death row be permitted access if they were so inclined. A number of them accepted the invitation and soon, it became a focal point to most of their individual needs of survival. The Warden even had bookshelves mounted on walls and a small table was bolted to the floor, where the bunk used to be. It became their official Law Library, donated by Jonathan L. Childress II.

Jonathan received offers from prominent lawyers offering to represent him, but he would never relinquish control as he had mistakenly done once before.

The Warden advised him that staff in the mailroom at Thames reported that they were receiving Bibles, packages, stacks of letters and even money, for Jonathan. They wanted to know what to do with it all. Jonathan came up with a solution that suited everyone. Father Birney distributed the Bibles and books among the men on the row. When everyone had what they needed, he would store them at the chapel for others to use at the main prison.

He was more creative with the letters. Anyone on the row who wished to read the letters and materials were given stacks of letters. The row hummed with J2 *esprit de corps*. Occasionally, one of the cons would tell Jonathan that some naysayer wished him eternal life in hell or that he should be hanged on Court TV, but for the most part, the letters supported him and his endeavors. The cons enjoyed the mail and the distraction it afforded them. It afforded Jonathan the time he required to complete his research. He was rapidly becoming an expert in forensic psychology and the finer points of writing. His seemingly insatiable thirst for legal theory, substantive law and the constitution was slowly being quenched. The priest would help him, giving Jonathan a sense that Father Birney had adopted his mission statement in life and abandoned the remainder of his flock at the prison. Then Jonathan learned that there was a volunteer Deacon who serviced the needs of the general population at the prison. Father Birney was his *aide-de-camp*, so to speak, and he was greatly appreciative.

The row had become a better place, a more peaceful place despite the serious consequences each of them faced by being there. A fortunate aspect is that none of the men on the row was facing imminent threat of being executed, as their legal battles devoured the months and years of judicial maneuvering.

"I think the Cardinal told him about you and your fight. Can I tell him you approve?"

"As long as it's not a reporter, Father."

Chapter 16

"People of the State of Illinois versus Johnny Lee Childress," the courtroom clerk said solemnly. And so began the gruesome rendition of events of the crimes for which he stood accused.

Rachael sat through the entire trial, as the State's Attorney wanted her there to maintain the flow of evidence because she was the "case officer" and because she seemed to have an adverse affect on the killer. Scott Schroeder wanted the jury to see that threatening interaction from the man he sought to convict and execute. He did not want the guy found insane. Anyone who would do that to those two girls could easily be found insane just because of the rage and brutality of the wounds, with the proper jury that is. So, Rachael was there as a weapon against Johnny Lee. Besides, Rachael is pleasant to look at and the male jurors would appreciate that. Prosecutors have little tricks, too.

Like the first witness up was the uniform car that responded first to the crime scene. The officer, who would have been more comfortable in a suit on his day off, was told to wear his full uniform. "Call a friend, call a cop." The prosecutors want them in uniform because of the pristine image they're supposed to have as public servants.

"To Serve and Protect" is on the sides of every marked squad car. The officer's uniform, like Superman's cape, represents authority, power, integrity and above all, trust.

He described the carnage inside that little apartment. Schroeder did not introduce the dramatic color photographs he had enlarged and mounted. He would save that shock factor for the Medical Examiner. Instead, he used a simple diagram, as if describing the collision of two Toyotas at an intersection. Clean. Simple.

Schroeder's next witness was the venerable Medical Examiner, Tommy Dorf. Now is when those "living color" photos came out of the un-living and gasps of disbelief and horror were heard around the courtroom. Even from the jurors. Perfect. Prosecutors select the goriest photos for jury trials, as if they were produced to scare the Jurors into convicting the accused. Schroeder had received the exact effect he had counted on, as the photos were quite horrible. The prejudice from these photos would become an issue on appeal, as Johnny Lee's attorneys had offered to stipulate to the crimes being committed, but that Johnny was insane at the time. Schroeder was having none of that. He wanted the jury to see the horrendous slashes and damage done to those little girls.

Tommy Dorf testified as usual. Perfect. He described the initial bloodletting accounting for the splatter patterns on the living room walls. Schroeder produced a model of a human bust, showing muscles, trachea, arteries and bone. He had Dorf identify the wounds and asked if they would be consistent with People's Exhibit Number 9, the knife that Rachael caught Johnny Lee with and he said, "Yes." For dramatic effect, he handed that knife to Dorf and asked him to trace the angle and point of attack across the neck of the plastic model. Everyone could almost feel that blade at their own throat as Dorf pulled it across the transparent neck. One juror had to rub her throat at that time, as if she may see blood red when she pulled her hand away. And all the defense attorneys could do was to watch, because Schroeder had the right to have Dorf demonstrate how the injuries were inflicted.

A diagram was used to show the vaginal penetration and the tearing of the hymen on both girls. They were both virgins, as to be expected at age 9. Schroeder had a case once where the defendant argued that the eleven year old was promiscuous and sought a lesser degree in penalty. Schroeder was on a roll and despite having a slam-dunk conviction, was playing the role of razor-sharp trial tactician.

The same diagram was used to describe the genital mutilation. Schroeder actually thought about using enlargements of the girls' pubic areas. "He was such a pompous ass," Tommy had told him in response and advised Schroeder to find another expert for trial. Dorf was having nothing to do with that circus stunt. Schroeder thought better after Dorf's admonition.

Next up was Sergeant Rachael Hart, the second in command at Homicide. An artist sketched her on the stand, along with a faceless jury and a caricature of both, the Judge and

Schroeder.

Rachael described the events and how she came to subdue and to arrest Johnny Lee, who couldn't resist sneering at the skinny bitch that kicked his ass. The jurors saw that and Schroeder got the desired effect. They hated Johnny Lee.

Rachael described the arrest and the knife he had on him. She identified People's Exhibit Number 9 for the record and it was admitted into evidence.

When the State tendered Rachael for cross-examination to the defense, it was Nello Gamberino who led the charge. Smooth. Not confrontational. He was the real shark at the trial and Rachael knew it. Schroeder was a warm, rectal breeze compared to the man questioning her.

"Sergeant Hart, when you arrested the defendant, Mr. Childress, you testified he was armed with a knife, People's Exhibit 9."

"Yes, he was."

"You also testified that he was hiding under a porch at the house where you arrested him?"

"Correct."

"And you were several blocks away from the crime scene, weren't you?"

"About four or five blocks, yes."

"Did you have a canine there that day?"

"No, they were busy elsewhere at that time. I had thought of that."

"Well, then, Sergeant, what gave you probable cause to arrest the defendant way over there?"

"He was covered in blood, was carrying a knife, and the girls or victims appeared to be murdered with a knife."

"Have you had prior contact with the defendant before, Sergeant?"

"No, I haven't."

"Were you armed like you are today? You carry a sidearm, correct?"

"Yes sir."

"And was your weapon holstered at that time or did you have

it out and at the ready?"

Rachael thought she knew where this shark was headed with this line of questioning. "It was out."

"And when you first saw Mr. Childress, you were carrying your weapon in front of you, where Mr. Childress could see it?"

"Yes, I made sure he would see it."

"Was he carrying his knife where you could see it?"

"It was in his right hand at his side. Yes, I could see it."

"Did you order him to drop the knife?"

Rachael had anticipated this coming, but had hoped Gamberino would overlook it.

"No, I did not."

"What did you do, Sergeant?"

"I holstered my weapon." She saw eyebrows arch at the prosecutor's table, a couple of the jurors and elsewhere. Everyone wondered why this unusual maneuver was employed.

"If you believed Mr. Childress was a murderer, armed with a knife, why would you not order him to drop this knife with your weapon in hand?"

Ben had asked her pretty much the same question and she told him it was because she wanted to beat the hell out of him.

"Because I felt I could disarm him without the threat of lethal force."

"Sergeant Hart, is that standard police practice?"

"I would have to say no, but this was not a standard arrest, either."

His next question caught her completely off guard, as she had anticipated it going in another direction.

"Have you ever heard of 'suicide by cop' in your prior experience?"

"Yes, sir. That has been discussed in recent classes."

"Is it possible, Sgt. Hart that Mr. Childress wanted you to shoot him that day?" "Objection, calls for speculation," Schroeder shouted.

"The officer can testify to her observations. She has testified to holstering her weapon, which is contrary to customary police practice." Nello said as if he had practiced it a thousand times.

"Overruled," the Judge said.

"I don't believe that was his intent, but I guess anything is possible." She wanted to avoid appearing argumentative, yet give them only the slight possibility that the craven killer wanted Texas Justice that day.

"No, I felt I could disarm him myself."

"Did Mr. Childress drop the knife?"

"Yes, sir, after I twisted his arm," she said loudly, drawing snickers from a few spectators.

"I see. Isn't it true, Sergeant, that you are considered an expert in at least one form of martial arts?"

"Yes." She gave him only the concise answer to avoid being boastful or a bully.

"Is it safe to say, Sergeant Hart, that you wanted Mr. Childress to attack you?"

"I was prepared, counselor."

"You wanted to hurt my client here, didn't you, Sergeant?"

"That was his choice."

"Would you have hurt Mr. Childress that day?"

"Yes, if he would not have dropped the knife."

"You had already formed your opinion of the defendant by his appearance, having never had any contact with him before, departed from standard police procedure, not summoned any back-up, holstered your weapon and you are asking us to believe that you didn't want a physical confrontation with my client where you could harm him without witnesses?"

"Objection," Schroeder protested, "it sounds like a summation by counsel."

"Sustained."

Gamberino had made his point. The expression on Rachael's face betrayed her. She invited an attack and disliked someone she didn't have any knowledge of, who may have been imbalanced enough to invite her to kill him.

"No further question," Gamberino said as he looked at the jurors as if to say "Remember all this, people."

Dr. Jack Farmer, the Chief of Forensics walked the jury through each of the scientifically proven connections between the crimes and Johnny Lee Childress. The most damning is the semen found inside the girls matching Johnny Lee's DNA.

The last witness is Det. Emilio Ortiz who set the stage for the video-recording of the confession. After the chain of custody matters were settled, the courtroom was darkened and everyone began watching the glorious performance by the accused, along with Rachael's questioning, admit to the entire offense. When the lights came back up, the jury wanted to hang him right there in court.

"The State rests, Your Honor," Schroeder announced in a grand gesture.

Sam Amaranta began Johnny Lee's defense by calling the psychologist from Cermak Hospital who first saw Johnny Lee when he arrived at the Cook County Jail.

Qualifying Dr. Quinn was easy, as he is a State employee.

"Dr. Quinn, when Mr. Childress was first brought to the jail, you screened him for a psychological triage, correct?"

"Yes sir."

"And you noted that he appeared distraught, withdrawn and traumatized, I believe are your words, where you ordered him into isolation?"

"That about sums up my evaluation and yes, I did want him away from other prisoners."

"Do you know how long before you examined Mr. Childress, that he was arrested and held in custody?"

"I believe it was the day before, about twenty-four hours."

"Do you know where Mr. Childress was held in that prior time period?"

"Yes, the reports said he had been held at the Chicago Police Headquarters. In their lock-up."

"In your years of experience, have you ever known any prisoners at the lock–up to receive any mental health screening or treatment?"

"No. If they believe they have someone who is in need of mental health care, they bring them to us."

"And when you say 'they', Dr. Quinn, who are you referring to? Do they have psychologists there?"

"No. The 'they' would be police officers."

"So, if the officers chose not to bring an arrestee to Cermak

Hospital, they would not receive treatment.   Is that correct?" Amaranta had one more question.

"Correct."

"Is it possible that an arresting officer could intentionally decide not to transport an arrestee to Cermak so that you couldn't examine them and note their condition at the time of arrest?"

"Yes, that's possible."

Amaranta had made his point.   By keeping Johnny Lee at the headquarters instead of transporting him to the Cook County Jail, Rachael could effectively hide his psychological condition at the time of arrest, from the whole world.

However, it is not unusual that cops keep their prisoners close so they can interrogate them and capitalize on the initial shock of being arrested.   Rachael did want to keep Johnny Lee close to her and push him into a statement, which he made.

The star of the defense strategy was Dr. Mohammed Azam, a forensic psychologist who initially trained in India.   After arriving in the United States, he was required to serve an internship to gain certification here.   He was accepted at the Walter Reed Medical Center, near Washington's Capitol, where he attended the soldiers returning from combat situations around the globe.   He had seen the aftereffects of the bloodletting and the imprint such acts indelibly etched on those minds.

Post-Traumatic Stress Disorder, PTSD, gained national prominence after returning veterans of the Viet Nam conflict exhibited delusional tendencies, hearing or visualizing "gooks" attacking them or suffering from imaginary wounds.

"Dr. Azam, when someone is traumatized, what is the most critical period for psychological intervention and treatment?"   Nello Gamberino asked, as he and Amaranta switched positions, as in one of those professional wrestling events on TV.

"Without question, twenty-four hours."

The balance of the direct examination dealt with various personality disorders, psychosis, testing procedures and how a clinical, forensic psychologist determines the diagnosis in an objective fashion.

In Johnny Lee's case, Dr. Azam spent three days, over a

period of weeks, during which he observed him and questioned him about his past history, childhood, likes/dislikes, relationships and the crimes for which he was there. He also administered similar tests as had Dr. Quinn, and the numerical scores were almost identical, but the interpretive portions varied.

In the end, Dr. Azam believed that Johnny Lee Childress possessed an adolescent thinking ability, somewhere around pre-high school, was incapable of maintaining a long-term heterosexual relationship, suffered PTSD, along with sociopathic beliefs, and had no wish to continue life. For these reasons he lacked a specific degree of culpability to enable him to premeditatedly formulate such crimes.

At the time Rachael listened to his supposition, she believed it was only "hired gun" testimony to try to save his miserable life. Attorneys knew that was a long shot anyway when they argued it at trial. What they targeted was the penalty phase. Childress had never been convicted of such heinous acts. His prior criminal history was marred with a few crimes which may have alerted the professional in the criminal justice system that he was a cauldron of emotions, bubbling near the surface like a volcano. However, no one caught the red flags and he slipped through their clutches.

The acts he stood convicted of today were so uncharacteristic when compared to his priors, that defense counsels believed that the jury would have to consider that when deciding whether to impose the death penalty. Sometimes, juries don't travel the route you have plotted for them. In 1939, for example, a jury in New York decided to impose the electric chair for a man named Edward Gein from Friendship, Wisconsin. He was not the first recorded cannibal to stand trial. Albert Fish was. The jury in Fish's case concluded that he was utterly mad, yet too dangerous to ever permit a reoccurrence of his crimes. Fish had pushed needles deep into his abdomen and under his testicles. He would beat himself on the back and buttocks, with screws and nails protruding, until blood flowed freely down the backs of his legs. He was convicted of murdering a little girl and eating parts of her.

Nello Gamberino watched the jury closely during the penalty phase. Schroeder displayed his various photo enlargements like a monument to the Marquis de Sade. Those photos damned their client, especially when Schroeder placed the enlargements of the twins' school photos next to the tattered remnants of flesh, bone and blood Childress left behind.

The penalty phase in a capital case is like a mini-trial, in that prior to their second term of deliberations, they are given jury instructions again. These instructions, like those given during trial, must be accurate, succinct, and constitutionally sound. If the jury is inaccurately instructed, courts of appeals will generally strike down the death sentence and direct the trial court to amend the sentence to a term of imprisonment or life.

Juries are instructed to consider all forms of mitigating facts, after the Supreme Court decision in *Apprendi v. New Jersey* despite a state statutory construction otherwise. Illinois permits a jury to consider the diminished capacity of a defendant during the commission of a crime. This statutory scheme places the burden of persuasion on the defendant using a standard reserved for civil trials, "by the preponderance of the evidence." In other words, who tips the scales of justice slightly in their favor with the evidence?

It took the jury in Johnny Lee's case less than an hour to render their verdict of death. The next day, Johnny was sentenced by the Judge in accord with the jury's verdict and it was all over.

Chapter 17

Jonathan focused on two primary fronts. First, he resented the District Court's inference that he suffers delusions today and should not be executed because of that fact. All three psychologists found him lucid, well versed, and cognizant of his surroundings and of the perilous fight he faces. He had testified truthfully in District Court and the State of Illinois provided no expert testimony to contradict the formidable "Hannibal Lecter."

His second front of legal attack regarded the jury instructions at trial and sentencing. He intended to argue that the District Court glossed over the import and he had a secret weapon close to the vest.

The State, he presumed, would assail the federal court's decision based or predicated upon the "current" state of his mind. Jonathan couldn't explain the sources or quantity of legal knowledge he now possessed and practiced so easily. It frightened him at times that he could cite a theory of doctrine and give supporting case law, as if he had studied law all his life!

Jonathan had forgotten the exact date that the Cardinal had mentioned that he planned to visit. When Father Birney awoke him and hustled him to the shower, he had spent the large part of the night studying and was a little groggy.

The Cardinal arrived wearing the customary resplendent red robes, with another man dressed simply, except that he wore a purple sash around his waist. He looked tanned, a bit older than Cardinal Carroll, but conditioned. He had close cropped white hair and wire framed glasses. He was carrying a rather large briefcase of black leather, which looked very expensive. Father Birney watched them enter the administration building, with anticipation.

"Jonathan, it's good to see you again," Cardinal Carroll said as he shook his hand and then gave him a manly hug.

"This is a very dear friend of mine, Jonathan. I would like you to meet Cardinal Bavielli."

The second Cardinal extended his hand and gave him a hug as well. They were in the same conference room next to the Warden's office and Kindt remained in his office as before. He had two Cardinals in his prison and was impressed.

"Jonathan, Cardinal Bavielli is not only a priest, he is also an attorney. He would like to talk to you about your appeal and is willing to help you."

"I have read your file thus far and I admire your work. I have some ideas for you and I'm willing to answer questions for you, if you wish."

At that, the second Cardinal placed several folders on the table. Jonathan could see his name all over them.

"I appreciate the help, sir, but I only have two issues I'm raising," Jonathan responded.

"Perhaps we can work on them together? I would like to get to know you better." He looked into Jonathan's eyes and immediately made an alliance he would later appreciate greatly.

"I think I would like that very much. Thank you."

With the Warden's approval and the promise from Father Birney that they were safe locked in the room with Jonathan while an officer sat outside in the corridor, Jonathan and his appellate team began to work. Cardinal Carroll excused himself after lunch and Jonathan marveled at the working knowledge Cardinal Bavielli had of his case.

By four o'clock, they were both ready to break for the night. The Cardinal and Father Birney left and Jonathan went to his cell to digest all that he had learned that day.

Throughout the day, intermittently, Bavielli had asked him about life after death and the testimony he had given in the federal court. His eyes got moist as Jonathan explained his return from limbo and the Reaper's mistake.

When Father Birney dropped off the Cardinal at a local hotel, he failed to notice that the Cardinal had no luggage whatsoever. When Father Birney was gone, the Cardinal hailed a cab and went to a nearby church where Cardinal Carroll waited. The resident priest, delighted to have such a distinguished guest, made them comfortable in the rectory and left for a meeting.

"What do you think of Robert?" Cardinal Carroll asked.

"The man I was with all day definitely isn't the same creature that murdered those two girls. I think you're right, John. Jonathan is polite, educated beyond that ever attainable by the killer and he has an ability to convert people. John, he has an innate power of influence to change people. Father Birney tells me that the men on death row are different now, more peaceful and believe in this guy. There's something very special about Jonathan."

"I didn't bring you from Rome to visit a prisoner. If what Jonathan says is true about his voyage back to life, we should not stand idle while these people try to destroy him."

Cardinal Bavielli thought about that and knew his brother Cardinal was right. "I need to make some calls, John. Let's see what we can do."

As Carroll walked past the room where Bavielli was seated on the bed, he overheard him on the phone. "Your Eminence..." was all he needed to hear. Jonathan was about to receive a helping hand.

The next morning when Jonathan was led to the Warden's conference room, he was utterly shocked. So was the Warden a half hour earlier, when Cardinal Bavielli appeared and brought a friend.

"Good morning, Jonathan," Bavielli said. "I'd like you to meet..."

"I recognize him, Cardinal." Jonathan interrupted. "I'm sorry, Cardinal, but I don't get visits by former U.S. Attorney Generals every day. What brings you here, Mr. Adelman?"

"It's nice to meet you Jonathan," the recently resigned Attorney General said as he shook hands. "Cardinal Bavielli and I go way back. He called me and said that he needed a little help here. I wasn't busy, so here I am."

Jonathan was not naive enough to believe that this man was "not busy" and just happened to be passing through. Adelman just left his position as Attorney general of the United States, when the President was elected to a second term. He said on TV that he regretted leaving the President, but wished to spend time with his family who he had been neglecting the last four years. And now he was here with him.

"J2, isn't that what they call you?" Adelman inquired.

"Yes, sir."

"Well, J2, I've read your case and Bob, ah, Cardinal Bavielli rather, went over some interesting things with me last night. I'd like to help."

"You want to help me, Mr. Adelman? I mean, aren't you worried about bad publicity helping me?"

"Nonsense, Jonathan. I believe that what you say is supported by credible evidence that has gone unrebutted by the State of Illinois. My friend here believes in you, too, and he's always been tough to sell. So, can I help?"

"Yes, sir. I appreciate all the help I can get, but I've pretty much made my mind up what I'm going to argue. I'm not insane and not going to let them argue otherwise. I meant what I said in court and if I have to die again to keep them from making me appear like some lunatic, then I will. Do you still want to help, Mr. Adelman?"

"J2," he said and paused, "I agree with my friend here and agree to your terms. Let's see what we can put together. Shall we?"

While the Warden was in and out of his office and Father Birney brought coffee and English muffins to the conference room, officers and staff stole glimpses of the prestigious guests. Adleman had removed his suit coat and rolled up his sleeves. The Cardinal was listening to them and making notes.

Father Birney brought sandwiches for lunch, as the men refused to break their concentration and tempo. When they finally decided that they could accomplish no more for the day, the conversation turned light, and about Jonathan's plans for the future.

"Jonathan, if you'd like, I'd be happy to argue your case for you," Adelman said.

"I appreciate that Mr. Adelman, but I think the Judges need to hear it from me. I want them to realize that I'm not Johnny Lee Childress. Do you understand, sir?"

"If they are half as impressed with you and your sincerity as I am, you'll win handily. If you change your mind, call me. Will you do that?"

"Yes sir," he said as he gathered up copies of cases the men had brought and his own notes. "I think your ideas will help. Thank you."

He turned to Cardinal Bavielli. "I'm kind of curious though, why I have a Roman Catholic Cardinal and ex-attorney General so interested in me and my case?"

"I'll answer that question for you," the Cardinal said as he looked towards the window. "Jonathan, I'll be honest with you. You deserve no less. Some of us are convinced that you are very, very special. The Reaper, as you called him, does not make mistakes and let people return. You are living proof that our religious beliefs, the Bible, are true. If we stand mute and let non-believers destroy you, we are as ignorant as they are. We don't know if you're an angel or the Messiah himself, but we do know that no one has refuted your testimony or given us a viable explanation otherwise. Does that answer your question?"

"I don't think I'm any angel, Cardinal. I do find myself wondering who I really am or why I'm here like this, but I don't think I'm an angel. I wish I had those gossamer wings so I could simply fly away from all of this."

"Christ found himself in a life and death trial, Jonathan. He lost that trial. We want to make sure you win this one." Adelman added. "I agree with Bob here. Until someone can prove otherwise, the evidence before me suggests that you are telling the truth."

"And what if we find out I'm no angel?"

"We'll cross that bridge when we come to it," the Cardinal interposed.

Jonathan had a lot to mull over and to think about that night, as he lay awake on his bunk and abandoned any thoughts of sleep. He found himself trying to recall anything about his past that would give him a clue of who he was before, but nothing came to him. He had no answers as to how he would explain his resurrection and all, if the Judges were to question him. He finally fell asleep near sunrise.

Chapter 18

"Showdown is Mounting in Court of Appeals as Big Guns Appeal in Childress Case"

Rachael began reading Mordeci's column on the pending appeal of convicted murderer Johnny Lee Childress, who even the affable reporter now refers to as Jonathan Childress.

The newspaper is delivered every day, compliments of Mr. Mordeci Habush. She cannot resist the urge to call him about these "Big Guns" he refers to this morning, but doesn't name.

"Good morning Sergeant Hart," he said after answering on the first ring.

"How did you know it was me?"

"Caller ID says 'Chicago Police' and I figure you're reading the paper right now, so it makes perfect sense that it's you."

"You should work for us, Mordeci."

"When I retire from here, I'm all yours. What can I do for you this morning, Rachael?"

"Who are these big guns you refer to in your article Mort?"

"You mean you haven't heard? One of the biggest gunfights in legal history is lining up. We have the Illinois Attorney General on one side and on the other, we have the ex-United States Attorney General, Adelman."

"What are you talking about?" Rachael said, not believing her ears.

"He was spotted at the prison yesterday, Rachael. He spent the day with Jonathan and appears interested in this case. He was accompanied by a man dressed as a Cardinal, although my source didn't recognize him."

"What do you think is going on, Mort?"

"I'm not sure, Rachael, but it looks like some really big players are lining up on both sides here. I can't imagine why a Catholic cardinal would be involved here, but they were there."

"Maybe they should just declare Childress a saint and build a shrine for him. Come on, Mort, this guy's a killer. He confessed to it. Why don't you print that and remind everyone of what he did. Why not print a picture of the gravestones of the twins? Come on, Mort, print both sides!" she challenged.

"Hold on there, Rachael. I report the news. I don't take sides unless I have to. If Adelman files an appearance in the appeal, maybe I'll take you up on the challenge. I've gotta run as I have a boss who wants to know about all this, too."

When Rachael hung up, she saw that her hands were clenched. Seething with anger, she stomped off to find some coffee and a file to work on. In Chicago, there was never a shortage of homicides to distract her from reality. She needed that right now. She didn't want to think about the Catholic Church, her church, getting into the fray. What would a Cardinal be doing with Childress?

As Rachael was trying to figure out why a Cardinal was visiting Childress, the Illinois Attorney General was shouting at an assistant. He wanted to be absolutely positive it was the ex-Attorney General of the United States who was there at the prison to see Childress. When he called the Cook County State's Attorney with the news, he also gave him a warning. If Schroeder lost the appeal in Chicago, he would not have the Governor's support or his, in the next election.

Schroeder had filed the State's Initial Brief and felt confident that it aptly set forth the law and would win a reversal. In fact, Childress should be receiving his two copies shortly. As yet, no one had filed an appearance on Childress's behalf. There was no way that a man sitting in a cell on death row, without a lawyer, could defeat the prosecutorial machine. The first time was luck. The Seventh Circuit Court of Appeals was very different. It's where the real sharks swim.

Jonathan had received his two copies of Schroeder's brief the night before. Father Birney borrowed one to read over and was returning it. As Jonathan had anticipated, the State argued that in essence, the District Court erred in making a de facto determination of Jonathan's competency and was well beyond its limitations in doing so.

Mr. Adelman had advised him to file his brief in a consolidated fashion, making it his Initial Brief and his Answer Brief all in one. He saw wisdom in that maneuver. Besides, he did not have unlimited resources for copying and such. The money he had received from supporters was used to buy needed items among the men on the row, such as hygiene supplies and stamps so they could write letters to family, friends or counsel. So, one brief was all he would file.

The cases the Cardinal and Adelman had given him were very convincing. The Supreme Court, forever in flux and swaying to the desires of the current administration or public sentiment, was in the process of swinging to the left again, after years of right-wing decisions under Justice Rehnquist. As the ailing Chief Justice was in the throes of cancer and dying, the high court issued a decision that mandated prosecutors to plead each and every element of an offense upon which an enhanced penalty could be imposed in the Indictment, and submit those elements to a jury for a finding of guilt beyond a reasonable doubt. And therein lay the epicenter of Jonathan's case.

Not one time was his jury admonished that the State bore the burden of proof beyond a reasonable doubt. When Mr. Adelman and the Cardinal pointed this out to him, he understood completely. In fact, the instructions given to the jury stated that the Defendant, Jonathan, bore the burden of proof that he was not competent at the time of the commission of the offenses. This instruction followed decisions in that vein or reasoning after John Hinkley was found not guilty by reason of insanity after shooting down President Reagan.

Congress immediately passed a Bill called the "Insanity Defense Reform Act" and it took effect immediately. It shifted the burden of proof to the defendant seeking relief from conviction, based upon his mental condition. Prior to that Act, once a defendant made a threshold showing of his suffering mental disorders or defects which rendered him irresponsible, it was incumbent upon prosecutors to overcome that presumption and to prove otherwise. Now, the judicial pendulum was swinging back towards defendant's rights and the prosecutors always having the burden. The Court had ruled that to hold otherwise would in today's legal market, violate the Constitution. Jonathan had a good chance at that issue.

He and Father Birney worked about ten hours a day for the next three days. Jonathan had written and rewritten his brief several times. When he had it as refined as possible, he began typing and when Jonathan was done, he had twenty copies. He provided the State with two, the Court of Appeals with twelve and two to the attorneys Amaranta and Gamberino who were still "friends of the court." Father Birney had one which, with Jonathan's permission, he shared with the man who had come to see him and received his approval. The brief was faxed to three numbers. One was overseas.

Jonathan's brief was mailed to the Seventh Circuit Court of Appeals, along with the parties, well within the twenty day period allotted in the Schedule.

"He used our suggestion, Bob," Adelman said in the overseas call.

"I see. Will he win, though?" Cardinal Bavielli asked.

"If the panel follows the law, yes. Do you want me to file as an amicus?"

"Jonathan was fairly adamant on that. I guess we have to wait. Can you be at the oral argument, in case it all overwhelms Jonathan?"

"I'll have my secretary find out if or when they have oral arguments scheduled and juggle my calendar around. I'll be there. Maybe my being there will make it easier for him to ask me?"

"Make sure you sit directly behind him. Let the world know who you support! It can't hurt to have such a powerful man behind you."

They both laughed at that line. As the Pontiff's counsel, he appeared alongside the Pope wherever he went.

"When are you announcing the Pope's visit to the United States?"

"That release went out this morning. His Eminence is visiting 22 countries on this trip. We'll only be in the U.S. two days before going to Guatemala, where he'll call for an end to the bloodshed for the political positions. We'll be gone for two months on this trip."

"Call me, huh?"

"You've got it."

The State's reply brief was due in seven days after receiving Jonathan's brief, if the State's Attorney chose to file a Reply. The case was on the fast track program in the Court of Appeals. It was a high profile case and hotly contested. The panel was not going to let it linger or stagnate. It had scheduled oral argument and had issued a sealed order for the Marshals to produce Jonathan on that date and time. Once again, the world would get the opportunity to see and hear Jonathan L. Childress II in an open courtroom. The major networks were sending their most popular faces. The gallery would be star studded and artists would be among them, since cameras are not permitted in any federal court.

As the hearing date for the arguments grew closer, the cards and letters to Jonathan increased. Thousands of people were writing. He received marriage proposals, job offers, book deals, personal appearances, and opportunities for just about every conceivable method to generate money or fame. It was in another stack of letters that Jonathan opened an envelope whose address appeared to be in a child's writing, or printing was more like it. Both really, as the child tried to learn how to write. Jonathan sat back on his bunk and began to read.

The envelope said that it was from Sacramento, California. It was from a little girl named Krystan Dunbar. She was nine years old and saw his story in the local newspaper.

Dear Jonathan,

My name is Krystan and I am nine years old. I read about you in

the paper and I believe that you must be an angel. I talk to God every

night, and I asked. My Daddy told me that I could talk to him whenever I   wanted. My Daddy is an angel now. Mommy says God needed him to

be his attorney. If you come to California, I will make you some cookies.

Love,
Krystan Dunbar

Jonathan laid the letter aside and considered writing the little girl a letter and then wondered if people would be upset, given the conviction and all. He decided to ask Father Birney to respond for him, as he would avoid unwarranted scrutiny. He would ask the priest when he saw him. The letter had a haunting affect on him though, and he found himself wondering why.

Later that morning while reading the materials Adelman had left him, Father Birney bounced into his cell announcing a glorious day outside and asked Jonathan if he would like to go outside in the prison yard. Jonathan hadn't been outside in the sun for some time and accepted the offer. As they were walking out, Jonathan retrieved the letter from Krystan.

"Father Birney," he began as he placed the girl's letter on a concrete bench outside. "Would you mind writing a letter for me? I received this from a girl whose father must be dead. She thinks I am an angel and that God told her so. Would you tell her I'm sorry about her father and that I appreciate the letter?"

"You're concerned about appearances? You believe someone will think badly of you if you write her yourself?"

"Yes. She sounds sincere and very kind. I wouldn't want the press to get a hold of that."

"I'll compromise. You write the letter and I will put it in one of my envelopes so that no one sees it. I think the Warden would understand."

"OK," Jonathan said as he stood up and invited the priest to join him for a round on the small yard there. He had a lightness to his step and he was looking towards the sky. The priest wondered if Jonathan talked to God as he did, and he made the sign of the cross.

They walked for almost an hour. Jonathan had also been reading his Bible and found several references quite interesting.

"Do you consider yourself a Christian, J2?" Father Birney asked.

"I think that goes without saying, Father. I made a voyage that is specifically portrayed in the Bible. I was there, Father! I know that there is something that continues on after the body expires. That's what the Bible says. How could I not believe?"

"Exactly, Jonathan. Exactly."

The Warden was waiting for them when they returned from their walk.

"Good morning, Father Birney, Jonathan," Kindt said. Both men responded likewise and entered the newly appointed library on the row.

"Jonathan, the U.S. Marshals sent me a message which partly goes to you. They said that whatever legal materials you have for court, will be taken when you go. They will be taking you to the place you were before, at the Metropolis Correctional Center. You can tell your lawyers they can see you there. You can't have any other visitors while you're there. Is there anything you need for me to ask them?"

"Can I take my Bible? Tell them I intend to use it as an exhibit."

"I think you should get your materials together soon, tonight, actually. You can figure out what I mean."

"Yes, sir."

At one o'clock in the morning, Jonathan was placed in a dark blue sedan and whisked north towards Chicago. The Marshals insisted that he don a bulletproof vest, as he had become a national figure and it was for his safety.

He was placed in isolation with nothing but the bedding and clothes they had given him. He had to stay focused and not let the solitude attack him. He found himself wondering about the little girl and her mother. Krystan said her Daddy was an attorney. God's attorney. An angel.

Jonathan was getting washed up for his trip to the Dirksen Building, at 219 South Dearborn Street, the federal courthouse, when an officer told him he had to hurry. His argument was scheduled for nine o'clock and it was only four in the morning. As he was preparing to leave, the Marshals gave Jonathan a dark blue suit, a white shirt and black shoes. When he was ready, the clothes fit rather well and he looked presentable.

As he was approaching the Dirksen Building, he saw a man selling T-shirts with:

"Christ Wasn't Crucified Twice" on the front with a photo of Jesus on the cross inside a red circle with a line through the photo.

What he did not see was the backside of the shirt which read:

Free Jonathan
God Sent Him Back for a Reason

Sam Amaranta was quite pleased with the artwork and was told that the shirts and other knick-knacks were selling like programs at the Super Bowl. Nello did not partake in Amaranta's sensationalistic marketing plan, although he believed Sam had good intentions to win public support for Jonathan. At least Sam didn't list his phone number on them.

The courtroom where the main event was to occur, sits well above most buildings in Chicago's Loop. When Jonathan was led into the rather large room, he noticed how intimidating it was with its oak paneled walls, seating, railings, tables and expansive bench which spanned almost the width of the room. Behind the elevated, ornately carved bench sat three high backed leather chairs and the seal of the United States Court of Appeals for the Seventh Circuit. On each end of the bench were flags, one an American flag, fringed in gold and the other was the flag of the State of Illinois. Most attorneys who appear in cases before the bench here are overwhelmed with the splendor and the consequences of their being here. What surprised Jonathan more than any of this, is that he was not intimidated or even uncomfortable at being there. It was as if he was at home or someplace familiar to him.

He organized his notes for his argument, as the State's Attorney sneered at him. He had been in courtrooms before and faced opponents like Schroeder. Strange. He could almost recall, but not quite. It was like a photograph that never was in focus completely, just a blur but enough to identify shapes.

Jonathan's thoughts were broken at the arrival of Amaranta and Gamberino. With a flourish, they swept into the room carrying briefcases large enough for weekend vacations. They began laying out files on the table in front of Jonathan. That is when he saw the artwork.

"Where did you get that, Mr. Amaranta?"

"Nice, huh? I had it done. People are buying stuff with this logo like mad. People like you, Jonathan. Wattyathink?" Amaranta posed like some carnival hawker.

"What I think is this. You will move your things from this table, immediately. This table is reserved for me. Take your freshman tactics and twisted marketing someplace else. Get away from me."

Jonathan picked up the artwork with "Christ Wasn't Crucified Twice" on it and faced the reporters in the gallery.

"This drawing and saying was not done on my behalf. I played no part in the huckster gimmicks created by Mr. Amaranta. I urge everyone not to purchase this sacrilege and make this man a profit." Jonathan boomed this announcement and reporters caught every word.

He threw the artwork at Amaranta. "Now, get away from me." Nello was utterly embarrassed by the whole matter. As the Marshals surrounded Jonathan, the clerk entered and explained that the Judges would be in momentarily. As Nello returned the files to his briefcase and moved behind to the table and the row of chairs antecedent to the railing, the clerk reviewed the signaling system of the red/green/yellow lights at the podium.

"When the green light is on, your time is running. Ten minutes before your time expires, the yellow light will come on. And when your time is up, the red will flash," she said. "Mr. Schroeder, you will go first, then Mr. Childress. The amicus will go last. If the panel has questions, they'll ask you at the end. Any questions?"

When no one said "yes," she returned to the front at the bench. That is when the reporters went into a frenzy and the Marshals moved quickly to hush them. Whenever the Attorney General of the United States, even recently resigned ones, enters a courtroom, it is an instant media event. Amidst the stars of newsreel pomp stood Adelman, in the flesh. The man who advised the most powerful man in the world and was the nation's chief law enforcement officer for over four years, commanded attention. He stifled all questions by raising his hand.

"Good morning, Jonathan," Adelman said as he approached and extended his hand to him.

"Good morning, sir," Jonathan replied.

"May I join you? I see you have a few empty chairs here,"

Adelman said with a smile.

"Do you think that's a good idea, sir?"

"Absolutely."

"Then, I would be pleased to have you join me," Jonathan said as he moved to the middle of the three chairs at his table.

The courtroom artists would include the Adelman profile in every sketch and Amaranta seethed as if his thunder had been stolen. It had.

When the panel entered, the presence of the ex-Attorney General was immediately noted on their expressions. When a member of the panel asked if he was appearing in the case, Adelman rose.

"Your Honors, I am stand by counsel for the Appellee, Mr. Jonathan L. Childress the Second."

"Very well. Welcome to Chicago Mr. Adelman."

"Thank you, Your Honor," he replied as he sat back down.

The appearances of the State's Attorney and even Jonathan himself, paled at Adelman's countenance in the room. He was impeccably dressed in the deepest blue suit Jonathan had ever seen and he believed he had been doing this for a long time. The suit had razor-sharp creases and sat perfectly on Adelman's frame. He was a man who dressed well, not like some who look like an ape dressed in a suit. Adelman belonged in that suit.

The presentations by Schroeder and Jonathan went as expected. Surprisingly, Jonathan was relaxed at the podium, spoke clearly into the microphone and stood erect. To some of the spectators, they believed he presented his case better than the State Attorney, who was upstaged by the presence of the distinguished gent at the opposite table, and that may have had an impact.

Nello Gamberino argued as amicus and tried not to offend Jonathan's position, until he reached the point of contention regarding the State of Illinois wishing to execute a man who may not be competent.

When Nello looked at Jonathan, whose hands were clenched beneath the table, he knew that he had alienated Jonathan and felt a pang of regret that he would never again be able to sit down and talk to him. He had crossed a line now.

At the beginning of questions from the appeals panel, Schroeder was the target vessel. The Judges demanded authority or proof that the reports of the three psychologists were somehow misplaced or lacking. Schroeder, who had obviously prepared well, countered with the general rule that jury verdicts are presumed to be accurate and to rest solely in their collective province.

When the panel decided they had had enough banter with the State's Attorney, they turned their sights towards Jonathan.

"Mr. Childress," Judge Kane began, "it's curious that you appeal your sweeping victory in the district court. Would you tell us why you think the decision was erroneous?"

"Certainly, Your Honor," Jonathan said as he rose from his chair and buttoned his suit coat and every eye and ear was directed towards him.

"The decision by Judge Echols leaves a lingering pall over the question of my sanity and fitness. I resent that patina or tarnish on my psychological make-up. I testified truthfully and accurately in the District Court. I am not the convicted murderer of those children. Unfortunately, and I cannot explain why I ended up in his body. I am not insane.

"Mr. Childress, are you aware of the descriptive term, savant?" Judge Kane asked.

Indeed Jonathan had encountered that term in his search.

"Savant. "

The implications associated with this term to Jonathan's case were complex and completely outside the record at this point. It was a major league curveball by the panel.

"Your Honor, although this expression was never raised by the Appellant or the forensic psychologists that examined me, I'll address that contention." Jonathan looked at Adelman as if he had to ask permission and Adelman nodded his approval as if Jonathan had asked the question aloud.

"The imputed argument derived from the careless use of the term savant, carries a dangerous overtone. If I am savant, which I categorically deny, the reasoning is that the coma, induced by the overload of deadly chemicals in the system, triggered a dramatic alteration in how I act, think and speak. However, that would mean that I am the murderer of those girls and I am slightly different. The area of savant is one of little research, as only a few examples of this phenomenon have ever been presented. The unavoidable flaw in that attack is that no one has come before any court and explained how a man with a seventh grade education could ever attain the lofty appearance of suddenly possessing vast amounts of knowledge."

Jonathan paused and looked at Adelman who had a brief smile on his face. "You're doing splendidly," his expression said.

"The Presentence Investigation prepared by a probation officer for the trial court, determined that Johnny Lee Childress had an I.Q. hedging slightly beyond the retarded level of 70. The current scores, affirmed at times and by separate entities, has my I.Q. well beyond twice the amount established by that probation officer. Unless Mr. Schroeder can present the testimony or evidence of a creditable person or source to explain how the old Johnny Lee Childress could acquire such an I.Q., and retain and relate such knowledge, wisdom and experience, the term savant is grossly misplaced." His point made, Jonathan looked around the room and saw that his point was well taken.

"Thank you, gentlemen. We will take this case under advisement and issue our decision in due course," Kane said.

When the panel had gone, Jonathan turned to face Adelman. "Well?" was all he said.

"Beautifully handled, J2. Any time you want a job, come see me," Adelman said as he beamed and shook his hand. Schroeder even nodded at Jonathan as the Marshals led him away.

Pandemonium resided outside the courtroom and was a full fledged feeding frenzy outside the Dirksen Building as Adelman left. He stopped just outside in the plaza and agreed to make a statement.

"OK, here you go," Adelman said as he acquiesced to the reporters who clamored for his statement and rationale for being there.

"I believe that Jonathan, the man all of you just witnessed in the courtroom upstairs, is very special to all of us. He just proved that he is a refined and eloquent man and definitely not the maniacal killer of children. When I served this country as Attorney

General, I said that I am a man of God, yet placed those deeply rooted beliefs aside as Attorney General and fulfilled my official duties without the Bible as my guide. Instead, the Constitution guided me. However, now that I am just a citizen again, I can speak more freely. Jonathan is not Johnny Lee Childress and I am convinced that God sent him to us for a reason and that reason is not to try to kill him."

"Mr. Adelman, are you saying he's an angel or the second coming of Christ?" the perfectly coiffed anchorman from CNN News asked.

"Perhaps you can tell me if you have a more creditable explanation as to how he is even here today and is so remarkably different. I'm, listening."

"Sir, are you going to represent Childress in the Supreme court?" the woman with a mic with 'Channel 7' printed on it, asked.

"If he wishes me to argue his case to the Supreme Court, I would be honored." At that Adelman was escorted out of the crowded plaza by uniformed officers from the Chicago Police Department.

The nation was abuzz with Jonathan's case. Every news channel, talk show and network presented some segment about him. Jay Leno had one of the shirts hawked on the Internet and held it up for the camera on the Tonight Show. "This is the current fashion in Chicago, the newly proclaimed City of Angels. Rumor has it that Jonathan Childress will run for President as soon as Illinois tires of trying to execute him."

When Jonathan was returned to his cell at Thames, the cons went wild with praise as he walked the row. He was home. Or, at least the only home he had known so far.

Every newspaper had the drawings of him, the three Judges and the ex-Attorney General of the United States by his side. The State's Attorney didn't appear in any of them and he was not happy at how he was outclassed in his own backyard.

"Good afternoon, Jonathan," Father Birney said as he sauntered into the cell. "Have you had enough rest to face another walk in the Sun?"

"Sure. I have something I'd like to ask you and discuss."

When they were walking slowly along the beaten circle on the tiny yard behind the prison, Jonathan was deep in contemplation. "Father, can I ask you a favor?"

"Anything, within reason, of course."

"Would you mind asking the Cardinal to find out what he can on the Dunbar family in Sacramento? The girl's Father died and there are times that I can't stop wondering about them. Would you mind doing that for me?"

"I can't see any harm in that. I'll call him this afternoon."

"The newspapers said I did pretty well in court and that Mr. Adelman next to me was a significant influence. Would you thank both Cardinals for me?"

"Certainly, but I'm sure they already know you're grateful," the priest responded kindly.

"Father, I've been thinking a lot lately. The Bible says God has His reasons for what He does. What do you think His reasons are for me? Am I to come back here and endure all this, just to get executed again? Why am I here?"

"Jonathan, I believe God wants you to set an example for all of us. The hardships you're going through now were similar to those Jesus suffered at the hands of Pontius Pilate. Jesus was promised his freedom if he'd renounce his faith, just like you being asked to admit you're insane and escape execution if you would. There are similarities between your situation and the one Jesus found himself in. I believe God is showing us what He coped with. I don't know if you're an angel, Jonathan. We, the Cardinals and I, agree that you are very special and prove that the Bible is correct. You're a symbol of our religion, Jonathan."

"It's all pretty confusing, Father. I wish God would tell me what He wants me to do."

"Perhaps He is and you haven't recognized it yet? There seem to be signs, Jonathan. Listen to your heart. It will lead you in the right direction and never lose your faith."

Jonathan wondered if they taught "ephemeral sayings" in seminaries. What the priest had just told him was thinly veiled, yet gossamer by design. It did little to quell his concerns as to why he was back on Earth.

In the two months subsequent to the oral arguments,

Jonathan kept busy as he began exercising every day, and began jogging. Father Birney would sit on the bench and count the laps and give him encouragement. Jonathan became tanned from his daily regimen in the southern Illinois sun and the warmer temperatures, compared to Chicago.

The quantities of mail, books, Bibles, photos of "available" women, cards and money sent to him mounted. A publisher offered three million dollars for the book and movie rights. However, Jonathan knew that under Illinois law, a criminal is prohibited from such profiteering, so any book deals would have to wait.

His account with the prison where they hold money sent to the prisoners, swelled to over forty-seven thousand dollars. It came from people who wished him success and wanted to help with legal expenses.

When Jimmy Baker was serving his federal sentence of seven years in Rochester, Minnesota, people sent him money every day. On the average, he was sending thousands of dollars out every month. Jonathan was a celebrity now and some people had faith in him. The money poured in. The Warden suggested that he open a savings account and that they would handle the paperwork for him as they did for other prisoners. Except, the others had release dates, and Jonathan did not.

Father Birney brought Jonathan a white envelope from the Court of Appeals. It was a large one, with that indestructible material you can't tear.

"Jonathan, the mail room just gave me this, for you. I think this is what you've been waiting for."

Jonathan hefted the nine-by-twelve envelope in his hands. "It's a long decision, Father. Do you think I won?"

"I can only hope so, Jonathan," the little priest said as he pensively waited for a sign. He watched Jonathan read. The wait seemed interminable as he watched page after page and Jonathan's expression was tense and concerned.

"They ruled against me, Father. They reversed the Judge down here and reinstated my conviction. One of the Judges disagreed with them though but he was outnumbered. I'm back on death row, Father."

"Oh my. I must call the Cardinal, Jonathan. He'll know what to do."

Jonathan didn't hear anything the priest said. He was facing the wall and preserving his strength. He never heard the priest leave.

The Warden came by to tell him he was sorry about the decision. He had just heard about it from the Director. What he told the Director but not Jonathan, is that before he would execute Jonathan, he would transfer to another prison first.

"They said the prosecutor was not required to prove my sanity as part of the charges. They also said that I'm fit for execution. How long before they set another date for that, Mr. Kindt?"

Kindt swallowed hard and pursed his lips. Then, wetting his lips with his tongue, he had built the strength to speak again. "Within thirty days, Jonathan. The State's Attorney is asking your trial Judge to set a new date already."

"Mr. Kindt, I think I need to be alone. Would you mind, sir?"

"Certainly. I'm sorry Jonathan," Kindt said as he left. He had become emotionally involved in this prisoner twice now, and he contemplated leaving Thames for another post, as he should never be involved in the life and death struggles of those he may have to kill later on. He was not neutral in Jonathan's case.

Jonathan kept two books in his cell, as he used the Law Library on the row whenever he wanted. The Bible rested on his bunk and was open to a spot where he was reading when the priest came to see him.

The second book is a Bible of sorts as well, the "Federal Rules of Civil Procedure," which contains all the rules and regulations governing civil cases, appeals and even Supreme Court Rules, is the practical guide of attorneys. He wanted to see if there is a provision on how long it takes before the trial Judge would receive the decision from the Court of Appeals. He read carefully, his hands slightly trembling. Then he stopped reading and shaking.

"I'd like to use the library, please," he told an officer walking past.

A short time later he was inside his personal library, which now sported a brand new electric typewriter, which he had paid for from his own account. He began typing and worked late into the night.

"Good morning, Father," Jonathan said, surprising the priest and beating him to the punch.

Are you feeling all right, Jonathan?"

"Fine. Are you ready to go outside?" Jonathan asked.

"Absolutely. It's a fine day outside," Father Birney said.

"Would you mind making some photocopies later, Father? It's for the Court of Appeals."

"Certainly. What is it?" the Priest inquired.

"I'll explain it to you on the way outside," Jonathan said. And so he did. When he finished, the priest needed to make another phone call to Chicago.

"Your Eminence," Father Birney began. "I am faxing you a copy of Jonathan's latest document for the appeal. He is quite at ease and believes this will derail everything the State is doing."

"Fine, Father, I'll pass it on as soon as I get it. Thank you and tell Jonathan that God will not turn His back on him."

"Yes sir."

Meanwhile, gloating over the good fortune in the appellate court, Schroeder had filed his motion in the trial court and was waiting for the Judge to schedule a new execution date. He wanted this killer put down once and for all. He decided to attend the next execution and make certain that he was dead. That revelry was extinguished two days later.

Schroeder was meeting with his top aide who gave him the news.

"Yes sir, " the assistant said, "Childress filed a Request for Rehearing en Banc and the dissenting Judge on that panel will call for a vote."

What Jonathan had done, after discovering the rule in the civil procedure book, was to ask the panel to present the case to all of the Judges on the Court of Appeals. If a member of the panel goes against the majority on a panel in deciding a case, he or she can submit the decision to all of the Judges and then they all vote whether or not the case is important enough for the entire Court to decide the controversy, and not just the three Judges representing the court.

"Judge Kane," who was the dissenter, "will go to all of the Judges for a vote," Schroeder lamented.

As it turned out, Judge Kane had done exactly that, and had anticipated or hoped, that Jonathan would file such a request. By closing hours that day, Judge Kane had garnered enough votes to support a full consideration of the case, and the decision by the panel reinstating Jonathan's conviction and sentence, was vacated.

"Things move quickly when they want them to," Jonathan off-handedly remarked when both Father Birney and Warden Kindt had faxed copies of the latest order from the Court of Appeals.

Kindt and the priest laughed outside Jonathan's cell when they each realized what the other had in hand, and how they both wished to surprise him. They doubted that theirs were the only fax machines working hard that day, either.

"It seems that Judge Kane is prepared to fight his brothers on the panel. How Biblical," the priest said, an expression of 'I told you so,' plastered squarely on his face.

"All we can do now is wait to see who wins," Jonathan said. "Would you let the Cardinal know, Father? And Mr. Kindt, I want to thank you for making our time here in the building a little more bearable."

The priest nodded assent and Tom Kindt looked at Jonathan a moment. In that fleeting time, he made the decision that killing people for the State of Illinois was not in his blood. He was going to transfer out of Thames. "You're welcome, Jonathan. You men have acted fairly reasonable here and I respect that."

When the priest and Kindt had left, Jonathan went back to studying civil procedure.

Chapter 19

"In a stunning upset, convicted murderer Jonathan Childress II has won yet again. In a majority opinion from the entire Court of Appeals, the initial decision by the reviewing panel was reversed. In affirming the District Court's decision and granting a new trial, the majority said that prosecutors must prove Childress sane beyond a reasonable doubt, once he had made a substantial showing otherwise," Rachael read to Ben Ori.

"Either this guy has nine lives and is using them up rapidly, or he is one helluva lawyer," she said as he listened intently.

Mordeci's article had arrived on their fax machine. He wanted her and Ben to hear it from him first.

"Rachael, I think you should pay the Polacheks a visit and see how they're doing," Ben said as if he were a big brother.

"They've got to be going through hell with all of this."

"I'll swing by there on my way home."

"And Sergeant, as your commanding officer, I'm ordering you not to let all this get to you, please."

"It's like God really is protecting this guy, Ben. It's tiring. I'll be ok with it."

While Rachael and Ben were discussing the front page news in Chicago, Father Birney was announcing the victory to Jonathan, loud enough for everyone on the row to hear.

"God works in mysterious ways, Jonathan. He will never turn his back on those who believe."

As Jonathan was reading the fax the Cardinal had sent, the Warden silently listened, not wanting to interrupt the priest's revelations. Kindt had received the decision from his boss and he wanted to see how Jonathan was holding up on the rollercoaster ride of emotions.

"You seem to be the Energizer Bunny of law, Jonathan. You just keep going and going. The news of this is on every channel. You're in the news more than the President."

"They're going to appeal to the Supreme Court, Mr. Kindt. They're not going to let this go."

Those words of prophesy by Jonathan were actually being

manifested in the State's Attorney's Office in Chicago. Schroeder had directed his top assistants to prepare a petition seeking relief in the U.S. Supreme Court. The odds of that being granted played against Schroder, but he would be known as the Defender of Justice and tenacious, if nothing else.

Cardinal Carroll called Adelman, who had heard the news and had already talked to Cardinal Bavielle. He was planning a visit with Jonathan, to discuss the possibility of representing him in the Supreme Court. Adelman also agreed to meet with both Cardinals in Chicago, where the Pope had scheduled a mass at Cardinal Carroll's cathedral. Cardinal Carroll is still considered the premier replacement for the aging Pontiff and would be the first American to assume command of the Catholic Church. Under the circumstances, the visit is a prudent measure and Carroll was to accompany the Pope for the remainder of his visit to the United States.

Schroeder wasted no time, as his petition to the Supreme Court was filed a mere four days after the Court of Appeals robbed him of victory. The case was now the most controversial case that the nine justices had to contend with on the docket. A decision had to be made if they were going to hear the case or let the decision stand from the appellate court. The threads and tendrils of politics and public sentiment seemed to cast Jonathan's case to the forefront. There was literally no chance that the Supreme Court would not accept the challenge. After all, they were dealing with an angel.

Chapter 20

"Are you joking around, Father Birney?" the burly Warden said as he stood behind his battle-scarred desk.

"No, sir. The Cardinal said they would be here Saturday and would like to use the chapel here. May I tell them you approve?" the priest asked reservedly.

"Of course. I want this coordinated with the Captain. I don't want any problems. You give me two days lead time for this? How long have you known, Father?"

"I was informed by Cardinal Carroll this morning. I came right here to you. If he says a mass here, I believe it will be a first time in history that I know of. We should get plenty of pictures."

"You handle the arrangements, Father. I'll tell Jonathan about the Cardinal's visit."

"I will tell Jonathan the Cardinal is coming to see him on Saturday, but not about the mass. I will let that be a surprise. Besides, I have some things the Cardinal faxed me this morning for him and he'll look forward to seeing Cardinal Carroll again."

"Thanks, Father. After you see the Captain, tell him I'd like to see him about this, will you?"

"Certainly," the priest said as he turned and headed for the door.

Kindt watched the Chaplain leave and looked at the ceiling. He had to figure out how to tell his wife she would be coming to the prison with him and to dress up in her Sunday best. He couldn't tell her anything more than that they were attending a mass together.

"Good morning, Jonathan," Father Birney said as he entered Jonathan's law library where he had been researching for hours.

"Oh, good morning, Father. What time is it?"

"It's after nine o'clock. How long have you been here?"

"Since I found Supreme Court Rule 10. It's a rule permitting the Supreme Court to take cases in which different district courts have made conflicting decisions and settles the dispute." Realizing that the priest understood very little of what he referred to, Jonathan then admitted that he had been there since five o'clock.

"I have some stuff the Cardinal faxed to me a little while ago.

I think it's something that you requested about the little girl in California."

"Thank you," Jonathan said as he accepted the pages and looked at them as if he had just been handed the Holy Grail.

"Jonathan, the Cardinal said he would like to see you on Saturday morning. OK with you? Oh, and it would be in the chapel. He said he would like to see it. Any problem with that, Jonathan?"

"I'll be ready. Tell him that I'm looking forward to it."

"I'm sure you will find it special. I'll see you later. I have to call the Cardinal and let him know." In an instant, Father Birney was gone and Jonathan began to read the documents given to him by the priest.

There was a cover page from a priest in Sacramento, addressed to Cardinal Carroll, which recited the request for information on the Dunbar family, who are current parishioners in good standing, of Our Lady of Fatima's congregation.

Krystan's mother is a Registered Nurse and returned to the nursing service when Krystan's father died. Krystan's father was a prominent tax attorney who represented celebrities and political figures.

He was returning from a social gathering with a client, alone, not wanting to keep Krystan up late and suffer boring chatter about various shelters in the Tax Code. It was raining, which is not uncommon in northern California for this time of year. As he rounded a curve, he struck a camping trailer which had come loose from the rear of a pickup truck and lay sideways across the road. Without the electrical connection to the truck, it had no lights whatsoever. The truck was on the shoulder next to it and a man was trying to raise the tongue of the trailer using the jack from the truck. He was doing his best to recover the trailer when Krystan's father struck it, killing the trailer's owner when the steel tongue suddenly smashed into his head and face.

The police arrived shortly after receiving a 911 call, where they found Krystan's father trapped inside the mangled Acura. The impact crushed the front end, sending the father into the steering column and ruptured his spleen, along with a grocery list of other organs shredded, torn or otherwise obliterated. Before the paramedics could extract him from the wreckage, he had asked the men to tell is wife and daughter that he loved them. He expired immediately thereafter.

Jonathan wondered why the police officer who wrote the accident report would include such a personal note about the victim's last words. He memorialized the love he had for his family, sure, but it remained strange to him nonetheless. While Jonathan pondered that question, is eyes continued to read. Abruptly, he stopped reading and his pulse began to race. Jonathan's hands trembled as he gently laid the pages on the desk before him. He needed to see Father Birney and requested the officer in the corridor to locate him as soon as possible.

"Father, the officer who wrote the traffic report put the man's last words in there to establish the time of death. Look at the time, Father. It's 12:18! That would be 12:18 in the morning, Father."

Krystan's father died the same morning that Johnny Lee Childress was receiving his just rewards from the State of Illinois into his femoral artery.

"Oh my! Jonathan, are you asking me if it's possible you are the girl's father? That God let you return so that you could reunite with your family in a body that's not crushed?" The priest made the sign of the cross as he asked these questions. He had to admit that the timing was perfect.

"Father, answer me this then? Why did Krystan write me? How do you explain my education and knowledge? The time of death coincides with the moment Johnny Lee began his private journey to Hell. Is it possible, Father?"

"Jonathan, I'm sure there was more than that poor man who died then. I wouldn't jump to any hasty conclusions. There are coincidences, yes, but there are no facts or evidence, as you say in your legal stuff."

"You're right, Father. I'm searching for an identity besides this one." But what Jonathan said and what he believed were diametrically opposed. He thought that he should not press or the priest might think he was crazy after all.

"I'll be ready Saturday morning when you come to get me. Anything special I should wear?" he said and both men began to laugh. All they wore on the row were those jumpsuits of Orange

Blaze material, and the joke brought levity to the conversation.

What Jonathan and Father Birney didn't know at the time, was that Tom Kindt had a better plan. Friday night, he showed up at Jonathan's door with a dark gray suit, white shirt, black Oxford shoes and one of his favorite silk ties of blue and silver stripes.

"Thank you, Mr. Kindt. I feel like a teenager getting ready for prom night."

"I had the guys here get this together. When we release someone or send them to court, we have suits for them. I hope the fit is okay or I'll have to scrounge up a tailor from one of the units here."

When Jonathan tried on the slacks and suit coat, they fit him just fine. Somehow, the Warden noticed, Jonathan belonged in a suit. He was comfortable in one, unlike some guys who have one suit for funerals and spend the rest of the year in jeans. Johny Lee would have looked like a fool in a suit.

"Monday, Jonathan, you're going to see the dentist here. We'll see what we can do about the gap up front there."

Jonathan was always cognizant of the missing tooth but refused to let it embarrass him. That did not, however, diminish his desire to do something about it.

"Thank you," he answered as his tongue wondered to the gap the Warden referred to.

Jonathan did not sleep well again, as he could not shake the thoughts swirling in his mind about the possibilities in California, while he struggled with a recalcitrant memory. By sunrise on Saturday, he was no closer to any answers than when he started. He decided to ask Cardinal Carroll.

Having showered and shaved, along with his military "high and tight" hair cut, Jonathan stood in the front of the mirror on the wall in his cell. He was leaner than he first was. He even had definition to his muscles. The jogging had slimmed him, the sun gave a golden hue to his skin and the exercises sculpted him. There was only one lingering resemblance to Johnny Lee's appearance and that was the missing tooth that Rachael had removed with her shin. And even that was soon to depart, as the dentist would fix that. With that repair, the transformation would be complete.

He dressed slowly, savoring the feel of real clothes against his flesh. As he was finishing up the Windsor knot to the expensive silk tie, Father Birney entered his cell.

"My!" the little priest said as he skidded to a halt. "You look great in the suit, Jonathan. You must have worked all night, by the red in your eyes." It was more of a statement than a question.

"I didn't sleep well."

"You have a huge day ahead of you, Jonathan Childress. The Warden is waiting for us in his office."

When Jonathan stepped out of his cell, with no handcuffs, his suit set squarely on his shoulders, he felt like a million bucks. Every con on the row was watching him as he passed by. Something big was happening at the prison but no one betrayed the secret. Whatever it was, even the Captain appeared wearing a blue suit that must have cost him a thousand dollars.

When they walked into the Warden's conference room, the oak warhorse table was resplendent with a white linen cloth and a cornucopia of food.

"Jonathan," the Warden said as he guided him around the table, "I'd like you to meet my wife."

He took her hand gently in his and was amazed at the poise she displayed! "Good morning. It's a pleasure and a surprise to meet you."

"My husband speaks well of you, Jonathan. He rarely does that, especially in his position. I've also heard a lot about you. You're quite a celebrity. Thomas said I would like you. So far, my husband has been correct. It's nice to meet the man whose name has become a household word."

"Thank you. I'm not sure I deserve all the notoriety, though. After all, I'm just another guy."

"Jonathan," the Warden intoned, "You are far from being ordinary or just another guy. You are now an international figure. You weren't told of today's events at my orders. I did not want this place to become some circus act."

Jonathan had a puzzled look now as he listened to Kindt. The Captain and the priest were beaming for some reason and he ached to learn the secret.

"In a few moments, Jonathan, a white van, escorted by

several cars as I understand, is going to arrive here. The Cardinals Carroll and Bavielli will be in the van. Accompanying them, especially to meet you, just another guy, is the Pope."

Jonathan's mouth was agape, his eyes wide with wonderment.

"The Pope is coming to see me?" he croaked, and his vocal chords didn't seem to work.

"Yes, Jonathan. He is due any moment now," Father Birney answered.

"In the meantime, help yourself to something to eat and try the coffee," the Warden offered.

"I don't think I can eat, Mr. Kindt. Some coffee would be great, though."

While Jonathan sat in a chair, nervously sipping his hot coffee, the entourage of vehicles entered the grounds. The Captain was waiting at the front gate and shook hands with the head of the Pontiff's security detail.

The van was not the famous "Pope mobile" seen on television. Instead, it was an armored vehicle constructed for the Swiss soldiers who were sworn to protect the Pontiff with their lives.

The Captain had seen a "special" on the soldiers beneath their ornate brightly colored uniforms around the Vatican. Garishly suited as they are, the men beneath these striped outfits are an elite force, a military branch which trains its men no less than the Navy SEALs or Delta Force. They were special forces troops that should not be under-estimated by apparel. Although these men were dressed in casual suits, the Captain admired the fit and trim appearance of all of them. The head of the security detail had a vise-like grip to his handshake and the thick neck of a bodybuilder.

A tower guard at the prison called the control center to find out what was happening at the front of the prison and was politely told to mind his post, stay off the radio and shut up.

When the side door to the van slid open, Cardinal Carroll was the first to exit. The Captain shook his hand. He was followed by Cardinal Bavielli, who stayed by the door and waited, looking inside and not towards the Captain.

Amid an abundance of white linen, was Pope John Paul, the world's leader of the Catholic Church. Cardinal Bavielli helped him into the motorized wheelchair one of the Swiss guards had produced. The Captain spoke into his walkie talkie and the group proceeded through the front gates. The two guards next to the van were handed firearms by the leader of the detail and one other, as they accompanied the Captain.

Everyone in the Warden's conference room had watched the whole scene. Jonathan was so nervous, he spilled coffee on the floor. He was not alone in emotional displays. The little priest was so excited he began to pray to calm himself.

"Shall we go to the Chapel, everyone?" the Warden invited, leading the way.

They were all standing in front of the Chapel's entrance as the entourage approached. The halls of the prison had been cleared and locked after serving breakfast. The only prisoner within hundreds of feet on either side was Jonathan.

Leading the way was the Captain. On each side of Pope John Paul was a Cardinal and bringing up the rear were the Swiss guards.

Cardinal Carroll took the lead as the group reached the Chapel and Father Birney stepped forward first. The little priest approached the Pontiff and as the Pope struggled to his feet, the priest knelt before him and kissed the ring upon his right hand.

"Good morning, Your Eminence," he said as he bowed his head.

In a wispy voice, the Pope asked him to rise and when Father Birney stood, stepped aside so that Cardinal Carroll could introduce everyone.

"Your Eminence, may I introduce you to the person you came to meet?" he said as he waved Jonathan forward.

"This is Jonathan, the young man we have mentioned to you."

"Your Eminence," Jonathan said as he shook the Pope's frail hand reverently. He somehow knew he should not follow the priest's genuflection or kissing of the ring, instead opting for the hand shake instead.

"It is a special opportunity to meet you, Jonathan. I can recognize God's work in you. I believe you are very important to all of us."

Not knowing how to respond to the plaudit by the Pope, he introduced the Warden and his wife.

"Your Eminence, this is Mr. and Mrs. Kindt, they're friends of mine."

When Kindt and his wife had each shaken the Pope's hand, Cardinal Carroll suggested that they enter the Chapel. With a Cardinal on each side, the aged Pontiff ambled towards the altar.

The Chapel, religiously ornate and conspicuously Christian in motif, had stained glass windows of the Virgin Mary and the Christ child. Even though the Chapel served all denominations, Christianity dominated the design. The altar was made of granite, with a tabernacle of bronze colored gold. It was carpeted in a rich, deep wine carpet, while the wood used for pews, railings and pulpit were a light oak or maybe ash.

The Pope knelt, made the sign of the cross and then proceeded to chairs placed a short distance from the altar. He waved for Jonathan to join him and they sat quietly until Cardinal Carroll had donned his vestments for mass.

"Jonathan, do you believe in God?" the Pope asked as he looked into his eyes.

"Yes. It's impossible to deny otherwise. I mean, my being here, my return, is proof that there is life after death."

"It does, my son. It proves the Bible is true. It also means God has a reason for returning you to us."

"You mean like an angel, Your Eminence?"

"Jonathan, you may be an angel. You may be the Savior himself. Time will give us that wisdom."

During the brief mass by Cardinal Carroll, assisted by Cardinal Bavielli, the Pope himself served Holy Communion to the small group.

After the service, they retired to the Warden's conference room, where they ate sandwiches and sweet rolls.

"Jonathan," the Pope began as he nodded to his security chief, who handed him a blue velvet case from the inside pocket of his suit. "I would like you to have something," the Pontiff said. He blessed the case and handed it to Jonathan. When he unfolded the velvet, there was a solid gold crucifix and chain, which was identical to the one worn by His Eminence.

"It's beautiful," his eyes wide, Jonathan looked to the Warden. Prisoners are not permitted to retain expensive jewelry. A slight nod, imperceptible if you weren't watching for a sign, told him he could keep it.

"Thank you, Your Eminence."

"Nonsense, Jonathan. It is all of us who should thank you for making your journey back to us."

"All of us feel the same way, Jonathan," Cardinal Bavielli said. "I never explained what I am, Jonathan, but I am counsel to the Pontiff. When I first came here, I needed to know if you were real, as His Eminence heard about your journey. After that day, I was convinced that you are proof that there is life after death. We do not need to know why you returned to us. The truth is that you're here. God has chosen you for some reason. Perhaps to set an example for all of us. That makes you special."

"Jonathan," the Pope returned, "the press is going to learn of my visit today. I have prepared a statement myself, actually. I support you, Jonathan. The Church is behind you. Unless someone can prove differently, you are God's emissary." The room got quiet then.

"Will you pray with me, Jonathan?" the Pontiff asked.

"Certainly, Your Eminence." Together they recited the Lord's Prayer. Just the two men. The most influential religious figure in the world and a man facing another execution.

"Amen," the entire group said when the Pope and Jonathan had finished.

"I'm afraid I must be going, Jonathan. My days are not mine to control most times. I ask one favor from you, Jonathan, will you keep me in your prayers and in your heart, as you shall be in mine?" The Pope held Jonathan's hand tightly, as if energy transposed from one to the other.

"Always, Your Eminence."

The group departed from the conference room, not the Chapel, leaving the Warden and his wife.

"You're international news now, Jonathan. This meeting will be discussed all over the world. Be prepared, Jonathan. Things are about to heat up," Kindt explained.

Jonathan was barely listening, as he held the Pontiff's gift clenched in his hand and watched the procession leave the prison gates. He couldn't believe what had happened to him. He would later learn that the Pope's visit had severe implications on a vast number of powerful people. He only had to wait two days.

Chapter 21

The call to Ben's home interrupted dinner with his wife, but she was used to such intrusions.

"Ben," Mordeci said excitedly, "you are not going to guess who spent the day with Jonathan Childress?"

"OK, Mort. If I won't be able to guess, why don't you tell me, since that must be the reason for your call?"

"Ben, Pope John Paul was there to visit him. I've confirmed it. He was there this morning."

"Rachel's going to go ballistic over this news, Mort. She's Catholic. The idea that her church is supporting this guy is not going to sit well with her."

"Ben, the whole world will know about this in a little while. This whole thing is about to get much bigger. International!" the reporter exclaimed.

"If only he would have died, we wouldn't have all this. A doctor screws up and people want to make the killer a saint."

"When I contacted the media people for the Pope, they said that a statement is being prepared now and will be available shortly. I think John Paul is going to support Jonathan and call for his release. Then what?"

"The State and the Supreme Court will have a difficult time on their hands. I'll call Rachael and calm her down."

It was a futile mission on Ben's part.

"There are moments in history where God's will is not understood. As Catholics and believers, when we encounter an instance where the Lord's hand has obviously set to work, we are required to act. Battles are not new to Catholics. Throughout history we have fought to preserve our faith and the Holy Bible. We have such a fight today. I have met the man called Jonathan Childress where he is confined and crusading for his life. I am convinced that he has made a journey no man can make without our Savior's help and blessing. There is a lesson in all this that every Catholic should heed. The Bible is accurate and there is a life after death. A Heaven. Jonathan is the manifestation of God's existence.

I urge every Catholic to rally to support the struggle this man endures today, just as Jesus did before the Romans. Accept the truth he brings us and the everlasting and eternal life we seek in Heaven.

Jonathan shall be in my prayers and I ask that he be in the prayers of those who are members of the Catholic Church."

Rachael read the entire statement aloud, twice. She could not believe the Pope had called for the support of every Catholic for a convicted child killer. She was repulsed at the very notion.

Sergeant Hart was not the only person who read and reread the Pontiff's cry. The President, a Catholic himself, was transfixed by the Pope's message. He called his long time advisor and former Attorney General, Adelman. Over dinner that night he and the President discussed Jonathan, his case, the appeal and the significance of the Pope's involvement. When Adelman left the White House, he had an invitation to return six weeks later. And, he was asked to bring his file on Jonathan with him.

The Pope's call to gather round was sounded in churches across America. Amazingly, though, ancillary Christian sects viewed the situation with Jonathan quite similar. Since the State of Illinois could not produce any reasonable explanation for the quantum differences between the killer and the present man on death row, there is a powerful force behind it all. Whether they worshipped Allah, Christ or Jehovah, the facts remained static. There were pictures of Jonathan with wings, halos and flowing white robes. There were also pictures of him as the Devil. Very few people had no opinion about Jonathan, no matter where you asked.

"Jonathan," the Warden said as he shook his head, "I have just been forced to add two more people to work in our mailroom. Your mail alone fills bags each day. I don't know what to do with all your mail. It's mounting higher each day. Any ideas?"

"The guys here are doing what they can, Mr. Kindt. I don't know what else we can do," Jonathan said as he sat at the table in the law library on the row.

"And your savings account is over two hundred thousand dollars. Checks and money keep pouring in every day in increments of five to twenty dollars. You've become big business, J2," Kindt said as he smiled.

"I really don't know what to say, Warden, I never expected any of this. I'll ask Father Birney if he has any ideas."

"What are you working on now? Your acceptance speech for President?" Kindt said jokingly.

Jonathan smiled broadly. "Actually, I'm doing my homework for the Supreme Court. I want to argue the case myself. I believe I can handle it, but Mr. Adelman said he'll be there just in case."

"That reminds me. Did you see the dentist?"

"Yes, sir. He said it would be ready in a couple weeks. Thank you."

"Well, I have work to do, I can't stand here gabbing with you. I have my own pile of mail to cope with from every media network known to man. If they can't interview you, they want me or someone here. They want to know how you spend your days, what you eat and all sorts of things."

"What do you tell them?" Jonathan asked as he smiled broadly in anticipation.

"I have a form letter which says you spend your days training in our world class fitness center and eat noting but angel food cake."

Both men laughed heartily. The Warden found himself doing that more often, lately. Not only with Jonathan, but with the cons on the row and in the general population. Although the row posed life and death struggles, the pall of those fearsome battles failed to bring the depression associated with it. The cons were occupied with J2's mail and had become willing volunteers. The priest had become foreman, distributing stacks of letters to each of them. The staff that worked now seemed more at ease as well. With the men constructively occupied, the drain of dealing with condemned men who had no hope was erased. Jonathan's victories in the courts and media attention, gave rise to their own hopes of victories. Jonathan was infectious. When the Pope paid him a visit, the row was alight. After the Pontiff left. the food from the conference room was brought to the row and distributed among the cons. It was a very special moment for everyone.

The crucifix Jonathan had received from His Eminence was shown to each of the cons by Father Birney, as he passed out food.

The Warden reflected on the changes brought by Jonathan and how he seemed to touch the lives of everyone around him.

Kindt did not tell Jonathan that he had submitted his own request to the Director, for transfer to a different prison.

Chapter 22

The huge chamber where the nine justices meet to hear cases is described in a single word: Grand. Across the front is the long bench; nine black leather chairs rest serenely behind. Each chair is the same height as its neighbor, signifying the equality amongst the justices. Appearances are more important as you mount the ladder of administration.

Behind the justices, high on the wall is the great seal of the U.S. Supreme Court emblazoned on a circular crest. The ceilings are high, giving the room an aura of spaciousness, which is deceitful in a way. Chairs have been added at the back of the room, just inside the arched entrances, as more and more people want to see the workings of the Court.

There remain remnants of a bygone era, such as those droopy draped curtains you see in the yellowed photographs from the post Civil War Era. The Supreme Court clings to traditional decorum, design and protocol. It refuses to step into a contemporary world or risk losing its patriarchal position. Unlike the Houses of Congress, where a hundred or more people create a branch of authority under the Constitution, only nine people form the pinnacle of the Judicial Branch.

Although the justices are appointed for life, Congress must affirm the President's selection via hearings and ballots. To say that politics does not permeate the judiciary, tainting their alleged neutrality, is grossly misguided. The vein of political definition runs deep in each candidate for a position. This alliance to a particular party will shape and mold the justices' respective opinions on hotly contested issues such as abortion, civil rights and criminal prosecutions. The mettle of the justices was about to be tested in *Jonathan L. Childress II v State of Illinois*. The briefs of the parties had been distributed among them. They had denied participation to numerous requests by various organizations, Constitutional scholars, prominent attorneys and "concerned" parties. The sole appearances beyond Jonathan and State's Attorney Scott Schroeder, were those of the original attorneys,

Gamberino and Amaranta. They would be the only people permitted to address the high court when the case was called in a mere ten days' time.

The U.S. Marshals' Service had flown Jonathan aboard one of its aircraft and quietly moved him to the county jail in Alexandria, Virginia. He was provided his legal materials and the former Attorney General visited him twice in preparation for argument. Jonathan was eager and well prepared. The degree of confidence he displayed before the Court of Appeals had not abandoned him.

The Warden had provided Jonathan with an ocean blue suit with a sky blue shirt and his "lucky"" silk tie of blue and silver stripes. Before the Marshals took custody, Kindt, Father Birney, the cons on the row and even the Captain wished him good luck. When Jonathan had left the prison, a mist of depression descended on everyone. They missed him.

The morning his appearance was scheduled, he began to get nervous. Not because he would be the first person to argue his own capital case before the Supreme Court, but because this forum is known as the "Court of Last Resort." There were no other appeals from here. A loss here meant death within thirty days. He did not fear dying. He had already done that. No, what Jonathan feared was that he would never find out who he really was or if he was Krystan's father in California. He had an inner need to have his own identity.

Cameras are not permitted in federal courts, which include the Supreme Court. There would be no debacles here like the O.J. Simpson trial. However, the arguments were recorded, using a stenographer and a tape recorder. Tapes and transcripts were ordered by every major network, present or not. Networks were intending to interrupt regularly scheduled programming when their experts, who were fortunate enough to garner a place to stand or sit inside the chamber, came outside to stand in front of their camera crews.

At that time, four thousand five hundred miles away, only six hours later than the time in Washington, people were clustering in the Vatican Square. They expected the Pontiff to make a brief appearance from the famous balcony. Prayer cards were distributed among the throng with a brief prayer likening the hearing today to the tribunal which condemned Jesus. The Catholics were joined by Christians all over the world. All nine justices knew the gravamen of their decision.

The man responsible for this appeal, the Cook County State's Attorney, Scott Schroeder, basked in the attention. A dauntless believer that even bad press is good for elections, his radiant smile and his hauntingly classical look of a collegiate jock, made the cameras love him. Outside the Supreme Court Building he was fearless, while inside he was terrified. It was the first time he had appeared in the high court.

Jonathan was led into the chamber and the room fell deathly quiet. Not only was the man who created all the hubbub there, he was accompanied, stride for stride, by the former Attorney General of the United States. Jonathan looked good in the suit Tom Kindt arranged for him. Adelman, likewise, wore a dark blue Armani suit, white shirt and a power tie of red and blue stripes.

They both ignored the crowd as they proceeded to their table, where they spread the briefs and materials out. Jonathan had obtained 3 x 5 cards upon which he had made his notes. He was relaxed and ready. He wrote a note and asked the bailiff if he would mind handing it to the clerk. The woman read the note and looked at Jonathan before typing on her computer keyboard. She wrote something on the note and returned it to the bailiff who brought it back to Jonathan.

The nine justices entered from the left and were in order of their seats. The Chief Justice is always in the middle.

When the matter was called, Schroeder proudly announced that the People of Illinois were represented by his truly. Jonathan and Adelman stood together.

"The Appellee, Jonathan Childress II is present in open court and appears pro se and with standing counsel, Lynn Adelman."

"Good morning, Mr. Adelman. It's a pleasure to see you again."

"Thank you, Your Honor. It's good to be back."

This innocuous exchange made Schroeder very uncomfortable and feeling out of his league. He was. Jonathan and

Adelman had discussed the strategy in permitting the former Attorney General to make the official record and to set a tone for the Court.

Schroeder began his spiel about the State's interest with finality and how the jury represented the trier of fact's determination of the evidence. His sales pitch was meant to distract the justices from the legal challenges Jonathan had presented. Schroeder opted for the law school maxim, "If you can't argue the law, argue the facts." And so he did. Ad nauseum. He was not winning votes with anyone on the bench. When he was given the signal that his allotted time had expired, Schroeder strutted to his seat like some vaudeville dandy.

When Jonathan was called, Adelman stood along with him, gave him a confident smile and then sat back down. Adelman made it clear that he supported, championed really, his cause, but that it was Jonathan's show.

"Good morning," Jonathan began and every justice nodded. Their eyes were riveted on him. He had their attention completely. "In 2005, while this august Court rendered its decision in **Blakely v Washington**, my direct appeal was pending. In **Blakely**, this court held that any element of an offense which motored a sentence enhancement, must be set forth in the indictment, submitted to the jury and must be proven beyond a reasonable doubt." He took a sip of water from the glass before him. He wasn't thirsty, but it calmed him and gave everyone an opportunity to digest what he just said.

"My attorneys, Mr. Amaranta and Mr. Gamberino, both here today, overlooked the dramatic implications of **Blakely** to my case. In doing so, they both rendered the ineffective assistance of counsel, offending the Sixth Amendment." Everyone seemed to look at the two lawyers now and Amaranta let his shoulders slump.

"The jury instructions in my case were fatally defective, as my attorneys did or should have known, as they permitted the jury to transcend this Court's holdings in **Blakely** in two respects. First, the jury was permitted to shift the burden to me at the trial. I say 'me' as a metaphor only, as I am not the defendant in that case, but this body was present in that trial court. The attorneys failed to assert, both at trial and on direct appeal, that the State was permitted to shift the burden to me to prove my competence. This egregious error would mandate a new trial.

The second error manifested during the sentencing portion of the trial. As I indicated in district court, the Court of Appeals and in the dicta of my brief before you, there are no safety measures under the Rule of Lenity, where if the aggravation and the mitigation are in equipoise, the rule in favor of non-capital sentencing as the most lenient punishment. This error would necessitate a commutation from the capital sentence to a term of years in prison."

The courtroom belonged to Jonathan. He looked at the justices and he could see the agreement in their looks. He was winning. The reporters were frantically making notes and he could hear pages flip as his argument was memorialized.

"I will not belabor the point in this case, as they are accurately set forth in my brief. The argument put forth by Mr. Schroeder are factual in nature and in no way address the legal errors. This case should have been scrutinized under the **Blakely** regime while on direct appeal and it was not."

After only ten minutes of his allotted hour, Jonathan thanked the justices for their attention and returned to his seat. He and Adelman had discussed at length the wisdom of making his point and if it was apparent that he was winning, abbreviate his Argument and show his confidence by resting.

The justices looked at the time and two of them smiled. It was a clever maneuver. Nello Gamberino cautiously approached the podium, realizing the seriousness of Jonathan's allegations. He weighed the consequences of him denying the oversight of **Blakely's** application to the trial and appeal, or the morality of admitting the error and taking a drubbing later. Amaranta watched him through squinty eyes. They would be branded as screw-ups if they admitted botching Jonathan's trial and their practices would suffer the adversity. Gamberino could say that they did not believe that the **Blakely** decision applied in competency findings at trial or sentencing. That excuse would be an error in strategy, as they call it, and give them an escape hatch.

"Good morning, Your Honors. Let me make this brief and to the point. We are all here to see that justice prevails and not quibble over who is at fault, if indeed fault is discovered. The adage of 'practicing law,' not unlike 'practicing medicine,' permits those practitioners an innate ability to be human. To err, if you will." Gamberino took a deep breath and relaxed. Every eye and ear was waiting to see where this was leading.

I have read the **Blakely** decision that Jonathan refers to today and how it compels the prosecution to prove their case beyond a reasonable doubt." Nello turned to face Jonathan now, not the Court, and Amaranta held his breath.

"Regrettably, both Mr. Amaranta and I must accept the responsibility for overlooking the importance of the **Blakely** decision. Had we held Mr. Schroeder here to that significantly higher standard of proof, we probably wouldn't be here today. This man who is struggling for his life probably wouldn't have been convicted."

And there it was, an admission that should ring the death knell to Schroeder's whole case and the two attorneys would be fire branded in the media as fuck-ups.

"Mr. Amaranta and I express our deepest regrets for this fundamental error and ask this Court to not punish anyone for our ineffectiveness."

As Nello walked back to his seat, he did not walk the walk of the defeated, but as a gentleman who was capable of admitting he had made a mistake. He retained his honor, if not his lucrative criminal law practice.

While Sam Amaranta looked at the floor in defeat and pictured the scathing headlines of their blunders in a capital case, Schroeder was either too stupid to realize the shocking blow his arguments just sustained, or he would be a world class poker player. His expression was unremarkable. The bets were that he was too stupid.

The nine justices had pooled their questions and had given them to the Chief Justice so that the media would be denied any ability to focus on one particular justice who asked a particular question. Every question would be delivered by the Chief Justice only.

"Thank you," the newly appointed Chief Justice said. "We have a few questions for the parties before we take this matter under advisement. We will begin with you, Mr. Schroeder as representative of the State of Illinois."

Schroeder slowly rose to his feet and approached the podium once again. The State's Attorney was a good politician and a "fair" trial lawyer, but not a shark. He was not aloof or improvisational during spontaneous debates. He feared being asked pointed questions by the justices and it was readily apparent now.

The Chief Justice asked him to "Explain why the *Blakely* decision did not apply" in his case. Schroeder ambled through enough rhetoric to confuse Merriam-Webster, but never eluded the measured attention of the scholars who sat before him. Schroeder was asked a couple more questions about the drafting of the jury instructions and their submission for the jury's deliberations. The last question the high court had referred to the open admission of Nello Gamberino to being ineffective. This last question was impromptu, as no one had anticipated such a grievous admission beforehand.

Schroeder's response was weak and flaccid. He clung to the fabric of his argument that the jury had afforded the defendant a fair trial and a just verdict. They were done with this pompous ass who could not fathom the utter destruction of his case at the hands of the gentleman from Illinois who admitted his mistakes.

"Mr. Childress, we have a few questions for you, as well," the Chief Justice said.

"Your Honor, if it pleases the Court, I am a bit overwhelmed by all this. I ask that my standby counsel assume this case."

This was Jonathan's idea alone, and although he had just caught Adelman by surprise, the former Attorney General's face did not show it.

"Very well, that is always your option, and this Court is very familiar with your counsel and his ability to appear here. Mr. Adelman, would you approach the podium?"

When Adelman looked at Jonathan, there was the same ice-like look he wore a moment ago when Jonathan dropped the case on him.

"Mr. Adelman, would you explain why the court should not determine that in light of the overwhelming evidence against your client, any error under **Blakely** would not be harmless?"

Adelman had helped Jonathan prepare his argument on this topic and was well prepared to inundate the justices with facts and case law that all but mandated them to require a new trial. His answer was replete and required almost fifteen minutes. The justices were busy scribbling notes as he spoke.

"Mr. Adelman, your client asserts that he is not the person convicted of the offenses which resulted in a capital sentence. Please explain why the capital sentence does not apply to the body of the condemned and requires a second execution?"

This was the question everyone had been anticipating. The reporters and justices flipped to virgin pages on their respective note pads. Adelman took this respite to drink some water himself. He was playing to the world now. It was a role with which he was quite familiar.

"A death warrant directs the termination of an identifiable source of evil. In this case, a child killer. An illiterate child killer. Once that resident evil is destroyed, justice has been served. Never before has a case presented the fertile ground we walk upon here today. And why is that?" Adelman paused as he looked closely at the justices and thought about the impact of his words.

"Because God has never permitted man to juxtapose his spirit with that of another. God did not want the body to cease existing and for a very good reason. He had a plan to allow the spirit of the man before you, a good and decent man whose education, poise and demeanor speaks volumes for his character, to return. As mortals, we do not understand God's work or intentions. We, as a country, embrace the existence of God." Adelman let that settle as he sipped his water and decided to close his answer and deliver his punch line.

Our Pledge of Allegiance speaks of 'one nation under God' and our democracy is rooted in the mantra 'In God We Trust.' We cannot undo what God has set in motion."

The Chief Justice paused as if inviting the gallery an opportunity to stand and applaud. He looked to his fellow justices and all shook their heads except one, who passed a note to him.

"One last question, Mr. Adelman. Is your client claiming to be an angel or emissary from God?"

"I don't think Jonathan has ever claimed to be an angel or any other holy being. He has consistently testified as to how he managed to return from limbo or whatever the place is called where The Reaper or whatever, gathers the life forces. The State of Illinois has failed to posit any credible explanation for the antithetical appearance of this man here today. Whether or not Jonathan is an angel is not for us to decide. That would be the strict province of the jury and time."

Adelman turned to Jonathan, who smiled at him and nodded. They could all hear the pages being flipped and pens scratching across paper in an attempt to quote him accurately.

"We will now adjourn this hearing and take this case under advisement. We wish to thank all of you for appearing. Mr. Childress, or Jonathan, we have prepared the standard certificate we issue to attorneys who appear before the Court for the first time. You are the first to appear pro se in a case and my colleagues and I wish to congratulate you. You have conducted yourself in an exemplary manner and have presented your issues well. No matter the result here, we find you unique. Mr. Schroeder, you will likewise receive a certificate. Mr. Adelman, I believe you already have yours framed. At least it was the last time you were photographed in your office." The Chief Justice was smiling at Adelman. It was a good sign.

The experts hired by media moguls all proclaimed Jonathan the odds on favorite to win. The stories that resulted spoke of Adelman's Biblical approach and references to America's history in God's existence. Unanimously, the reporters called Adelman's delivery as nothing short of brilliant. On the steps outside the Supreme Court, the cameras surrounded Adelman as he descended and headed towards a waiting limo.

"Mr. Adelman, how do you think the arguments went today? Do you believe the court will give your client another victory?" one reporter from the Washington Post asked.

Adelman stopped and looked at the reporter. "You and I are no strangers. You've attended numerous briefings with me, so let me set the record clear here. The Supreme Court does not give victories as if they were trophies or belt buckles. The law does not require any criminal defendant to prove his innocence. That burden must always rest with prosecutors. If Jonathan prevails here it will be because the prosecutors failed to meet that burden and shifted it instead to Jonathan."

Adelman hoped the justices were watching this interview inside their chambers.

"That's all I have to say. You heard everything in the courtroom. Thank you."

Jonathan was returned to the Alexandria jail in a dark blue van, its windows so heavily tinted that you could not see the people inside. He had a quiet smile on his face. A smile that now had no gap where a certain police sergeant had knocked out a tooth. The sketches and photos now reflected a full set of facial teeth.

Schroeder basked in the media attention and downplayed the day's taciturn events. He gave the cameras his best profile and hoped that everyone in Illinois saw him on their televisions.

Cardinal Bavielle, who was in contact with Adelman from his car, was excited to hear the news and relayed the encouraging information to the Pontiff, who blessed the crowd and issued a written statement affirming his gratitude for and in the American justice system.

Tom Kindt and his wife watched the evening news and smiled at the anchor's comments about Jonathan's predicted victory over the State of Illinois. The anchorwoman asked, "Is Jonathan an angel?" and a picture appeared of Jonathan without the missing tooth and looking calm as he was led towards a van by marshals. Kindt wanted the man to win and wondered about the foundation of his own faith. If Jonathan was true, then there was a final judgment above and he wanted to be prepared.

The cons and staff on death row watched various news channels and Jonathan emerged from the Supreme Court Building a sure shot winner. The cons remarked to each other that the asshole State's Attorney never stood a fucking chance and Jonathan had kicked ass. The staff on the row admitted to each other that Jonathan was nothing like Johnny Lee Childress, but couldn't explain why.

Rachael was livid and almost shot her expensive high definition television. She felt like the world had forgotten the innocent blood that covered the sonofabitch's hands when she arrested him. She regretted now that she hadn't shot him that day and granted his wish of "suicide by cop" if that was his intent.

"Mort," Rachael said blandly, without any salutation whatsoever. "Do you want to do an interview?"

"You're upset Rachael. Calm down and talk to me," Mordeci Habush said in a soothing tone.

"Print this, Mort. I, as arresting officer, will meet with Childress, not Jonathan, Mort, Childress, where I will openly discuss the crimes. If I am convinced that he is not the killer I arrested, I will banner his cause for freedom."

"Rachael, you know he won't do that and especially not while he stands to obtain a new trial. I would, however, like an interview with you about your opinion on all this ecclesiastical talk of him?"

"How about tomorrow morning at my office? I'll clear it with Ben and we'll go from there. I think people are forgetting what this guy was convicted of, and his victims."

"I'll bring breakfast and you buy the coffee."

"That's a deal that's always open to you, Mort, with or without your bagels."

"Calm down, Rachael, and I'll see you tomorrow."

When Rachael hung up, she decided to go to the gym and work out her anger. Some poor bastard was in for the lesson of his life.

In the Polish community across town, was a father who seethed with anger and his need for vengeance resembled searing beefsteak on a red-hot grill. He had already forbidden Bibles in their home and banished all Catholics as friends. He hated them all, especially the Pope, who believed the killer of his two daughters was some angel. The Angel of Death, maybe. He had made the decision long ago that he would see Childress dead, with no miraculous resurrections, if he had to drive a wooden stake through his blackened heart.

There was no middle ground for people to park their opinions. Either they hated Johnny Lee or they liked Jonathan. Talk show hosts went with the ebb and flow. Whatever boosted Nielson ratings. Jay Leno enjoyed updates on Jonathan. It was almost a daily part of his opening monologue to mention him. He said one night that he had the perfect jury for Jonathan's next trial and held up a placard with a drawing of a jury box and twelve pictures of O.J. Simpson. Jonathan heard about it from several cons on the row who watched the tonight show, mostly to hear about Jonathan and his exploits. It kept them going and helped them avoid the trappings of their own plights. Indeed, Jonathan was infectious, but a wonderful strain, not a bad one.

Chapter 23

While Jonathan waited for the decision from the Supreme Court, he captured an idea that the Warden unleashed and then drafted a form letter for all the well-wishers who wrote to him. With Kindt's approval, his blessing actually, the letter was taken to a local printer and one hundred thousand copies were printed, boxed and delivered to Father Birney. There were envelopes too, all nicely typeset with "Jonathan L. Childress II," festooned in the upper left corner. In all, they had cost Jonathan almost three thousand dollars, but were necessary to meet the needs of the prison. Every day, several of the cons would get together and form one long assembly line. They would fold the letters, place them in envelopes, address the envelopes according to the return address from the letters received and put a stamp on each one before dropping them into boxes. The letters Jonathan received were then boxed and held for removal to an outside storage facility, which Jonathan also paid for every month. He even remunerated his workers with money every month. This was technically against the rules, but Jonathan selected those without family or friends to send them money for necessary hygiene items and put them to work. All was good on the row.

Jonathan was hurried to the library on the row where staff had quickly plugged in a small television. A reporter Jonathan recognized instantly from the evening news was standing before the Supreme Court Building. "Special Report" was in bold letters in the upper right-hand corner of the screen.

"In a seven-to-two decision issued about an hour ago, actually, the Supreme Court struck down the conviction of convicted murderer Jonathan Childress. For the first time in the Court's history, every justice issued an individual opinion which agreed in part but dissented in part with their brother or sister jurists. Although each justice had a personal rationale for vacating the conviction, the majority agreed that Childress's conviction was unconstitutional," the anchor man said as if reporting on world affairs.

"What happens next, Wolf?" the newsroom reporter asked.

"Well, the mandate, or official Order of the Court, will issue in ten days. After that, Childress will go to Cook County where it will start all over again. It's as if he were just arrested."

"Can you tell us any specifics from the decision today?"

The man on the steps of the Supreme Court held up about a one-inch stack of papers. "Certainly. I have a copy of the almost two hundred page decision, one of the longest ever issued by the Court. The Chief Justice avoided the more argumentative questions about Childress, instead opting for the black letter law. It was that well defined law which formulated the majority opinion the State of Illinois simply avoided, proving their case of competency beyond a reasonable doubt, according to a 2004 decision called *Blakely v. Washington*. Other Justices believe Childress suffers some organic brain disorder, which may have been caused by the ill-fated attempt to execute him. One justice, however, wrote that if God had wanted Childress dead, he would have permitted the chemicals to work. In refusing to do so, the death warrant is no longer valid and it would be cruel and unusual punishment to attempt a second execution if Childress is again convicted. This justice, a distinguished lady who served on the Second Circuit Court of Appeals for years, stopped short of calling Jonathan, as he is now known, an angel or emissary of God."

"Is there any comment from the opposition or the former Attorney General?"

"I spoke with Mr. Adelman by phone a few moments ago and all he would say is that he was pleased with the outcome and would be meeting with Childress later in the week. I was advised that the Cook County State's Attorney is holding a conference later this afternoon. Back to you in the studio."

Jonathan felt as if the weight of the world had been lifted from his chest. The incredible string of victories now brought him full circle and he was headed back to Chicago, where it all began years ago.

The cons cheered, banged on doors, and shouted their versions of "attaboy" as Jonathan walked past each cell and thanked them for their help.

Father Birney swooped onto the row and caught up with him after hearing the news. He was standing in front of a prisoner's cell, where he was watching a soap opera and the Special Report interrupted the soap. Hearing Jonathan's name, the priest asked the man to turn the volume up and listened to the full report before rushing off, and he even failed to say good-bye to the prisoner. He found Jonathan doing a victory tour past the cells. Even the officer following Jonathan was smiling.

"Congratulations, Jonathan. I just saw the news."

"Thanks, Father. I need to talk to you if you have some time today."

"How about right now? Can we go to the library here?"

When they were in the little library on the row, Jonathan opened a notebook on the table where he watched the report about himself.

"When I was in the Supreme Court, Father, I wrote a note to the clerk. It felt as though I had been there before. Father, I was relaxed and somehow familiar with everything there. Anyhow, I asked the clerk if an attorney from Sacramento, California by the name of William Dunbar had ever appeared before the Supreme Court. Here is the note and her answer, Father. He did."

"Jonathan, are you insinuating that you are really William A. Dunbar, as this note reads?"

"I think it's possible, don't you?" Jonathan pleaded.

"I don't know, Jonathan. If God had a hand in all of this, it is certainly possible. He created life; I suppose He can move it around. I don't know. I can ask the Cardinal what he thinks," the priest said, avoiding a committal to Jonathan on this.

Rachael was incredulous. "Ben, how did we go three-hundred sixty degrees on this guy? He had exhausted every appeal. He was strapped down and his ticket punched for a one-way trip to hell and because some chemicals were bad or whatever, this guy gets a new trial? Can you explain any of this to me? You should have let me give Mort that interview."

"There's going to be a new trial and you are the key witness. It wouldn't have looked good if you appeared in the press spewing venom and were asked about it on the stand. That's why I said no," Ben returned.

"Damnit, Ben, this guy is being called an angel and stuff. I'd like to hold pictures up from the inside of that apartment and show the world, this 'angel's' work. Perhaps the Pope would like a set of photos for his collection?"

"Sergeant Hart, will you settle down? We're not Judges, we're cops. Besides, how is Childress going to argue that he's incompetent when he's arguing his own case in the Supreme Court? He'll get convicted again. The evidence remains the same. I think you should check with the parents of those girls, though. See if they're doing all right."

"I'll stop there tonight as their father is probably at work. He's not going to understand any of this either, Ben."

"Make sure that all the evidence on the Childress case is back in custody. See that whatever exhibits from the trial that went to the appellate court is personally picked up, signed for and returned here or to the State Attorney's office. I don't want any flaw in the chain-of-custody, ok?"

"I'll handle it myself since most of the stuff has my signature on it."

Ben watched Rachael amble out of his office without another word. It was hard for her to understand how the courts work. Hell, he didn't understand either, most of the time. He wondered how the family of those girls was going to hold up through another trial. He felt sorry for the roller-coaster ride of emotions they must be going through.

Chapter 24

Jonathan wrote very slowly, forming the letters in his words in his best cursive style. After all, the letter was going to a nine year old and he wanted her to be able to read it.

He asked her how she liked school, what she wanted to be when she grew up, if she had lots of friends and how she was planning to spend her summer. He closed by thanking her for her letter and told her that he had it hanging on the bulletin board in the library.

He gave the letter to Father Birney and insisted that he read it to make sure it wasn't pushy or misguided somehow. When the priest agreed that it looked quite appropriate, Jonathan smiled.

"Father, thank you for mailing that letter. If there is another letter from her, would you see that I get it?"

"Absolutely," he responded as he looked around the library they had crafted on the row.

"We have some matters to attend to, Father. I will be leaving here soon and we should decide what to do with my mail and how we'll keep in touch."

"Yes, the Warden said you'll be leaving soon. He said they're making arrangements now. Something about a quarrel with the Cook County Sheriff. The Sheriff wants the State to transport you back and the State's telling the Sheriff it's their responsibility. Silly, really, and all about money. Who pays the tab? I'll keep in touch with you and if something urgent comes up, I'll get it to the Cardinal. He'll know what to do."

"Thank you for everything, Father. You've been a Godsend to me and I know the men here appreciate you, as well."

"I must admit that I'm going to miss you, Jonathan. I believe that knowing you has been the most exciting time in my life. I know everyone here will miss you, but will root for you in court."

Without waiting for a reply, the little priest turned and hurriedly left in a swoosh of robes. As he passed the Warden, there were tears in his eyes and Kindt believed he knew why.

"Jonathan," Kindt started as he walked into the little library, "the arrangements have been finally made for your trip back to

Chicago. You can take your legal materials with you, your Bible and keep the cross the Pope gave to you. We'll keep the rest of your things in storage here."

There was a pregnant pause as both men realized the implications of that statement. The inference of "you'll be back" definitely struck a nerve.

"I meant that we'll keep everything until you tell us where to send it." Kindt said as he hoped to lighten his poor choice of wording earlier.

"What will become of the library here, Mr. Kindt? Will it remain?"

"Well, technically, everything here belongs to you. It was all sent to you or you paid for it. If you wish to donate it to the prison, you can. But, I have to tell you that the next warden may not approve of it and dispose of it."

"What do you mean, 'the next warden?' Are you leaving here, too?"

"I don't want this spread, so please keep it to yourself. I'm moving on, Jonathan. I'm transferring to a little facility called Sheridan. It's up near Joliet. I can't stay here, Jonathan. You showed me that."

"I want these guys to have it, Mr. Kindt. They need it. They need the hope in these books."

"Jonathan, the books are not the inspiration around here. You are. Your victories in court, the Pope himself coming to see you, and what you give to people. These guys will miss you." As an afterthought, Kindt said, "And so will I."

Jonathan looked at the Warden and realized that this place was the only home he had known. It was as if he was born on death row. What an oxymoron that was.

"Thank you, Mr. Kindt. I guess it sounds strange, but I'll miss this place. It's kind of scary, not knowing where I'm from or where I belong. I think I have a destiny or mission to fulfill. I'm not sure where this journey is taking me or why I'm here. In a way though, I think we're all a little like that. Aren't we?"

"I think you're right. I never thought I would ever say this to you, but good luck, Jonathan. You've changed us all around here."

"Thank you."

"By the way, my wife wanted me to give you this. It's against the rules so eat it in here. That's a direct order," Kindt said, smiling, as he handed Jonathan a bag of homemade fudge.

"Tell your wife, thank you for me. I think this will ruin my lunch, but I'll risk it!"

"I'm not supposed to tell you this, but who can you call anyhow. You're leaving here tonight." Kindt then left, almost as quickly as Father Birney did.

Later, after savoring the fudge, Jonathan packed his meager belongings. He had never bought a television, at least not for himself. He had bought a few for others on the row, but never had time to watch television, so he didn't waste the money. He did have a radio, however, which he wanted to give to the newest arrival on the row. It was a young guy who had murdered his parents and was full of rage. Jonathan was sorry for the guy in a way. His parents must have done something to him to die at their son's hand. So, he wanted this radio to go to him.

What remained of Jonathan's worldly possessions was primarily documented in nature. His T-shirt with J2 was neatly folded on his bunk and would be placed in storage. That was all he wanted saved for him.

He sat on his bunk and was lost in deep, sullen thought. He was leaving his sanctuary and going to a strange place. He was going to undergo the emotional complexities of a trial and it all frightened him.

The State plane turned out to be a Beechcraft King Air. The ten passenger twin engine aircraft flew at over three hundred fifty miles per hour. Jonathan, chained and shackled, was on-board with two Department of Corrections officers who transported prisoners full time. It took little more than an hour for the corporate craft to land at Midway Airport on Chicago's South Side, where a Cook County Sheriff's Department van awaited. He was spirited away from the airport and thirty minutes later, entered a new world at the Cook County Jail.

The portion of the jail where Jonathan was taken is old. Very old. In fact, it was the original jail decades before. Because he faced the death penalty, he would automatically be placed in the maximum security section called ABO, in "Division One."

Since the original jail was built over seventy years earlier, the Cook County Jail had expanded dramatically. It now housed over four thousand prisoners and encompassed two city blocks. It resembles a prison, in that thirty foot high walls with gun towers establish the perimeter defenses. It is also known as one of the toughest jails in the country. Haven to various street gangs, it is now standard procedure to ask every prisoner who he "rides with," so that they're not housed with rival factions and someone gets hurt. Even staff members are asked similar questions before being hired.

In Jonathan's case, being extremely high profile, he was placed in maximum security, in a single man cell and right next to the officers' station. The cell was nothing like the one at Thames. It is smaller and the walls were not concrete block, but poured concrete. It bore the years of repeated paintings and had numerous names gouged into the thick layers of paint, memorializing the patrons in the past.

Jonathan sat on the bunk. The mattress was old, dingy yellow and smelled of urine. A small bedroll rested on the foot of the bunk, which held a torn sheet and a blanket which wasn't fit for a horse. It was a dreary place and reeked of fear from the men who preceded him. His new home. Jonathan drew his legs up on the bunk and placed his head on his knees. That is how he rested that night. That is how the Sheriff himself found him the next morning when he walked into his cell. He wanted to meet his celebrity prisoner and Jonathan disliked the man, immediately.

When the Sheriff had puffed enough and finally left, the Chaplain appeared. He brought word from the Cardinal, who had personally called him the day before, and said that he was planning a visit. Cardinal Carroll also requested that the Chaplain make him as comfortable as possible, and to let him know if Jonathan needed to talk to him. The Chaplain, who is not a priest, agreed to help and had brought new sheets, blankets and even a pillow from the jail's warehouse. A mattress was being brought and Jonathan thanked him. It all made his cloistered world much better.

Jonathan's legal materials arrived that afternoon, having been inspected for contraband or weapons first. He began to arrange the documents in the folders. Having read the transcripts from the first trial, he knew the precise order in which the State's Attorney would present its evidence. When evening fell, exhaustion overcame him, and he slept on his new mattress and bedding.

His initial appearance before the same Judge who presided over his first trial was a media event. The courtroom sported bullet proof glass dividers which separated the spectators from the defendant and the attorneys.

The minute Jonathan was led into the courtroom, the gallery fell silent. He seemed to have that affect wherever he went, he lamented.

The Judge entered and his case was called.

"Mr. Childress, this case has been remanded for a new trial. Do you wish me to appoint counsel?"

"No, Your Honor," Jonathan announced.

"Mr. Childress, you have a right to represent yourself. The Court notes that you have done so in your case thus far, and you appear quite familiar with the judicial system. However, there are complexities associated with charges such as in this case and I strongly urge you to reconsider representing yourself."

"I realize the consequences, Your Honor," Jonathan said solemnly.

"The Court notes that counsel was appointed for the first trial. I would be willing to review your financial situation and appoint counsel. Would you consider that?"

There was a commotion in the gallery and Jonathan noticed the Judge's expression. When he turned, he realized why.

"Sorry I'm late, Your Honor. My plane was delayed. May it please the Court, Jonathan L. Childress II appears in person and with counsel, Lynn Adelman. Good Morning."

"Mr. Adelman, it is a pleasure to meet you and I welcome your participation in this matter. Mr. Childress, is Mr. Adleman your counsel?"

"Yes, Your Honor, he is." He said, beaming with joy and the welcome sight of his trusted confidante.

The State's Attorney was not particularly pleased to see the former Attorney General appear in his backyard. The morose expression on his face betrayed Schroeder and the media noted it.

"How much time will you need to prepare for trial, Mr. Adelman?"

"The defense is ready to begin immediately, Your Honor."

This statement caught the Judge off guard as cases of this magnitude generally required months of preparation. It was not unusual in Cook County courts for murder trials to take as much as years before proceeding to trial.

"Are you sure, Mr. Adelman? Once I schedule this matter for trial, I will be reluctant to delay it."

"As the Court is probably aware, I am quite familiar with this case and have worked extensively with the Defendant. We're ready for trial."

Under Illinois law, as in every state, a defendant charged with a crime has a right to a speedy trial. If he or she is not brought to trial within the prescribed period of time, the charges must be dismissed. The Judge had no alternative but to comply and hope that the State would be prepared.

"I set this matter for trial in eight weeks, as number one on my calendar. Any pretrial motions will be filed within ten days of today. Since prior counsel in this case filed a comprehensive motion for Discovery, I will direct the State to provide all materials requested therein. Likewise, I will direct the defense to reciprocate and to provide all discoverable materials to the State. I want this accomplished within thirty days of today. Anything further?"

"No, Your Honor," Schroeder said as he continued to note the dates on his yellow pad.

"None, your Honor," Adelman said, not needing to make notes.

From where Mordeci sat, he could see several of the artists' renditions of the real players in this courtroom drama and in each of the ones he saw, all omitted the State's Attorney. He gave one of the artists his card and requested her to contact him immediately. He wanted to purchase her drawing for the newspaper. The attention would focus on the appearance of the former Attorney General and he understood the import of that focal point. Mordeci had a hunch that the media was about to play an integral role in the re-trial. His employer would require him to capitalize on events and perspectives that would sell papers. The color drawing would help, even if he spent the thousand dollars for it.

Although Jonathan had looked directly at her, there was not the slightest hint of recognition, unlike when she had testified at his first trial. Rachael believed that sitting directly behind the defense table, in the first row no less, would evoke some form of emotion from the man she had arrested for murder. She wanted to expose him as a fraud as he cursed her, for if he did so, he would be admitting his culpability through recognition. If he were truly a different man, then he would have no recollection of her whatsoever. Her litmus test had failed, but she would not give up that easily. Rachael opened the door in the courtroom divide and approached the defense table.

"Good Morning, Mr. Adelman," Rachael said, extending her hand.

Believing she was an attorney, given the cut and fit of her business suit, he shook her hand. "Good Morning, Ms....?" He asked.

"Hart, Rachael Hart." She watched for any aggressive movement by the man she had disarmed and arrested years earlier.

"I believe you're a Sergeant now, aren't you, Ms. Hart?" Adelman responded, remembering her name from the transcripts.

"Your client knows me, Mr. Adelman. Don't you, Johnny Lee?" she said laconically.

Jonathan looked at the tall redhead, but gave no sign of emotion.

"Ah, is this some primitive test, Sergeant? You want to see if Jonathan remembers you? Well, I assure you, Sergeant, he does not. If you are quite finished with the sophomoric test of yours, I have a trial to prepare for."

Jonathan accompanied the deputies in the courtroom out the door he had entered. As he walked, he had reviewed the encounter with Rachael in his mind. She had tested him, even before Adelman arrived. That explained why she sat directly behind him. She was shrewd and would be a formidable witness for the prosecution. He remembered from the trial transcript that she was responsible for his missing front tooth.

"Ben," Rachael began after returning to the Homicide offices.

"I was in Childress's face and I gotta tell you, he played his role well. He didn't let on that he knew who I was. His mouthpiece did all the talking."

"Is it possible that he didn't recognize you?"

"Aw, come on Ben. Not you, too? Are you gonna tell me he's an angel too?"

"Nothing of the sort. What if his mind refuses to remember? Blocked it all out somehow? Is his mind mixed up by all those chemicals they put into him?"

"This is going to confuse the jury, Ben. Even if Schroeder gets a conviction, he won't get the death penalty. It's kinda hard to believe that some screw-up during the execution gets the guy off. I would think, and I am not alone here, that they would just mix another batch of those chemicals and keep pumping it in until he finally died. How did a screw-up get him all these new rights and a new trial?"

Ben noticed that Rachael was sullen and not her vibrant self. This whole thing was grating on her.

"Have you checked on the parents, Rachael?"

"I stopped by their house last week. The mother is comatose. The father seems distant, though. He isn't doing well, Ben. He doesn't understand and, quite frankly, I can't sooth him because I don't understand, either."

"Maybe you can get someone from the State's Attorney's office to talk to them and reassure them that everything will work out?"

Ben and Rachael looked at each other after he said that.

"Ah, hell, I don't understand all this either. You made a good bust. The guy had a fair trial and was given the punishment which of course, he didn't like. I don't like this any more than you, Rachael, but this went all the way to the U.S. Supreme Court. Short of shooting Childress that morning like the mob does to make sure someone is dead, we were just spectators. Try to explain to the parents that in America, the wheels of justice turn slowly, but eventually those wheels are gonna grind this guy up. We'll all attend his last execution."

Chapter 25

Time went by slowly for Jonathan. He couldn't go outside, visit his little library or even just sit and talk to Father Birney. If it weren't for the books the Chaplain brought him, he would have nothing to do.

"Father Birney says hello, Jonathan, and this letter is for you. He asked me to deliver it personally," the Chaplain said as he reached into his jacket pocket and handed him the tri-folded letter.

"Thank you," Jonathan said, as he returned the gaze of the officer sitting a few feet from him. Then he saw the postmark and the child's scrawl on the envelope.

Dear Jonathan,
My Mommy says you may not have a window where you are,
so I drew one for you. Now you can see the flowers and birds
Outside. I really like school and when I grow up I want to be doctor, I think. In Sunday School, they tell us about angels and Mommy says people think you might be one. Do you have wings? Can you fly? You are in my prayers at night.
Krystan

Jonathan was elated at receiving the letter from the little girl. He unfolded the second page in the envelope and there was Krystan's "window." It was tastefully done in crayon, with a brown frame and dividers, leaving four small panes of glass. In Krystan's yard there were brightly colored flowers and some bluebirds, or at least the birds were in blue crayon. And next to the flowers were the child's version of her and her Mom, holding hands. Each had yellow streaks representing blond hair. They were both waving and smiling.

He hung up his "window" out of sight from the guards or others who looked inside his cell. Only he could look out Krystan's window and he wondered about the chain of events and the coincidences they shared. "Couldn't possibly be..." he said aloud. He smiled at the prospect.

Across the street from Jonathan, Scott Schroeder was having a strategy session with his Criminal Division and Appellate Division chiefs. Adelman had filed a preposterous defense notice. Under the "alibi" provisions of Illinois and federal laws, any criminal defendant must give Notice to the Court and the prosecution that they intend to argue that it was not them who committed the offense, and they were some place when the offense occurred.

"This is bullshit, boss. The notice Adelman filed says that it isn't Childress who killed the girls but fails to identify where he was at the time. The Judge can't allow this defense," the Criminal Chief said to Schroeder.

"And what if he permits it? We're not talking about the average defendant here. I want an ironclad response to this thing." Schroeder said as he slammed the alibi notice on the desk.

"We're going to argue this thing tomorrow, as the Judge wants no delays here. I want the response on my desk by two o'clock today."

Schroeder was tired of losing to Childress and now the killer had one of the most notable attorneys in the world representing him. "Star Power" was a mounting phenomenon where famous defendants like O.J. Simpson, Robert Blake and Michael Jackson seemed to escape justice because of their popularity. Johnny Lee Childress, now renowned as Jonathan L. Childress II, was an international event now. His counsel, the former Attorney General, not only had significant media exposure but maintained close ties with the current President. Each surpassed Schroeder in the international and national arenas, but not in Illinois - and certainly not in Cook County. He would not permit these two rapscallions to upstage him on his own turf. The Criminal Court Building belonged to him. When he walked its corridors, he was immediately recognized and greeted by almost everyone he passed. He is the State's Attorney and elected by the People. So, why did he worry about this "Star Power" influence? Because Childress and his counsel were equally famous in Cook County and he knew it.

A million times, Schroeder cursed the doctor who flubbed the simple task of overdosing the sonofabitch who killed two kids. He had heard that the doctor resigned afterwards and moved. "Maybe he was in cahoots with Childress?" He asked himself. Then he shook that ridiculous defense from his mind. It was a simple case of ineptitude which had blossomed into a new trial. Amazing!

Schroeder had another murderer who haunted his career. A man named Eddie Veins, pronounced "Vee-ins," who had hunted down and brutally executed an entire jury. That case had almost demolished his career. Someone even wrote a book about the Veins escapades, called it "Jury Duty" and there is talk of a famous producer who intends to make the book into a movie. He escaped the Sword of Damocles by blaming everything on federal investigators and prosecutors. He counted on the feds employing their S.O.P. or standard operating procedure, and simply answering media questions with "no comment." This evasive response motored infinite speculation and clouded Schroeder's culpability in the attempted cover-up.

The Childress case presented no such opportunities to skirt direct responsibility. If Childress managed to survive this prosecution, Schroeder's career would not. Like in the game "Texas Hold'em," all Schroeder's chips were in the middle of the table. The problem was that the other side had aces, too.

Downtown, in the heart of Chicago, or the Loop as it's called, Adelman was sharing office space with an attorney who also wrote books. The author/lawyer was on the location where a new movie was being filmed, based on one of his novels and he would be gone for at least three months. His partners covered for him in such instances and he had told Adelman that he could use his office and staff to prepare for the high profile jury trial.

Adelman, after gaining Jonathan's approval, had carefully crafted the alibi notice. If Jonathan were believable, then he, not Johnny Lee Childress, was in another place. It would give the jury another method of finding him not guilty. This is especially critical if Jonathan were not found to be legally insane. In a black and white world, where a jury would have only two options, yes or no, he hoped to introduce a gray area. The alibi.

Adelman hoped that Schroeder wouldn't see it for what it was and argue the reality to the court. There is a term in the legal profession called "jury nullification." It is rarely encountered, but it is where the jury declines to convict the defendant, even when the evidence is overwhelming. There are reported cases where this phenomenon has occurred but is potentially existent in cases with celebrities who juries just don't wish to see convicted. Jonathan is a celebrity and so is Adelman. The paralegals at his temporary office could not locate a similar case with such notoriety ending in nullification. He hoped Schroeder didn't see the angle.

Ben invited Rachael to lunch as an effort to help relieve her of the sullenness she was laboring with as a result of the Childress case. Since she carried an active caseload of homicides, Ben could not afford Rachael being distracted. She had just made another arrest in a case where a drug dealer had murdered one of his girlfriends, who was also an informant for the Chicago Police Department. She had spotted the killer while on her way to the scene where he had just run the girlfriend down on a cross-walk. Someone using their cell phone had called in a description of the car and Rachael happened to spot a vehicle matching the description. When she attempted to stop the car, a high speed chase ensued. The suspect lost control of his car, which shot up a guy wire on a utility pole and somersaulted through the air like a scene from "Too Fast, Too Furious," and Rachael was there when the guy was extricated from the wreckage by the firemen. It was very dramatic and was shown on the evening news. There was Rachael, those distinctive Irish features, dangling handcuffs while she watched the firemen use the "Jaws of Life" to pry the guy out of his vehicle.

That was the Rachael needed, not the woman who was so distraught over the Childress case that Ben had actually considered telling her to meet with the Department psychologist, who usually attended to officers who had shot suspects during an arrest and were in need of emotional help to get them through.

Rachael was dangerously on the edge. She was having difficulty accepting the turn of events and the stress of a second trial. Ben would see her gazing out of the office windows or simply staring at the box on the floor next to her desk, which held the Childress file. Once, he saw her staring at the Death Warrant that took them to Thames that night. It was as if she expected to find wording that everyone had missed and end the new trial.

Yet, Ben knew that the referral to a Department psychologist would forever smudge her exemplary record and deter her from future promotions. He did not want to risk that, so he opted to watch her for signs of fatigue or stress which would detrimentally affect her performance as a cop.

"Rachael, are you all right with this case? I don't want you on the edge with this."

She looked at Ben over her glass of orange juice. "Is that why we're here at lunch, Ben? Because you think I'm losing it and a cheeseburger is the cure? Or are you just playing big brother?"

"A little of each, I suppose. I don't want you out there on me. The squad and I need you in your usual form."

"I'll be fine, Lieutenant, as soon as that sonofabitch is dead and his head is carted off so his body can't find it." That said, Rachael set her glass down and got up.

"Thanks for believing in me." Then she just walked away. She had never done that to him before.

Chapter 26

Because Jonathan was not needed nor expected to appear, the gallery was not crowded with the national news types. The local reporters would be used on link-ups to the national networks if something noteworthy transpired. Mordeci would appear for the national media group which owned the Chicago Tribune. He would use the drawing he purchased from the initial appearance for his column.

Schroeder and two of his subordinates were at their table, a yellow pad resting squarely before each of them.

Fashionably late, as ever, Adelman strode into the room and immediately became the epicenter of attention. He placed his briefcase on the table and removed a single manila folder, which he placed in front of the middle chair. He stood until the Judge entered and sat when everyone else did.

"Good Morning," the Judge began. "We're here because the State contests the filing of an Alibi Defense Notice. Is that accurate, Mr. Schroeder?"

"Yes, Your Honor. The notice is insufficient on its face and denies the State an opportunity to prepare and defend against this defense." Schroeder waited for the Judge to say something, but when he didn't, he continued.

"The applicable provisions, your Honor, require the defendant to give the State specific details, locations and witnesses which the defendant will seek to introduce in invoking this defense. The notice which Mr. Adelman filed omits any such details, locations and witnesses. We ask that the notice be stricken and have filed our brief in support."

"Not too shabby," Adelman thought. "But..."

"Good Morning, Your Honor," the former Attorney General beamed. "The defendant has filed his brief as well. Mr. Schroeder is correct in that our notice fails to give exacting details and locations. However, it does state that Jonathan Childress II will testify in this matter." Adelman let that sink into the crowd of note-takers and the Judge.

"In regards to the details and the location components of the notice requirements, the Defendant contends that one of two, or a combination of both, the lethal chemicals which were methodically pumped into him during the fated execution or the existence of an organic brain disorder have eradicated the Defendant's ability to recall the details and locations the State seeks today.

The Defendant is willing, your Honor, to provide every detail and location his debilitated memory will permit. The State cannot escape culpability in this, Your Honor. We will demonstrate that the chemicals used on the Defendant are designed to destroy the brain and in a non-discriminatory fashion. We believe the Defendant has met his burden."

Adelman continued to stand at the defense table as if to invite questions. The Judge looked at him for almost a minute before he ruled.

"Mr. Schroeder, I'm going to deny your request at this time. However, and I underscore that, Mr. Adelman, I am going to hold you to the offer of proof you have set forth today. In other words, you will have to present credible evidence which will demonstrate the lethality of those chemicals on the Defendant's lack of memory. If you fail to do so, I will deny you the use of the jury instructions on the Alibi Defense and preclude you from arguing that during closing arguments. Am I perfectly clear?"

"Perfectly, Judge," Adelman said with a wide grin. All he needed to do now was to add a name to his witness list. A forensic chemist who recently retired from the FBI Crime Lab in Washington was going to testify regarding the side effects of even minimal doses of those drugs. His credentials were impeccable, too.

The news was not good for Schroeder, but not fatal to his case. Once this jury saw those horrible photos of those gorgeous little girls, they would convict the Pope himself.

Adelman went directly from court to the jail where he met with Jonathan. He had yet to tell his client his plan for a nullification or even what that was. In fact, when he first breeched the alibi topic to Jonathan, he wasn't certain he would understand. He was surprised when his client began citing premises upon which they could approach how he would testify.

They also had one more tactic for Mr. Schroeder at trial.

Chapter 27

As the new trial got closer and Rachael was rehearsed by Schroeder, she became even more irritable. She had not had lunch with Ben since the afternoon she walked away from him. She had not come by the house to visit, as she usually did, as she was very close to Ben's wife as well. At work, she reported to Ben as a superior, not as a friend, especially one who was like family. She hardly talked to him and it was worrying him. Because she referred to him as Lieutenant, not Ben, he took to calling her Sergeant, not Rachael.

Not only was Rachael standoffish with Ben, she shunned Emilio, her partner, and avoided the rest of the officers when they wanted to talk.

Ben really began to worry when Emilio Ortiz requested a new partner.

"Emilio, what's happening with Rachael? Is it the Childress trial?"

"Ben, her and I have been partners for a while and we've been through some rough cases. This thing is eating at her. She's not the same Rachael. I don't want a new partner, but I don't know where her head's at. I'm worried that she's stretched out."

"What about after the trial? Do you think she'll be ok?"

"Possibly. I think that will depend on how it turns out." Emilio said guardedly.

"I think I am going to deny your request for a new partner. Instead, I'm going to get her to take a week off. She has vacation time and if I have to, I'll give her leave time to prepare for Trial. How's your case load?"

"I can use some help, Ben."

"You got it," Ben said as he reached for the phone and arranged for a temporary partner for the eager detective.

Meanwhile, he had left a message for Rachael that he needed to see her when she returned.

"I got your message, Lieutenant. What's up?" Rachael said, as she entered his office.

"Sergeant, how's your case load?"

"Average. Why?"

"I want you to take the rest of the week off and get ready for the new trial. I'll arrange for vacation time for you to begin immediately."

Rachael paced a moment, her arms folded across her chest and her head down. Then she stopped.

"Lieutenant, if this is your half-assed way at inferring that I'm not fit for duty, at least have the cajones to say it. I don't need to use my vacation time to prepare for this trial. If you're ordering me out of here, you're going to have to suspend me, which you have no reason to do, or you'll have to give me a 'leave.' Which is it?"

Rachael's face was aglow with Irish anger right then. She looked like she wanted to attack him. Ben did not want to push her any further or offend her, so he was careful in his wording.

"Sergeant, I'm giving you administrative leave. I want you to prepare for this trial. In doing so, you will work with the State Attorney's Office. You don't need to report here. If they need you at Schroeder's office, then I want you there. Your partner will cover your cases until this new trial is over. OK?"

"You sonofabitch. You're relieving me without even a hearing. Why?"

"Rachael, you're edgy. I think this new trial and all is wearing you down. I want you to take a few days off and come back the Rachael Hart we all know. I'm not relieving you and only Emilio will know anything and that will be very little." Ben did not want to tell her that Emilio didn't trust her any more. That would probably get his ass kicked by this fiery Irish energy source before him.

"Do you want my star, lieutenant? The Glock is mine, not the Department's."

"No, I do not." he said emphatically.

"Piss off, lieutenant," she said as she spun and like an Irish meteor, she streaked out of his office leaving a trail of anger and shame behind.

When she had gone, Ben, wondered whether or not he had erred in not asking her for her badge. He had to admit that he had never seen her like this before. He hoped he had made the right decision to exclude any Department psychologist at that point. He was rooting for Rachael to recover, herself.

"Shit," Ben said loudly and a number of detectives looked at him. When he noticed them, he glared back and they understood immediately. They went back to work.

When the Cardinal came to see Jonathan, he came under cover of darkness. Reporters lurked around the front gate of the jail, expecting Adelman or maybe even the Pope disguised as Elvis, in the Pope mobile.

The Cardinal was given special privileges and they were permitted to meet in the attorney's room, where there was no divider and Jonathan was not handcuffed. One wall was all Plexiglas like they were on display. The Cardinal did not tell Jonathan that the room was once used to house the throne-backed electric chair where Cook County officials carried out their own executions. At one time in Chicago's periodical history, the County hung people in the same basement.

"Good morning, Jonathan," Carroll said, a smile across his face. "Mr. Adelman tells me that things are going well in your case." The Cardinal omitted that for the money Adelman was receiving from the Vatican, he could have gotten Saddam Hussein off on genocide.

"Hi, Cardinal Carroll. I'm glad you came. I have something I'd like your opinion on."

The Cardinal settled back in the wooden chair and listened to Jonathan's explanation or take, rather, on the events which had occurred on the night Johnny Lee was executed and how Krystan's father was crushed in his Acura two thousand miles away.

When Jonathan finished he had a myriad of questions, including why did he have such a working knowledge of law? Why did Krystan write him in the first place, and why he felt so relaxed in the Supreme Court hearing?

"So you believe you're Krystan's father?" the Cardinal asked in a serious tone, not sarcastic.

"Cardinal Carroll, would you please get me the background on her father, his education, photo, and possibly pictures of Krystan and her mother? If I see something familiar, it may trigger my mind. It would help and I need to know who I really am - or was."

The Cardinal looked at him for a long moment before he answered. "All right, but I don't want any disclosure of this or the press getting wind of it. I don't want Adelman to hear about it. It will remain between you and I or it's no deal. Do I have your word on that?"

"I already mentioned this to Father Birney," Jonathan said squeamishly.

"Him, I can handle!" the Cardinal said forcefully. "Do we have an understanding?"

"Yes, sir."

The two of them talked about the cards and letters pouring into the Vatican and the Cathedral in Chicago.

"You have a lot of believers, Jonathan. Also, no one can explain a number of facts about you and the incredible string of legal victories you have amassed thus far. If God wants you free, Jonathan, He certainly is making His wishes clear. We have even heard that you may be the second coming of Christ. It's all very intriguing and could be construed as Biblical. Christ's turning to us as a criminal would not be a surprise as He was branded a criminal when crucified. You see what I mean?"

"Cardinal, I don't know anything about all that. I don't know who or what I am." Then he added, "Yet."

The Cardinal held Jonathan's hands in his, piled like a sandwich and he said a prayer for God to look upon Jonathan for the new trial.

The irony of the prayer struck the Cardinal as he was seated in the back seat of the Lincoln, on his way back to the Cathedral. He laughed to himself. "As if God isn't already watching over him," he mumbled, watching the buildings go past the windows. If people were right, and Jonathan was an angel or the Savior, he should be asking Jonathan for his blessing, not vice versa.

Chapter 28

"Your Honor," Schroeder began, "the State has a motion for an expanded venire."

"Mr. Schroeder," the Judge answered, "this Court has already anticipated problems with selecting the jury and I have ordered one hundred potential jurors and another hundred on standby."

It required a week to select twelve jurors and the State's Attorney was not pleased. Schroeder wanted any potential juror from the venire, pronounced ven-eye-ree, or jury pool, who believed in God, discharged. When that approach failed, he was relegated to the Judge removing potential jurors if they had a predisposition. In the end, the Court directed that one juror at a time be questioned, after a woman who was being asked questions to determine her spirituality as a juror, blurted out that she believed Jonathon was an angel and Schroeder was going to Hell for prosecuting him.

In the end, they had twelve people and four more as alternatives. They would begin on Monday morning at eight o'clock sharp. The Judge advised the jurors to have clothes packed as he was sequestering them in a local hotel under strict security by the Sheriff. He was taking no chances.

Ben had attempted to keep track of Rachael and her whereabouts, but had no luck. He called the State Attorney's Office to check on her, but no one had seen her after she dropped off all the "evidence" bags and obtained a receipt for them. The head of the Criminal Division told Ben that she called in once and asked if he had anything he needed done, but he said "no," and he never heard from her again.

"Emilio, I want you to drop in on Rachael and see how she's doing. As her friend and partner, Detective. Not a spy. I want to know how she is. I don't want any report, either. I just want to know she's handling this okay."

"Ben, she's gonna know why I'm there and she's gonna be pissed. If she breaks my arm, I want comp pay and time," Emilio said as he sauntered out the door. He did not look forward to this. He knew Rachael and her temper.

The Homicide Chief considered sending backup with Rachael's partner, but that would only make it worse. Ortiz would be fine.

Chapter 29

At the beginning of the new trial, Schroeder gave a flawless opening argument. He avoided any mention of an alibi and smartly so, as the defense had to meet a burden of proof regarding organic brain damage in order to introduce the defense. He did not need to help them with that idea of theirs and he had his own plans. For twenty minutes he hammered away with the ferocity of the attacks and the jury reacted similarly to the first one.

When the Judge asked Adelman if he would like to make his opening statement, Adelman gave them his first surprise.

"If it pleases the Court, the Defendant wishes to reserve opening until the close of proofs by the State."

In most states and the federal system, a criminal defendant may employ such a tactic, but rarely does. The prosecution sets a tempo from opening statements and generally a defendant uses the opening to disrupt that rhythm and plant seeds of distrust or reasonable doubt in their minds. A good trial advocate will elicit a tacit agreement with the jury to hold the prosecution to their burden of proof. Proof of guilt beyond a reasonable doubt is a difficult and ephemeral notion of fairness, but the State has to meet or exceed that standard.

The prosecution's case followed the identical game plan as the first trial. Every witness, every exhibit was exactly the same. Adelman did not object to a single exhibit. In fact, to the chagrin of the State's Attorney, Adelman did not make a single objection. Schroeder got away with prosecutorial murder, using leading questions and almost testifying himself.

On several occasions, when Schroeder's theatrics got out of hand, the Judge looked at Adelman as if inviting some objection so he could curtail the abuse. But no objection came. It required great restraint by Adelman to remain calm and not give away any hint of the rage beneath his exterior.

On the third day, just after the jury was sent out for lunch, the Judge advised Adelman that he had a telephone message in his chambers and asked him to accompany him. Just Adelman.

"Counselor," the Judge said sarcastically, "I know you're

familiar with evidentiary rules, so I feel the need to ask you what in the hell you're doing out there? If letting the State run rampant is some ploy of yours to gain a mistrial, it won't work. What are you doing?"

"It's no ploy, Judge. My client and I have discussed all this and we have agreed to let the prosecution get their case on and over with as quickly as possible. We're willing to let them have a wider latitude to achieve that goal."

"I don't believe that bullshit for an instant, Counselor. If you are setting this up for an appeal on ineffective counsel and a third trial, you won't get it. I am going to memorialize our conversation here in a letter, which you will sign and I will hold under seal. Schroeder will not be privy to it, unless the issue is raised on appeal by your client that you fucked up this trial. Is that clear, Mr. Adelman?"

"Perfectly, Your Honor. But you won't need the letter."

"Why's that?" the Judge said sneeringly.

"Because there will be no appeal from my client," Adelman said as he walked towards the exit.

"Oh?" the Judge said, his eyebrows almost reaching his receding hairline.

"There won't be a conviction to appeal," the former Attorney General said with that famous smile of his, looking over his shoulder on the way out. He left the door open so the Judge could hear him. "Asshole."

When the horrible pictures hit the easel, some of the jurors cried. Schroeder was slaughtering Jonathon and the reporters who frequent trials made comment in their respective reports that they had never seen a trial where not one objection was made by defense counsel and the prosecution seemed to run the courtroom. The latter comments perturbed the Judge as he wanted the whole world to know who the boss was in his court. So he decided to rein in the prosecution himself and advised Schroeder to reduce or curtail the theatrical crap. Even if the defense didn't object, as Schroeder aptly noted.

To the inquisitive eyes of reporters and the jury, Jonathan wept in the courtroom. One reporter noted Jonathan looking at his hands, front and back, as if those little girls' blood had indelibly stained them somehow.

When Rachael took the stand, she was sure that Jonathan would break his silence, just as he did in the first trial. He didn't and that had an impact on her psyche. She answered many of Schroeder's questions in narrative form and no objections came from the experienced Adelman. She testified to her search and finally the physical arrest of the Defendant.

Everyone was captivated now, as to the defense's posture to permit the prosecution unfettered and unchecked questioning. Veteran reporters shook their heads wondering how Adelman ever gained prominence as a trial lawyer and he made not one objection. Schroeder didn't care, as he was getting his way and the conviction assured. When Rachael was finished and again Adelman had no objections to the bloody knife and clothing, Rachael was tendered to Adelman's cross-examination.

For the first time in the trial thus far, Adelman rose to ask questions. He had not asked one witness a question thus far, so every eye and ear was his now.

"Sergeant Hart, for the record, you have testified that my client is the man you arrested that day."

"That's correct," she said sharply.

"And you interviewed my client on video the night of the arrest. Is that correct?"

"Yes, that's the tape of the confession," she added.

"Have you interviewed the Defendant since that time?"

"No. I have no reason to. He admitted to the murders and I don't care to be around him."

"We've all heard about the attempt by the State to execute my client. That's no secret here. You attended that ill-fated execution, didn't you?"

"Yes, I was there. I was shocked when they told me the next morning that he was still alive."

"Is it safe to say that you don't like my client very much, Sergeant?"

Rachael took a deep breath and calmed herself before answering. "No, counselor. I don't like your client. I don't like murderers, period. Especially child killers." Rachael let the venom drip from her answer.

Rachael waited for the same bullshit idea that came up during the first trial about "suicide by cop" and how Johnny Lee wanted her to shoot him that day. A million times recently, she found herself wishing that she had given him his wish that day if that is what he wanted. Had she shot him, she would have been a hero and none of this would be taking its toll on her or anyone else.

"Sergeant, I see that you're armed today in the courtroom. Were you similarly armed the day of the arrest?"

"Yes, I was."

"Yet you testified that when my client had the knife in his hand, with blood all over him, you did not aim your weapon at him and order him to drop the knife. Is that correct as well?"

"Yes," she said exasperated. She knew what was coming next. She was wrong.

"Sergeant, you attended the execution, so you wanted to see my client die. That's why you were there, after all, to witness his death. With all that has transpired since that time and this new trial, have you ever found yourself regretting not using your weapon that day and shooting my client when he failed to surrender the knife?"

Rachael realized the concealed treachery in that question. If she said "yes," she would be admitting that she would have employed excessive force necessary to effect an arrest. If she said "no," she would be saying that she didn't want to hurt him, yet attended his execution, which made little sense. She would also be lying.

"Yes, I have. If I were making the arrest today, I would do it differently."

"Thank you for being honest. No further questions, Your Honor." Adelman sat down tenuously and made a brief note to himself.

The prosecution rested its case on that note and it was Adelman's show next.

"Your Honor, the defense asks that the jury be excused for a moment so we can address a matter."

Being almost four in the afternoon, the Judge excused them for the day and that is exactly what Adelman wanted. It would give them time to erase those horrible pictures from their minds.

"The defense would like to call Dr. Neal Whitehurst, Your Honor, a forensic chemist, to establish the effects of those chemicals so that we may proceed with our defense."

And so Dr. Whitehurst, his education and credentials substantial and immaculate, testified that the chemicals, individually and combined, beyond a reasonable degree of medical certainty, damaged fragile brain cells.

Despite a gallant effort and some theatrics anticipated by Adelman, Whitehurst's expert testimony was bullet proof. Adelman could now argue the ridiculous alibi defense. Schroeder just knew the jury was his and wouldn't buy the dog and pony show the defense intended.

"Ladies and gentlemen of the jury," Adelman said as he walked to and fro before the jury, "it is the Defendant's turn to present their defense. You will hear from the Defendant himself, as I'm sure we all need to hear from him. I know what he is going to testify to, an advantage that will be shared with all of you very soon. I never tire of hearing him explain certain events, as I'm sure you won't, either. As incredible as it may sound, you will also hear expert testimony that substantiates his testimony and is unrebutted by the prosecution. Do you all remember that tape referred to by Sergeant Hart when she testified? She interviewed Johnny Lee Childress. You heard the man on that recording. That man is not in this courtroom today. In fact, the man in that recording is quite dead. Gone forever. The man sitting next to me these past days is articulate, compassionate and most importantly, his education is remarkable. His aptitude scores in the genius range, as you will hear from highly respected professionals, who work for State and federal agencies, I might add, and are not hired guns for the defense."

Adelman went to the defense table and picked up a sheet of paper and walked to the podium. "The Judge is going to instruct you about 'reasonable doubt' and I'd like to explain that a little before we get started. In a nutshell, reasonable doubt is where reasonable people are not reasonably convinced that the State has proven its case. The exact legal definition is contained in the instruction.

We have been authorized to argue what is called the 'alibi defense.' My client did not commit these vicious crimes because he was not here. You'll understand when we present our witnesses, but remember that you were all advised by the Court at the start of this trial to keep an open mind and make no predispositions. That is the law and not a request. That is a fundamental tenet of our American jurisprudence. It's what we stand for in this world and it's what makes this country unique.

When you have heard the evidence and reviewed each of the exhibits, there will be only one conclusion. I am confident that you will all find that the State has not met its burden and acquit Jonathan of these charges."

The reporters frantically wrote notes and a few went outside to phone their stories in to their employers. Jonathan listened to the eloquent statement and could see the jurors watch the famous attorney. He had captured their attention and they were starving for this evidence Adelman claimed would convince them. They challenged him, it was in their eyes. Jonathan finally had a real attorney.

Rachael listened to Adelman's drivel, seething with emotion. To her, it was a preposterous argument from a creative mind that P.T. Barnum would have envied. Yet, Adelman had piqued the interest of a number of jurors. She could read their expressions and body language. She also watched the father of those girls, as he sat day after day behind the State's Attorney. She saw him once at night leaving the courthouse where he must, she presumed, have met with the prosecutors. What was left of him after the first trial was assuredly destroyed by the new trial going on. She could see the blank and darkened look in his eyes and they reminded her of a shark. Black orbs, devoid of color; devoid of life itself. A whole family was murdered that day. Rachael was on administrative leave as Ben had directed, so she would watch the entire trial, as she would the next execution.

Chapter 30

Adelman's first witness was the soothing and affable Dr. Warren Clifford.

"Dr. Clifford, you are employed by the State of Illinois, are you not?"

"That's correct. I work for the Department of Corrections."

"The report you prepared regarding my client, was that the product of observing and testing him?"

"That is also correct," Clifford said guardedly. Clifford had testified many times, but generally as a prosecutor's witness where he was engrained with the concept of never volunteering information.

"When prisoners arrive at the prison, do you screen them and write a report for the file?"

"Yes, sir. That's policy."

"Do you have a copy of your initial report and evaluation of the Defendant?" Adelman knew he did, as he had obtained his client's entire file from the Department of Corrections.

"Yes, I do." Clifford opened a file folder he had brought with him. It was part of the order with the subpoena he had received.

"And that evaluation, Dr. Clifford, is not very flattering is it? It has terms like sociopath and dissociative behavior, does it not?"

"Yes, sir, it does."

"Dr. Clifford, when you compare your initial evaluation with the latest one you prepared upon direction of the federal court, if you removed the subject's name, in your professional opinion now, would you say they were the same person in both reports?"

"Only if they were authored by different psychologists," Clifford said demurely.

"But they weren't written by different psychologists, where they? They were written by you. No further questions, Your Honor."

Schroeder could not assail the State's own expert and passed him on without any cross-examination. The two evaluations spoke for themselves.

Dr. Sebastian, the federal psychologist, was Adelman's next victim.

"Doctor, you authored a report which was submitted to the federal court, pursuant to a court order. Is that correct?"

"Yes, sir, it is."

"In your report, you use colorful terminology such as schizophrenia to describe my client. Is that correct?"

"Yes, sir," Sebastian said proudly.

"Your evaluation omits any mention of voices, Doctor. Can you explain that to us?"

"Voices? I'm not sure I understand your question."

"Isn't it a fact that people suffering from schizophrenia or what is called schizophreniform tendencies, hear or act upon voices heard only by them?"

"Generally, yes," Sebastian said as he carefully observed the prosecutors.

"Can you direct us to your notations of what voices or commands my client claimed to hear?"

"No."

"You are not the Chief in your department in the federal detention center, are you?"

"No."

"Do you know Dr. Ann Lechman?"

"Yes. She is the Chief Psychologist there," Sebastian said. He always kissed a little ass when he could. It never hurt when trying to work your way up in the federal Bureau of Prisons.

"Is she more experienced that you, Dr. Sebastian?"

"Yes." He wanted to say "no," but that would mean the ass kissing he just did was for nothing. In reality, Sebastian felt like the number two quarterback behind Joe Montana and deserved a chance to star himself, only as long as she was there, he would always be the number two man.

"No further questions, Your Honor," Adelman said as he turned his back on Sebastian and walked away. He had just accomplished the total destruction of the only report that Schroeder could have hung his hat on. Schroeder knew it, too.

Adelman's next witness was Dr. Ann Lechman.

"Dr. Lechman, you have testified in many cases?"

"I would say at least a thousand times." She was the

epitome of the appearance one would conjure up in casting a movie about Jonathan's case. She would star in the role as herself. Her Saks Fifth Avenue suit fit like a second skin. She sat erect in the witness chair and answered clearly, while looking Adelman directly in the eye. "Venerable" was only one word to describe her. Adelman was about to elicit more descriptions.

"And primarily, Doctor, you also testify on behalf of prosecutors in state and federal courts?"

"Yes, Mr. Adelman. I do."

"Is it also an accurate statement that most of these times that you testified for those prosecutors that your evaluations did not aid the defendants?"

"Yes. That would probably be accurate."

"Have you ever been referred to as 'Hannibal Lecter,' a slight gleaned from the killer in *Silence of the Lambs*?"

She smiled and said that she had heard herself referred to as that and found it humorous. To Rachael, though, she could see the building blocks Adelman was using to achieve his goal and the State's Attorney was all but helpless.

"Dr. Lechman, you wrote an evaluation of the man sitting there next to me, did you not?"

"Yes, I did."

"Would you please read your conclusion for us?" Adelman asked as he faced the jury. He wanted to see their expressions when "Hannibal Lecter" spoke.

Lechman cleared her throat and began.

"In conclusion, it is my opinion, based upon a degree of medical certainty, employing the standard practices that are generally acceptable in the psychological community, that Jonathan L. Childress II is no longer a danger to society and will, without question, remain so for life."

Adelman looked at the jurors. A few of them looked at Jonathan. Schroeder looked at the table before him. Adelman had just assured the jury that they could release Jonathan and not fear him.

"Would you mind my client living next door to you, Dr. Lechman?"

She realized the snare Adelman hid within this question. If she said "yes," she would be contradicting her threat assessment.

"No, Mr. Adelman, as long as he kept his dog out of my yard."

A few people actually chuckled at that. More smiled at the levity she had given the otherwise horrific trial. To Rachael, though, the woman had bestowed a new personality to a killer and the promise that he would behave himself if the jury let him go.

"No further questions, Your Honor," Adelman said as he walked past the prosecutor's table.

Schroeder thought for a moment and only when the Judge got impatient and asked if he had any cross-examination, did he respond.

"No questions, Your Honor."

Schroeder was biding his time until he could shred Childress on cross-examination and expose the sham.

The Judge adjourned for the day. It was fairly certain that the main event would come the next day. Jonathan would take the stand and the courtroom would be an international meeting place for the most notable media stars.

Rachael wanted to talk to the victims' father again. She wanted to reassure him that the killer of his family would not avoid justice. She walked behind him, wondering if she should approach him and where. He was standing down the hall, leaning against a door, weeping. She could see his shoulders bouncing as the great sobs of grief racked his body. She decided better of it and continued on, leaving the poor man to his personal agony.

Almost every television and newspaper headlined the testimony from that day. Even Mordeci had to admit that Adelman skillfully demonstrated substantial admissions from unfriendly sources, that the man seated at the defense table was very different from the killer who faced the jurors in the first trial.

Rachael remained at home that night. She had no appetite for food and had wine, instead, while she dismantled her Glock and cleaned it. She would go to bed early. She would have to be in the court early for the grand finale.

Chapter 31

When Rachael arrived the next morning, hours before the trial was to resume, she found that a metal detector had been set up at the entrance to the courtroom. Deputies were stationed outside and a couple officers were looking under the pews in the courtroom itself. When she cleared the metal detector, producing her identification again, having already done so to enter the building before it officially opened, she was asked by the bailiff to be careful of her weapon, lest someone grab it and begin shooting. She wondered if he gave that same warning to the male police officers, or was that reserved for females only? She put that out of her mind and took a seat behind Schroeder in the rear of the Courtroom, where she could watch most of the room, not in front where she usually sat. She sipped the coffee the bailiff had brought her, perhaps as a peace offering and the slight about the alternative outcomes that this trial could have. She still could not believe how they were even there at another trial. There was the insanity of it all! Adelman, fashionably late as always, arrived and asked the bailiff to set up the audio-visual equipment.

"Your Honor, our next witness is Johnny Lee Childress."

All were expecting the Defendant to rise. Instead the lights were dimmed and the ninety minute recording of the killer's confession with Rachael appeared on the overhead screen. People around Rachael began to look from the screen to her, realizing, if they had not known from before, that she was the arresting officer.

The jury, of course, had seen the tape before, when Schroeder introduced it, but not in the light cast by Adelman. When the recording ended and the lights returned to their normal luminescence, she saw Ben on the other side of the courtroom. She had not seen the Homicide Chief enter, as she was engrossed in watching the jurors, instead. He only looked at her and nodded, before returning his attention to the trial.

"Your Honor, my next witness is Mr. Jonathan L. Childress, II, the Defendant."

Reporters fidgeted, arranging notepads and attempting to focus their attention on every word.

When he was sworn and seated, in an even, clear voice,

Jonathan recited exactly what he had told Judge Lucius Echols in the federal courtroom that rocked the world. Not one word or sentence misplaced. Simply stated, the Reaper had opened the gate and he slipped past.

"Have you ever murdered anyone, Jonathan?"

"No, sir. I could never do what I've seen in crime scene pictures here.

"Where were you when those girls were murdered, Jonathan?"

"I'm not certain. I only have a hunch, but I know that was not me."

"Have you ever committed a crime?"

"No, sir. I don't recall ever being charged or convicted of any crime."

"Are you the man we saw a short time ago in that recording?"

"No, sir."

"I have no further questions, Your Honor."

Adelman sat down at the defense table and turned to a fresh page of his yellow pad. He anticipated Schroeder's grilling of Jonathan and had brought one of the attorneys from the firm where he used an office, to the County Jail. She was a former Assistant U.S. Attorney and had a perfect conviction rate. For hours they pounded him relentlessly and she never wavered in her voracious attack. Jonathan was unflappable.

"Good morning, Jonathan Lee, how would you explain this miraculous adventure you claim to have made?"

"It's Jonathan, Mr. Schroeder, and I really can't explain why I'm back."

"I'm sorry, but we all know you as Johnny Lee Childress. That's the name you used when you were arrested, confessed to killing these two girls and the name you were indicted under. Now, you want us to believe that this Reaper or Guardian of the souls or spirits, simply left this gate open and you flee?"

"Well, sir, only the jurors here have to decide if I'm telling the truth. No matter what I tell you, Mr. Schroeder, you're not going to listen. It's the truth, though."

"If you're someone different, why do you use the Childress name?"

"Because, Mr. Schroeder, I have not had the opportunity to discover who I really am or why I'm here. I've been kind of tied up." Jonathan let the last sentence roll slowly off his tongue to give a little levity. It worked, too.

"You've been on death row haven't you?" At this, Adelman could have objected and would have won the objection based on prejudice because another jury had convicted him to die. But then again, the whole world already knew that.

"Yes, sir, I have."

"And you really don't want to die, do you?"

"Mr. Schroeder, I've already died once and it's nothing to fear. However, I would like the opportunity to find out who I am and why I'm here. Then again, if these people truly believe I'm the monster that murdered those two girls, then I'd deserve to die."

"Have you ever died?"

"Well, sir, I'm not sure. I can tell you that if I did, it must not have been too terrible, because I'm sure I was going to a better place when I fled back here."

"Are you an angel, Mr. Childress?" Schroeder asked as he faced the jury now.

The courtroom was so silent, you could hear the ballpoint pens scurrying across paper and a couple of spectators make the sign of the cross.

"Mr. Schroeder, I am not sure how to answer that. I mean, I have no wings and I cannot fly. I have no super powers. I am a man, just like you. The only difference between us is that I've been given a second chance."

"I beg to differ with you. Jonny Lee there is a huge difference between you and I. You see, I have never confessed to butchering two little girls and then concocted a lie to save myself," Schroeder said as he looked at Jonathan as if he could literally melt him where he sat.

Realizing that the questioning was not going to produce a new confession or provoke a display of aggression or threats, Schroeder decided to terminate the examination.

"Your Honor, the defense rests," Adelman said as if he were

an undertaker sealing a casket. The trial of the century was a wrap. All that remained were closing arguments, the jury instructions and a verdict. It would all start after lunch.

Chapter 32

During the lunch recess, the television airwaves crackled with opinions on what side had won. Cardinal Bavielli entered the Pope's office to quietly advise him that all that remained now was a verdict. The Pontiff only nodded in understanding.

Schroeder's strategy was to touch the salient points and evidence during his initial closing argument. The defense would have its say and then Schroeder would have the final word. That is when he would drag out those vivid color photos of the mutilated bodies and vilify Jonathan.

As Rachael sat in the rear of the courtroom, she watched Ben silently leave. She caught him looking her way a couple of times, as if she would shuffle over to him and apologize for her huffy behavior. She refused to subject herself to that. She had every right to be upset with him. Besides, Rachael was far more worried about Mr. Polachek, who looked as if he had aged twenty years the past year alone. His shoulders were slumped and he shuffled his feet more than walked. Stress and depression oozed from every pore, as one could easily recognize his defeated expression. He was suffering and no medicine could dull the pain. Schroeder never called him as a witness, as he didn't believe he could endure the additional strain and he would contribute very little anyhow. Schroeder would use him during sentencing when he asked the new jury for the death penalty.

When Rachael went for coffee, after having the bailiff reserve her seat in the back of the courtroom, Ben was nowhere to be seen. She did, however, run into Emilio, who said he happened to be in the building and thought he would stop by. They shared coffee and then it was time to return to the finale. Emilio watched her leave and then made a call on his Department cell phone.

Everyone associated with the new trial was adamant about one thing; the closing arguments were going to decide the fate of a man revered and hated around the world. The entire block around the Criminal Courts Building was now barricaded by Chicago Police Officers. Every television network in the country had a van or truck parked outside, its antennae mast reaching skyward. No other trial had garnered such media attention in Cook County history. There were trailers parked and used as dressing rooms for the elite performers in news broadcasting. You would think the President himself was attending. That was a miserable time for commuters, but great for the local restaurants.

The President was not in attendance, but he did have eyes and ears in the courtroom. After all, he was a Catholic too, and wondered if Jonathan was truly unique and living proof that his faith was accurate. When Adelman had returned to the White House as invited, he brought Jonathan's file and the two of them discussed the complexities and unexplainable facts. When Adelman asked the President if he had thoughts of intervention, the Commander in Chief merely stated that he might if the need arose. The President did remark that he found the whole matter intriguing and disturbing, whatever that meant.

Chapter 33

When the Judge gave the floor to the State's Attorney to begin his summary of the evidence, Schroeder performed as expected. Methodically, he paraded the soft exhibits before the jury. He avoided mention of the preposterous alibi defense, not wanting to risk giving it added credence to the jury, and he didn't want to convey that message to them. From the one hour the Judge allowed each side, Schroeder wisely reserved half for his rebuttal. It was now up to Adelman.

"Ladies and gentlemen of the jury, Jonathan and I wish to thank you for sitting through this trial. We appreciate the inconvenience you have endured in order to fulfill your civic duty. Juries are one of the most important aspects of our legal system. They are integral to our sense of fairness and many fine men and women have shed their lifeblood in order to preserve our way of life. By serving as jurors, you thank them for their sacrifices as well."

Adelman liked the patriotic flavor he put on jury trials. As a prosecutor, he reminded every jury that they were following in the dreams the framers of the Constitution had in mind when they labored to craft that document. It was like he invoked their private allegiance to him as a representative of their government. He wanted that same allegiance today.

"This is probably the most difficult case to decide in American jurisprudence. We have a mixture of Heaven and Hell. As the former Attorney General of the United States, I championed the separation between Church and State. I realize now that I may have been mistaken in that cause, when I became involved in this case. I believe in God, but I felt He had no place in our courts. I was wrong. When a witness is sworn before taking the stand, he swears before God. As a nation we embrace the existence and omnipotence of God.

I won't take but a few minutes to present this case to you. I know you want to get home to your families. There is no question in my mind that this man at the defense table with me is a product of God. Not one witness got up here to explain the stark contrasts between this man and the killer, Johnny Lee Childress. You witnessed Johnny Lee testify in that video recording. You saw

Jonathan testify. This trial is not about who murdered those precious girls. It's about the existence and power of God. If you believe that God permitted this man to return and fulfill some destiny, then this man is not guilty. To believe in God and then convict this man, you will offend our Creator and face your own judgment before Him."

Adelman sounded more like a fire and brimstone evangelist than an attorney. When he walked back to his seat, he looked at the jurors as if challenging their own fate when their day came. He was magnificent. He was right, actually, in that the trial was not about who killed the twins. It was about God and whether the State was able to overcome the facts supporting Jonathan's testimony.

Schroeder marched out the shocking photos, which may have elicited the opposite effect from some jurors according to the majority of trial experts hired by the networks. Was the soft-spoken, finely educated man who appeared before them as Jonathan, capable of such a gruesome act?

The prosecutor was careful not to deny the existence of God, or risk offending the Christian senses of the jurors. When he finally thanked the jurors for their service and called for the only reasonable verdict of guilty on all counts, he did so with more grace and style than anyone had seen him exhibit before. He was the panacea or elixir to the whole problem; convict the man and let's go home.

While the Judge read the jury instructions, the reporters filed out, sure that deliberation would take time and they wanted to be on the air.

Rachael sat in her seat and calmly listened to the Almighty speech by Adelman. Grudgingly, she had to admit that he was good. His advocacy abilities earned him a trust position with the current President and he would be Attorney General yet today, if he hadn't chosen to be a family man instead. She was just overwhelmed at how this pedestrian murder trial, of a confessed killer, had metamorphed into a trial over the existence of God.

Mr. Polachek sat closer to the front, yet not in the first row where he had a seat reserved. He was wasting away. Since Rachael had last visited the Polacheks, his wife was a walking catatonic and he had surrendered all hope. His face looked like melting wax, the once sharp features now sliding into slack skin. That is why she watched him one night after work and began to worry about him.

The jury was taken to the study where they would deliberate. If they had failed to reach a verdict by six o'clock, they would be returned to the hotel. The study was large and was equipped with a bathroom, coffee maker, and a small refrigerator with bottled water and sodas along with a microwave for light sandwiches to tide them over till dinner. There were armed deputies in the hallway outside the door and in the courtroom.

All they could do now is to wait. The world held its collective breath.

Chapter 34

After four solid days of deliberations, the jury had still not reached a unanimous verdict and speculation ran high that there was going to be a mistrial if the jurors were hopelessly deadlocked.

Defense attorneys across the land heralded the lengthy deliberations as a tacit victory and that Adelman had made an Oscar winning performance. Indeed, he had, Jonathan admitted to himself as he awaited the decision in his cell. The Chaplain had brought him a small black and white television to help him pass time. He saw his old attorney on the evening news, as if they were experts in his defense and the interview appalled him. They were marketing themselves, plain and simple.

It warmed Jonathan's inner being to see the reports where people lighted votive candles for him in churches and the Cathedral in Chicago. Whatever he was, people believed in him. Evidently, someone or some people on the jury believed likewise.

At six o'clock on Friday night, the Judge excused the jury for the weekend. The Sheriff's vans then moved them to the hotel, where they were under tight security, as if a visiting dignitary were there. Their immediate family members were permitted to visit them, but they were reminded that they were not to discuss the case. They were prisoners themselves.

The Judge had plans for the attorneys in the case. On Monday morning, he wanted briefs from both sides, relating to motivation and resolution of what seemed a deadlocked jury. He wanted no reason for a Court of Appeals to direct a third trial and caution ruled the day. Adelman had a vast network of resources at his disposal. His successor as Attorney General was a man he had hired and molded for that position and he owed Adelman. The Department of Justice prepares and maintains various manuals for federal prosecutors. A phone call and the related materials were faxed to him. It was a matter of dictating his brief, using the extensive brief from his friend.

Schroeder had minions, who he quickly delegated to handle the task and headed for interviews on talk shows and the need to bolster his public image. He is an international figure for the moment and when he seeks the death sentence again, he would like to suggest a public hanging and let the cameras roll on that. But, that would be too crass even for him and his atavistic concepts of punishment.

Chapter 35

"Gentlemen," the Judge said as he sat smugly behind his desk in chambers, "I am considering an *Allen* charge in this case. There is no reason why the jury couldn't reach a verdict here and I want your positions."

An *Allen* charge, otherwise known as the "dynamite jury instruction," is a scary tactic where a Judge will berate a jury for not returning a verdict and in a thumbnail sketch, tells them to go get one. It is an intimidating moment for any juror.

"The State has no objection," Schroeder announced.

"The defense is going to object, Judge, simply because it's too soon. The jury has been out for a week and this is a complex case. Further, it would prejudice the Defendant by implying that the evidence is overwhelming and they should convict. If you give them the dynamite instruction in a capital case, this early, I think that the Illinois Supreme Court will look severely on the prudence."

And there were the magic words that every Judge fears. They may be reversed by a higher court. Even the Supreme Court can be overruled by Congress.

The Judge, his adipose veins protruding across his nose aglow with anger because Adelman was quite right. And, the Judge was not willing to risk a third trial because of an appellate court. Then again, he did not want a third trial because the present jury was unable to reach a unanimous verdict.

"On Thursday morning, gentlemen, if the jury has not reached a verdict, I will give them the *Allen* charge. Is that sufficient notice for both of you?"

Both attorneys nodded.

As if it were scripted, the bailiff appeared at the Judge's door.

"Judge, the jury has a question. It's on the note." The deputy sheriff handed the folded paper to the Judge and quickly left the office.

After reading the few lines twice, the Judge read the note for the Court Reporter to record.

"If the defendant is found mentally incompetent at the time of the murders, what will happen to him? Can he be executed?"

The questions were of grave concern to each of the three men, yet signaled a victory to both sides, simultaneously. The jury was not given an insanity defense during trial or in the instructions. They were being creative on their own. To Schroeder, the part about execution inferred the jury's willingness to impose such a sentence, even if they felt that someone was incompetent at the time of the offenses, but not now. That would be a jaundiced reading of that portion, but nevertheless a reasonable one.

To Adelman's more seasoned eye, the note portrayed quite a different picture. The jury was winging it and searching. Someone on the jury was leading them into uncharted waters.

"Any suggestions, gentlemen?" the Judge inquired.

Adelman beat Schroeder to the draw. "Your Honor, I suggest that you amend the instructions to allow the procedures for civil commitment in such cases, as related in the Illinois statutes."

Schroeder was beside himself at that suggestion.

"Your Honor, the Defendant has not put competency at issue when the murders were committed. To allow this constructive amendment now deprives the State the opportunity to rebut."

Adelman couldn't have said it better himself, so it came as no surprise when the Judge denied his request.

"I don't like it that the jury members are conceiving their own law, here. So, here is what I'm going to do. I'm going to direct them to re-read the instructions as I've given them."

A few minutes later, the Judge did exactly as he said, but there were faces on the jury that did not look pleased at his answer. The jurors would not even look at the State's Attorney. That is when Adelman knew the State was floundering.

Adelman decided to wait around to see if the jury reacted to the Judge's admonishment.

"How do you sleep at night?" Rachael said, startling him. He did not hear her come up behind him in the hall as he headed for the Men's Room.

"I'm not sure what you mean, Sergeant. I don't think I like the tone of your voice, though," he said as he stopped and turned to face her.

"Your client, counselor, murdered two innocent children. Do you have kids, Mr. Adelman?"

"Sergeant, I think your conduct is inappropriate and I will make a written complaint to your superiors. I suggest that you do yourself a favor and leave."

"He'll kill again. If you get him off this case, I mean. Are you willing to accept that?" Rachael was the same height as the former Attorney General and was mere inches from his face now.

"Perhaps, Sergeant Hart, you should solve some of the thousands of unsolved murders I understand Chicago has piled up and let the juries decide guilt? Now, if you'll excuse me."

Instead of walking away, Rachael joined him in the Men's Room and made sure they were alone. Adelman looked at her incredulously.

"Do you have some latent desire to be a man, Sergeant, or are you a voyeur?"

Rachael looked at the stalls and saw no feet where someone was seated on a commode. "Maybe I just wondered if you had any balls, Adelman?" And she was gone in a flash leaving the attorney to look at himself in the mirror. He was going to make her life miserable for this. While Adelman churned the wording in his mind for the official complaint regarding Rachael's conduct, the bailiff said the Judge wanted him ASAP.

"We have another note from the jury, gentlemen. This is beginning to remind me of the *Runaway Jury* movie. It seems the jurors have minds of their own, or someone is herding them like cattle. Here's the note."

Adelman and Schroeder read the note together.

"Must the State's Attorney prove that the defendant is not an angel?"

"Someone on that jury thinks they are very clever," the Judge said sarcastically. "What if we brought them in here one at a time and asked them if they believed the Defendant was the Easter Bunny as well?"

This remark drew a laugh from Schroeder, but Adelman was

larger than both of them. His savvy and experience rendered them freshmen.

"I will ask the Court Reporter here to immediately transcribe that remark, Judge, and I will file that with my complaint with the Supreme Court for their consideration. In response to the question, I suggest that you direct them to two institutions. The first, regarding the elements of the offense, as in the **Booker** decision which the Supreme Court recently announced, affirming **Blakely**. Second, I submit we remind them of reasonable doubt."

The Judge did not want to see this man from Washington file a complaint against him. It was just an off-handed joke. But, he wouldn't help him win the case, either. The jury was reminded again to reread all of the instructions and sent out again. The buzz in the courtroom gave some inaudible message to the news crews that the jury was active and a verdict could be about to come down. The anchor people began to mobilize and show up in the courtroom.

Rachael remained in the back of the room and watched. She saw the utterly destroyed father of the girls amble in and sit in the rear of the courtroom, near the door, as if he wanted to distance himself from the man who took his daughters' lives.

Then, the bailiff walked through hurriedly and said the jury had reached a verdict. It was as if the Hollywood lights were brought to Chicago. Life sprung up from every direction. Adelman came from the hidden rooms behind the courtroom, joined by his client and a half dozen uniformed deputies. Schroeder, two assistants in tow, gushed in and was all confidence.

The Judge arrived next and he directed the bailiff to bring in the jury.

"Has the jury reached a verdict?"

"Yes, Your Honor," the foreman said, who turned out to be a salesman and fairly well educated, as Adelman recalled.

The bailiff carried the form to the Judge, who read it slowly and looked at the jury defiantly. He gave the form back to the bailiff, who returned it to the foreman.

"Go ahead and read," the Judge directed, as if he were dismissing a child.

"We, the jury, find the defendant not guilty."

Reporters literally ran from the courtroom and the Judge

banged his gavel several times to restore order.

Rachael saw the Defendant sit down and was crying, while Adelman patted him on the back. The State's Attorney sat down, shaking his head in disbelief. When Rachael looked for the girls' father, he was gone.

Adelman stood by his client's side as he sobbed openly. The Judge dismissed the jury and released the Defendant, disgusted with the verdict himself and doing little to conceal it. Then, he too was gone. Rachael could not believe that the man she had arrested was now a free man and going to walk out of the courtroom.

Every network interrupted regular programming to announce the verdict and the cons on death row went wild. The Warden received the news from his wife and leaned back in his office chair, as if saying a silent prayer himself.

Father Birney called Cardinal Carroll, who had already learned the verdict and had called Cardinal Bavielli in Rome. "It was a glorious day for the Church," the little priest said.

When Adelman helped his client to his feet, he saw Rachael's glare and it made him uneasy. He kept a keen eye as they walked past her and opened the door. Rachael was not far behind them.

The hallway was crowded and reporters had tape recorders thrust in Jonathan's face. The elevators lay ahead in an alcove, forming a "T" from the hallway. A single deputy preceded Adelman and his client, as they moved slowly towards the elevators. Rachael did not see Ben or Emilio, who were approaching from down the hall. What she did notice, though, was the yellow mop bucket with sudsy water resting on the corner of the alcove and the hallway. She wondered why someone would leave that unattended, with no mop and just when the trial of the century was ended.

As the mob of reporters moved into the alcove, she saw a hand enter the sudsy water of the bucket and remove a zip-lock bag with a gun inside. Rachael yanked her Glock from its holster and stood at the alcove's entrance.

"Adelman," she shouted and when the reporters saw her weapon they dove to the floor.

Ben and Emilio, seeing Rachael draw and shout the former

Attorney General's name, drew their own weapons and went on opposite sides of the hallway.

"Rachael," Ben shouted, "drop the weapon." The Homicide Chief and Emilio cold not see what was before Rachael in the alcove, or they would have seen Mr. Polachek aiming his gun at the former Attorney General, who stood between him and Jonathan.

The sounds of weapons firing almost simultaneously filled the hallways. Immediately after firing, Rachael dove for cover behind a pew in the hallway.

"Damnit, Sergeant, push that goddam gun out in the hallway," Ben shouted and she complied. Then, she stood up, her hands clear of her body and darted to the alcove. When Ben and Emilio rushed around the corner of the alcove, expecting to see the elevator doors closing and Rachael nowhere in sight. Instead, she was bent down next to Adelman, who had a chest wound she was attending to. A few feet inside, lay Mr. Polachek, his head ruined and obviously dead.

Emilio, who had retrieved Rachael's Glock, cleared the alcove, while Ben identified themselves as police officers to the deputies responding and the first one who had gotten on an elevator expecting Adelman and Jonathan to join him, but didn't before the doors closed. Jonathan cradled his attorney's head, watching Rachael attempt to staunch the blood flow. Wisely, he remained stoic.

They said nothing to Rachael until paramedics arrived and they looked for a place where she could wash her hands. Strangely, they took her to the Men's Room where Rachael had confronted Adelman earlier. When her hands were clean, she turned to Ben.

"Would you have shot me, Lieutenant?"

"Reluctantly," was all he said. "Would you care to explain what happened or do we have to take you downtown for questioning?"

Instinct told Ben that there was a lot more to this story than met the eye. Even a trained one like his.

"I'll choose the trip downtown," she said smiling.

All right. You're under arrest. Detective, you will locate this suspect's vehicle and bring it to the office. I'll transport the prisoner here."

"Do I get handcuffed?" she chided as they walked away.

"No, but you almost got shot back there. Emilio has a hair trigger, you know," Emilio heard Ben say.

Over a late lunch of sandwiches from the "roach-coach" or roving vendor in a little truck, Rachael gave her official statement, recorded for later transcription.

When she had stopped by the Polachek house, she saw the father leaving and she decided, on a hunch really, to follow him. She wanted to know if he had become a heavy drinker lately. Instead, he drove to an indoor shooting range and when Rachael slipped inside, she saw him loading a semi automatic handgun.

She later questioned the proprietor of the range and learned that Mr. Polachek was a regular customer at least once a week and used a whole box of ammunition each time.

"So, that's why you looked and acted so damn weird?" Ben asked.

"Ben, I figured that poor man was going to try something and I was right. That whole family is dead. The mother will end up in an institution now that she has no one to care for her."

"I'm sorry, Rachael..." Ben began and she finished.

"For thinking I was planning to do something to Childress?"

"Yes," he responded bluntly. "You weren't yourself and I was concerned. You should have told me about Polachek."

"You never gave me a chance. Then you sent Emilio to check up on me and I almost whipped his ass. He's supposed to be my partner."

"For the record, Emilio said he wanted comp time if you hurt him." They laughed at that picture.

"So, you are officially reinstated to active status. I hope you're rested after your hiatus. The detectives handling the shooting at the courthouse want your official statement. By the way, how did Polachek get the gun into the courthouse?"

"When I went to court real early this morning the front entrances were locked. One deputy sitting at the rear door let me in. He asked why I was there and when I told him the Childress trial, he mentioned that a few people seemed to almost live there. He told me about the father who was there early every day. The deputy must have gotten used to seeing him and let him pass. He must have hidden the gun inside the courthouse somewhere and got it when the verdict was read. I'd bet he had it in a closet or washroom. When he pulled it out of the bucket, I wasn't surprised."

Ben and Rachael watched the news as they finished eating. The trial of the century and now the shooting that resulted was on every channel.

"Mr. Childress, any word on your attorney's condition?" the Eyewitness News reporter asked.

"I was just informed that he is out of surgery and is expected to recover completely, thanks to the quick actions of Sergeant Hart."

"What are your plans now, Jonathan?"

"I'm going to see a girl about some cookies," he responded.

"Shit" was all Rachael said as she threw the rest of her sandwich in the garbage.

Epilog

As a writer of fiction, I have the unique opportunity to create people and events. I do this to distract my readers from the doldrums of life and, more importantly, to cause them to think.

I am not a Christian, as I am Native American, but I believe that man did not walk from the sea. Something created the spark of life and it was not planets colliding with other objects in space. Be it God, Allah, Jehovah, Abraham or Great Spirit, there is a Creator.

Likewise, I have no personal knowledge if Grim Reaper exists, or whether a dark angel descends to collect the souls or spirits of the expired. If that is true, then there may be a place where those are detained and could present an opportunity for escape.

Would we call that fugitive an angel or something else? I leave that up to you, the reader.

daniel storm

Daniel Storm

Mr. Storm is Native American and ascribes to the Blackfoot heritage and ways. He grew up in Illinois and Wisconsin, where he attended the University of Wisconsin and ultimately studied law. After college, he participated in defending some of America's most notable crime figures, while associated with prestigious law firms.

As an author of numerous crime/fiction novels, he spends hours creating stories that compel readers to devote their undivided attention. Internationally, he is on the threshold of tremendous success, despite his retaining control of his stories, the production of his books and distribution.

He lives near Milwaukee with his German Shepherd, Merlin. He enjoys seeing the sites in Wisconsin on his Harley.

As a Viet Nam veteran, Storm works within the Wisconsin community to assist soldiers and military families, both of those in active service, and veterans and their families.

www.danielstormauthor.com